ENEMY OF THE STATE

THE ENEMY DUET
BOOK 1

B.H. EASTWOOD

www.bheastwood.com

For inquiries, please contact the Author through her website, www.bheastwood.com.

Cover Design: Ashes and Vellichor
Editing: Nice Girl Naughty Edits
Interior Formatting: Champagne Book Design

ISBN 979-8-218-60858-3

PLAYLIST

The Aisle of Fire—Orbit Culture
Antpile—Kublai Khan TX
Jaws—Sleep Token
Dance Macabre—Ghost
Slow Suicide—Cultist
The Path—Sylosis, Heriot
Join Me In Armageddon—Thy Art Is Murder
Monster—Skillet
Blood—Bad Omens
She is a Fire—Cradle Of Filth
Hands of Sin—Bleed From Within, Sylosis
Best Before: Death—Paleface Swiss
Rats—Ghost
A World Of Pain—Warmen
Say That You Will—Sleep Token
Demolisher—Slaughter to Prevail
Crows—The Plot In You
Hell—Filth
Come What May—Imminence
Keres—Thy Art Is Murder
The Cycle of Violence: Chapter 1—Varials
Cannibals—Of Virtue
A Bloodsoaked Symphony—Whitechapel
Whore—In This Moment
Wasp—Motionless In White
The Other Side of Anger—Crypta
Haunted By Guilt—Kalmah
Strangler—Orbit Culture
Belleville—Knocked Loose

If I'm There—Bad Omens
Drowning—Saltwound, Taylor Barber
Not Strong Enough—Apocalyptica, Brent Smith
Song of the Dusk—Insomnium
Reign of Darkness—Thy Art Is Murder
Bringer of Vengeance—Kataklysm
Death by a Thousand Cuts—Imminence
Bleed You Dry—Afterlife
CUT.BLEED.REPEAT—PROJECT: VENGEANCE, Left to Suffer
Hell Finds You Everywhere (feat. Noah Sebastian)—Thousand Below, Noah Sebastian
Darkness At The Heart Of My Love—Ghost
Kill or Be Killed—Spite
Extermination—Upon A Burning Body
Living Dead Girl—Rob Zombie
Wargod—Immortal
I Am Damnation—Bleed From Within
Telomeres—Sleep Token
Descent—Sylosis
Take Me Home—Knocked Loose
Rats—Motionless In White
Death Empress—Synestia, Disembodied Tyrant
Between Death and Dreams—Brand of Sacrifice
Boomslang—Kublai Khan TX
Walk With Me In Hell—Fit For An Autopsy

The full playlist is available on Spotify.

AUTHOR'S NOTE

Hello, friend!

Thank you so much for picking up *Enemy of the State,* book one in *The Enemy Duet.* I am truly grateful to you for giving this indie author a chance. It means so much to me.

Before you begin, I'd like to mention that this is a *dark* romance with depictions of graphic violence, death and torture. There are also on-page depictions of violent, rough sex with scenes involving dubious consent, as well as sexual and physical torture, making this book suitable only for mature audiences over the age of eighteen. Please proceed with caution if this subject matter could be upsetting for you.

This story and its characters are a work of complete *fiction,* wholly a figment of my imagination, and should be viewed as such. Moreover, this book is *not* to be used as a guide for...you know, anything. If you're looking for more information on any of the topics highlighted in this story, I'd encourage you to seek non-fiction resources.

As someone who appreciates going into a book with blinders on, I'll ask that you place your trust entirely in me. However, if you'd like a list of content warnings, they can be found on my website, bheastwood.com.

On a lighter note, when I'm deeply submerged in a book—both writing and reading—I love allowing a story's world, atmosphere and its characters to consume me. I find myself wondering what a book character's drink of choice would be or what foods they would eat if they could raid a kitchen. Or, what drink I would pair a book with. On the off chance that I'm not the only one who wonders about such things, I wanted to share what beverages I would pair this duet with.

If I was drinking (responsibly, of course), I would pair this book with a glass of French Bordeaux. If I preferred to keep things dry, I would pair this book with a triple shot of espresso.

These are simply my opinions, and you are, by no means, obligated to agree or even care, but I wanted to share in case there was someone out there interested.

Now that we've gotten that out of the way, it's my sincerest hope that you enjoy this wild ride you're about to embark on. Strap in, friend.

Without further ado, welcome to Exile Island...

KEY

Throughout the following story, you'll find several Finnish words. For easy reference, those words and their meanings have been included here. Most of these words will also be defined within the body of the text, for those that prefer not to have to reference a key.

Äiti: Mother
Äiti kusipää: Mother asshole
Äpärä: Bastard
Isä: Father
Kusipää: Cunt
Jeesus Kristus: Jesus Christ
Pilu: Twat
Vittu: Fuck

For those that dance in the dark.

ENEMY OF THE STATE

CHAPTER 1

Louhi

IT FEELS LIKE SOMEONE TOOK A BATTERING RAM TO THE INSIDE of my skull, my limbs heavy as I regain consciousness, though I don't dare open my eyes. I'm not prepared to let my captors know I'm back in the land of the living. Instead, I allow my other senses to speak.

The air is thick and damp against my skin, not wet, but humid. It's warm wherever I am, bordering on hot. It smells of tepid, stale piss and sweat, and I resist the urge to bring a hand up to my nose to block the smell or curl my lip in disgust. My mouth is dry from a combination of the drugs and the cloth gag. There's a faint metallic taste that lingers on my tongue from where I bit my cheek at some point.

My hearing is what screams at me the loudest, nearly overpowering my other senses. Heavy metal music blares through the speakers, filling the space of wherever I am, contributing to the throbbing in my head. Under drastically different conditions, I'd be jamming out, head-banging along to whatever song is playing, preferably smashed against the barricade of a festival or concert. From what I can make out through the haze of the drugs I've been pumped full of, it sounds like something I'd enjoy.

When the song ends, I catch the brief resonance of voices not far from where I lie on a hard surface. Another loud song booms, and I risk a deep, centering breath as I attempt to focus on the sounds beyond. I curse internally when the music prevents me from making out the content of any conversation, but based on the register, they're deep and male and not all that far away.

Despite the music, the thumping cadence of footsteps suddenly reaches my ears, growing louder. The footfalls give way to the grating of metal scraping against something hard and unyielding. *Concrete, maybe?*

A second later, something solid connects with the soft skin of my side, and I deduce that someone kicked me. *Kusipää. Cunt.*

"Wake up," a man growls.

There's no longer any reason to keep my eyes shut, so I blink a few times, the room coming into focus as a vicious scowl forms on my face. *Room* would be a generous word for where I am. There's no other way to describe it: it's a cell.

A moldy-looking substance covers the dank concrete surrounding me, climbing toward the ceiling like a revolting form of ivy. The only light is from the hallway, but I wouldn't need light to know there's nothing in here with me. No bed, no toilet, no sink, no cellmate. Just me and four concrete walls. A far cry from my cozy bedroom that I'll likely never see again, not even after I bust out of this joint.

I may as well make the most of my time here, though. While the conditions aren't ideal, fun can be made anywhere—especially *my* version.

The wanker rams a booted foot into me a second time, and I grunt as I roll over to protect my vulnerable side. Glaring up at him from where I lie prone on the floor, a string of insults and Finnish curses fly from my mouth, but they're closer to unintelligible noise due to the gag.

Fantasies of bloodletting, violence, and mayhem fill my mind, daring me to dip into the pool of violence where I prefer to exist. *What I wouldn't give for just thirty seconds alone with this äpärä. Bastard.*

His dodgy chuckle bounces off the walls around me as if he could determine exactly what I just said. Catching me by surprise—which is *not* easy to do—he squats down and slices through the zip tie holding my ankles together.

No matter how badly I want to kick this arsehole in the balls, I don't dare move my freed legs. Though, that's mostly because they still feel like they weigh eighty pounds apiece. Despite my lethargy, I don't know what they plan to do with me, so I study his next move. I'm nothing if not patient, even if the need to make him bleed is threatening to eat me alive.

He proceeds to snip through the plastic holding my wrists together in front of my body. The apprehension bubbling through me doesn't reach my face, though. I've spent years working to hide my emotions behind an irremovable blank mask.

My eyes dart to the second man in the room, who hasn't yet spoken, as he steps over to the entrance of my cell where he waits for his mate. The man beside me slaps my face in a way that would have me snorting smoke if I had been born a dragon. In a sense, I suppose I was; my scales just happen to be invisible.

"Welcome to Ex-I, sweetheart," he drawls, in a distinctly American accent. I clench my jaw, and he flees my cell as if he's on fire, likely knowing that if he lingered a second longer, I'd do much more than breathe smoke.

The barred door to my cage shuts with a reverberating *clang*, sending ripples through my brain, and I crane my neck, locking eyes with the two masked men clad in army uniforms on the other side. Yanking the gag from my mouth, I wad the cloth in my closed fist to keep for later, since it doesn't appear that this five-star government resort will be providing me a roll of toilet paper. The smile I give them through the bars is malicious, unnatural, feral even. It's an expression that promises death.

And I always keep my promises.

I wake sometime later, the drugs in my system to blame—or to thank—for my ability to have fallen back asleep. Much to my chagrin, I find that I'm still in the cell and the same deathcore music thrums loudly through the building. Carefully, I sit up, trying to control my movements so that I don't nauseate myself by moving too quickly. The last thing I need to do is puke in my new *home*. I doubt my captors would be so kind as to clean it for me.

Once I'm upright, I scoot my way to the back wall to prop myself against it. The lighting is low, and I glance up, noticing there's a single unlit light bulb dangling from the ceiling. I'm not sure if it's burned out or simply not turned on, but it doesn't matter. There's no switch on any of the walls, so it's controlled by a panel elsewhere, assuming it functions at all.

The same offensive smell from earlier lingers, and I breathe through my mouth to avoid making myself sick. I shouldn't be surprised that there's no window to open to access fresh air or sunlight.

I'm unsure how long I've been here, but if I had to guess, it's been less than twenty-four hours.

Suddenly, shrieks pierce through the heavy guitar riffs and harsh vocals of the metal music, that blare like a siren warning of an impending storm, coming from somewhere beyond the concrete walls of my *castle*.

Alright, so I'm not alone here. It's not as if I thought I'd be the only prisoner in devil-knows-where, but knowledge is power and paramount to my survival in this situation.

The lights flicker in the hallway beyond the barred door to my cell, giving off a spooky ambiance. I'm sure that's by design, but unfortunately for my jailers, I've always been a sucker for the eerie, preternatural parts of life.

Another scream slices through the music and I'm reminded of the earlier arsehole's parting words, *"Welcome to Ex-I, sweetheart."*

What the bloody hell is Ex-I? Where is it? And most importantly, what the fuck happens here?

CHAPTER 2

Louhi
24 Hours Earlier…

MOST CITIZENS CHOOSE TO BELIEVE THAT THE DARK, unsavory side of their government doesn't exist. They stick their heads in the sand and blind themselves. Even those that acknowledge the illicit affairs of their governing body are likely unaware of the depth and width of its depravity. That's a truth never more evident than within the United States of America.

American citizens seem to live in this bubble-wrapped world where their government is good and triumphs over evil. It's laughable, really. My situation is proof of that.

I'm being held in an underground prison somewhere in the bowels of Washington, D.C. I haven't been fed in at least two days, maybe longer, and I've only had a few sips of water in the same time frame. I'm thirsty, hungry, knackered, and dirty. I've been beaten, degraded, and interrogated in ways that are considered anything but humane.

I was prepared for this, though. I simply need to hang on.

Two soldiers in army uniforms and matching mesh masks stalk into my cell, grip me under the arms, and roughly haul me to my feet. I've only seen US Army soldiers since I arrived here a few days ago, but I'm not entirely sure who's running this show. It could be the CIA, US Military, FBI, Homeland Security, or someone else entirely. Maybe all of them. Ultimately, it makes no difference; they're all the same entity, the only distinguishing factor being the configuration of various letters of the alphabet.

I lick my split lip, internally wincing at the tinge of pain. My right eye is still swollen from where I was punched upon arrival. I certainly look my best; there's no doubt about that. All glammed up, for sure.

"Move," one of the brutes orders, before muttering under his breath, "British scum."

I suppose as far as insults go, it could be far worse.

Stumbling forward as a result of the shove he gives to my back, I toss a glare over my shoulder before continuing out of my cell. My wrists are now shackled in front of me with metal cuffs, along with my ankles, restricting my movements significantly. The metal cuts into my wrists harshly, making my skin seep tears of blood, the droplets tracking down my palms and fingers before falling to ground and staining the grey concrete floor crimson. I'm leaving my mark on this place as if it were the washroom stall of the dive bar I visited as a teen where I'd written *Louhi was here.*

The hallway is lined with more masked soldiers, and I smile confidently as I stride past them. It doesn't matter what they do to me here—or anywhere else, for that matter. This is not how I die. This is not the end of the road.

He's coming for me.

I'm led down the corridor, then around a corner and subsequent hallway that slopes upward. Eventually, our posse arrives at a loading dock. An armored military vehicle is parked at the rolled-up door, with the double doors of the boot open, and when I slow my steps, I'm shoved forward again. My intuition tells me that I should *not* get into that vehicle, but it doesn't appear I have much of a choice. I'm essentially chucked into the floorboard of the waiting transport vehicle's rear doors before four guards climb in after me.

"Sweet dreams," the brute from earlier taunts as he plunges a syringe into the soft skin of my neck.

Everything becomes hazy, as if a heavy cloud has descended upon me, but I have just enough clarity left in my heavy head to hear one of the men say, "Maybe Digs will have better luck pulling answers from her than we did."

My eyes drift closed of their own accord, but a few chuckles reach my ears as one of the men replies, "There's no 'maybe' about that. He has the highest success rate in history."

The men continue to talk about me and this Digs person, but I'm no longer conscious enough to understand what's being said as the darkness reaches up its boney hand to drag me under.

Present...

A tall, lean, muscular man dressed in another army uniform appears before my cell, holding a small metal tray with something that I *think* is supposed to resemble food.

An olive-green mesh mask is pulled over his entire head with holes that reveal his eyes—the shade of which I can't quite make out. Despite the dim lighting, I can tell that his eyes aren't cold like the orbs belonging to the guards from earlier. I can't help but wonder how the fuck this bloke ended up working at whatever this place is. As he moves subtly, I catch a glimpse of the skin around his eyes. It's a beautiful umber shade, and I consider what the rest of this man looks like. He's probably hot. And even if he isn't, I want to pretend he is, because that's more fun and I *love* fun.

We study each other for a long moment before he wordlessly bends, placing the tray on the floor and sliding it through the designated space between the bars at the bottom of my cage door. He holds my gaze before eventually backing away and disappearing in the direction he came, his footsteps eaten alive by the music that never seems to shut the fuck up.

Once alone, I glance at the so-called food. I don't feel hungry, but I'm certain that's because of the stress and, likely, extreme hunger I'm experiencing. I need to eat this slop. I have no idea when my next meal is coming or what's in store for me. Crawling over to the tray, I notice there aren't any utensils, no surprise there.

Scooping what I'm guessing is oatmeal into my mouth with my fingers, I choke it down. Next, I tear off a piece of bread and pop it into my mouth, ignoring its stale taste. What I would give for a flakey, tender piece of halibut right about now, with a crisp, chilled glass of Chablis. Maybe paired with some grilled vegetables and a side salad of spring greens topped with a fresh, light lemon vinaigrette.

Pretending that's what I'm eating, I tear a chunk off the semi-cold hamburger patty sitting next to the "oatmeal" and nearly hurl it back up when I swallow. Disgusting doesn't even cover it. *Evidently, the torture begins here.*

I'm not sure how I manage it, but I finish the entirety of the meal and shove the tray back through the miniscule opening as hard as I can, watching it slide across the floor and come to a stop in the middle of the hallway. It's harder for them to ignore a tray in the middle of the hallway than it is a tray in my cell. Besides, I don't want that nasty shit in here. Going against my very nature, but without the courtesy of a napkin, I lick any residue from my hands and fingers and wipe them on my black prison uniform. At least my clothes are black. That's a silver lining.

I stare at the hallway as a rat scurries out from who-bloody-knows-where and halts at the tray, nibbling on the crumbs. Rats are such fascinating creatures, the ultimate survivalists. I spend the next several minutes watching the rodent feast. Given the humidity and filthy living conditions of this place, I'm not surprised to find rats reside here, too.

The thumping music blasting through the speakers shuts off abruptly, and I sigh, soaking in the peace and quiet for a moment.

Through the bars, I notice I'm at the end of a dead-end hallway. There's a concrete wall to my left and no cells across from me, just another solid wall. When I get out of here, I'm never going to want to see concrete again.

Halfway up the solid wall across the way, a single shiny black camera stares back at me, and I make a mental note to take advantage of this situation once I get a better lay of the land.

The same man who brought me my dinner reappears sometime later to collect the tray in the center of the hall. He glances at me after retrieving the tray from the floor. I flash him a smile that borders on coquettish and speak for the first time in days, my voice hoarse with disuse.

"Would you mind terribly bringing me something to drink? Soda, water, wine, I'm not picky."

He snorts, gives me his back, then retreats down the hallway, and I call after him, making myself sound saccharine and innocent, when, in reality, I'm anything but. "Sir, that's no way to treat a lady."

Sitting cross-legged in the center of the cell, I sulk, desperately trying to think about anything other than my thirst.

To my utter shock, the guard returns a moment later, squats down, and holds out a paper cup through the bars for me to take. I blink at him, wondering for half a second if my brain has hallucinated him out of dehydration. Testing that theory, I reach out and tentatively grasp the cup, my fingers brushing against his.

This time, I smile gratefully, and he gives me a curt nod before departing. I'm left alone once again.

The cup was full when he brought it to me, and I don't want to drink it too quickly. Unsure of when I'll be awarded more water, I only take a few sips before placing the cup in the far corner of the room and lying on my side to try to sleep.

CHAPTER 3

Sean

"How are you, honey?" my mom asks, her slightly pixelated face lit up on the screen before me. Her smile is strained, lines of worry lacing her features. A ripple of guilt rolls across my mind, but I force it to evaporate before it can consume me.

"Good, Mom. How are you?" I ask casually, trying to ease her concern. I'm safer than she thinks, but I can't tell her that. I'm even closer to home than she realizes, but I can't tell her that either.

"Are you eating enough and drinking your water?" she asks, ignoring my question.

A short titter escapes me, but I confirm. The tension around her amber eyes eases, and she smiles at me through the screen. "Sorry, honey, you know I'm just worried."

"I know, but I'm okay. I promise." My military career has been hard on my mom; she tries to hide that fact, though she does a shit job of it sometimes.

"How's Jace?"

She's only asking about my best friend to try to match whatever Jace told his mom, and I suppress an eye roll. Our moms became fast friends six years ago and I'm glad they have each other, especially considering the secrecy of our whereabouts and classified jobs. I think they talk to each other more than Jace and I do, and our bunks are directly next to each other in the barracks.

"He's good too. He's eating, drinking, and wreaking the usual havoc."

She smiles, looking sheepish, knowing she's been caught out, and her face freezes as the connection shorts out for a second. "Have you met any nice girls wherever you are?"

"No, Mom. There's no girl."

I'm not celibate, but I'm certainly not dating by any stretch of the imagination. I'm all kinds of fucked up and have absolutely no business subjecting a woman to my madness—at least not on a permanent basis—but I wouldn't dare share that with my mom. Besides, there aren't exactly any women where I am. This place is barely suitable for me, much less a woman.

"You should keep an eye out. You never know when the girl of your dreams will fall into your lap. I'm not getting any younger, and I'd love some grandkids."

"You *have* grandkids, Mom. Or do Callie's boys not count?"

She laughs, her amber eyes sparkling on the screen. "You know I love your nephews more than anything, but you could start adding to the collection."

I give her a tight smile, not willing to crush her dreams. I don't see myself having kids, but this isn't the time nor the place to have that conversation. Although, my mom is amazing and would be nothing but supportive if I told her that's what I wanted. I make a mental note to broach the topic with her in person on my next leave—whenever that is.

Changing the subject, I ask, "How are things at home?"

I listen as she prattles on about my sister, and how she's considering early retirement. She's been talking about retiring from her successful advertising career for years, but she's never actually done it.

My mom is sweeter than a candy store, kindness radiating from her aura like fog floating up from the surface of a forest lake. She deserves a better son than me.

"Digs, Major Thompson wants to see you," Martinez states, drawing my attention to the doorway. I nod, then turn back to the computer on the desk in front of me. "I've got to go, Mom."

"I understand. Call me again when you can, okay? I love you."

"I love you, too," I echo before ending the video call and logging off the computer. I don my mask and stalk down the hallway toward the major's makeshift office.

Passing the closed door of the gym, I hear Ghost's "Dance Macabre" blaring, and I know without looking inside that Jace is in there. He's a rock fan and Ghost is always his first choice. I much prefer metal, enjoying the harder, more extreme musical elements. It also keeps the inmates awake and annoys the living fuck out of them, so no matter how you slice it, I win.

I make a left turn down the hallway that leads me past the entrance to the cages, the first of ten cell blocks, each housing eight cells. As far as I know, we've never had more than seventy-three prisoners at one time. We currently only have forty-one, but I get the sense that number will be dropping soon.

"Slow Suicide" by Cultist hammers through the speakers of all ten cell blocks and the barest whisper of a smirk tugs at the corner of my mouth. Fuck, I hope these walking pieces of filth are miserable. When I pass Borman, one of my guys, I decide to ask him to shut off the music for a few hours. I like to play with my food before I eat it and I'm getting hungry.

I haven't always been this way. I was made. Created. Molded like potter's clay. Reborn into the person I am today, like some kind of demonic phoenix. I used to be relatively normal; a strong man my mother was proud to call her son—a man *I* was proud of. It wasn't until the government got their hooks in me that things…changed. My mom doesn't know about the version of human I am now: the type that *craves* the hunt and *lives* for the scent of blood in the water.

I hope to God she never discovers my barmy penchant for torture.

My day-to-day role has become more than just my *duty* or my assignment—which it is—it's my goddamn *hobby*. The government knew what they were doing when I was given this post.

I continue down the corridor until I reach the major's temporary office. He's rarely here, and when he's not, I'm in charge. Knocking, I dutifully wait until I'm ordered to enter.

"You asked to see me, sir?" I ask, removing my mask and taking up my position across from his pitiful desk. He's a large man, with salt and pepper hair and lines marking his weathered face. He nods as he holds out a manila folder for me to take.

L. KOSKINEN is printed in bold, black ink along the side, and I slide it open and begin to scan the text, not making it much further than the second summary paragraph when the major interrupts me, "Koskinen is waiting for you in Cell Eight."

Only the worst of the worst criminals are sent here. Those kept at Ex-I are a national security threat, a danger to civilization, or simply too depraved for a maximum-security prison. The low number assigned to L. Koskinen tells me he's a threat to national security. The higher your number, the less of a security risk you are. Everyone in Cell Block One is a terrorist and has been on at least three watch lists at one time or another.

Prisoners here are usually unknown to society in the first place; so dangerous that the government shields them from public view. But when those criminals are eventually caught, they need a hell to make home for a while, and that's where I come in. I'm the gatekeeper of this hellhole, at least until I send you on to Lucifer for your next round of fiery damnation.

If you're here, you've already been pronounced dead, forgotten, thrown into the pits. The outside world doesn't know about this place, therefore offering more freedoms—and the potential for *creativity*—than a standard prison. We have our own set of rules, our own code, and believe me when I say that the list of rules is very short.

Rule number one: never reveal the existence of Ex-I. Rule number two: never kill a prisoner without orders. That's it. Everything beyond those two rules is on the table.

"I'll let you brief yourself later. I've got a chopper waiting, so let's make this quick. We believe Koskinen is the leader of a British terrorist cell. We thwarted their attack on the Federal Reserve, but we need intel on the next target and remaining members of the organization. You have six months. If you don't get answers by the end of February, Koskinen is to be eliminated. Do you have any questions?"

"No, sir. I'll get you what you need."

Sure, I have prisoners still holding out on me—like the behemoth in Cell One—but I rose the ranks faster than a bolt of lightning for a reason, and it's not because I can squat three times my weight. I get results.

"I know you will. You're dismissed."

I turn and start for the door, folder in hand, when the major stops me. "Diggory, keep your wits about you with this one. Koskinen is probably the most dangerous prisoner in this building."

With that omen, I nod once and stalk out of the room, tugging the mask back on and making a beeline straight for the barracks, where I hope I'll meet up with Jace. On my way, I stop and ask Borman to bring my new toy to what we refer to as the "playpen."

As I suspected, I find Jace fresh from a shower, pulling on a shirt, and I toss him the folder. I yank the mask from my head and take some deeper breaths as I give him a moment to briefly skim the text on the first page, which contains more than enough information for us to get started.

When he glances back up, a small smirk quirks the corner of his lips, and I have no doubt that my own face mirrors his. I jerk my head in the direction of the door and leave the barracks with Jace at my side, my mask dangling from my fingertips. Once outside the heavy metal door of the playpen, Jace asks, "How do you want to play this?"

His expression is cloudy now, but his eyes betray just how excited he is to sit down with some fresh meat. He's almost as unhinged and bloodthirsty as I am.

"I thought we'd start with the sprinklers."

He arches a dark eyebrow, his eyes widening slightly as he huffs, the sound somewhere between disbelief and humor. "Waterboarding, really?" he clarifies, as he crosses his arms over his broad chest, fisting his mask.

I shrug. "Baptism by fire."

"Bro, it's just plain baptism if there's water involved." Rolling my eyes, I tug my mask on, obscuring my identity.

A generous dose of excited adrenaline pulses in my veins as I blow into the room like a violent storm, letting the metal door rattle against the concrete wall behind it.

CHAPTER 4

Louhi

I'M BORED.

I wonder what day or time it is. There's no way for me to make markings on the wall or anything either, not that I would. None of that matters.

I've begun talking out loud to keep my mind from withering. I don't answer myself or anything—I'm not *nutty*—but I recite lyrics to my favorite songs, invent creative insults, and solve mental math equations. Considering my mind is the only weapon I have at my disposal, I need that blade to be sharper than ever.

The next few days—only marked by the tender-eyed soldier boy bringing me my meals—pass uneventfully. Every day is filled with heavy metal music, and if they don't cut that shit out soon, they'll manage to ruin my favorite genre, and we can't have that. I've been consistently fed two meals a day and given one cup of water. So far, this is vastly more pleasant than my previous arrangements. Nevertheless, I'm not naïve enough to think it will stay this civilized.

After being silently denied a loo, I made one in the corner of my cell. Certainly not ideal, but it's not as though I had other options. I have to assume that's what the small drain, no bigger than my palm carved into the floor of the corner, was for anyway. I've just finished relieving myself—adding to the grotesque smell of this hellhole that

I have yet to acclimate to—when a soldier I've never seen before appears in front of my cell, sans meal. The music covers any additional noises, so his approach was silent, which only irritates me.

Without giving away my vexation, I wink at him. "Well, hello. Nice of you to join me. I'd offer you tea, but I seem to be having some supply chain issues. Perhaps I should take that up with management."

His face is covered by a mouthless mask that extends down his neck, but I watch something that looks like amusement cross his exposed frosty green eyes, though it's gone in a flash. I cock an eyebrow as he pulls keys from his pocket and leans close to the wall next to my cell, just out of sight. I deduce that he's either using a retinal or fingerprint scanner because I hear a faint *click,* followed by him sliding the key into the lock and opening my cell.

My eyes track over his body, taking inventory of the assault rifle strapped across his back, the Glock holstered at his hip, and the tactical knives at his waist and his thigh. His assessing gaze combined with the fluidity in which he moves tells me this dude isn't some theater puppet. He would notice if I slid the knife from the sheath at his thigh, though I'm still tempted to try it. The only thing that stops me is the coldness behind his stare that warns me he would have no problem embedding it in my chest. Reminding myself to behave, I keep my twitchy hands at my sides.

With a politeness I forgot I possessed, I offer him my wrists, and he snaps on the cold iron cuffs. The chain is long and drags on the floor between my legs.

He takes a step backwards and holds the door open for me. I smile at my escort—*captor*—and chime, "How chivalrous of you."

"Move," he orders gruffly, jerking his head toward the other end of the hallway.

I take in my surroundings as we walk, evaluating the number of cells we pass—seven—and the fact that four of them are empty. It seems I'm the only woman, and the way the men in the other cells leer and spit vitriol like poison darts as I pass tells me they haven't seen the female species in a *long* time. None of them say anything I haven't heard before, but what I do notice is the varying ethnicities and accents of the three men jeering. One of them is clearly a Scotsman, another is from a Spanish-speaking place, but since my Spanish is shit, I'm not sure where he's from specifically. I pass an American next—from somewhere in the northeast, if I had to guess—and the last cell is empty, but the door is open, leading me to believe that it's usually occupied and its resident is simply absent.

Knowledge is power, Lou. You never know what might be useful. My brother's advice from years ago slithers into my mind as clearly as if he were here with me.

At the end of the hallway, there are several more masked guards armed to the teeth, and I can't help but smile broadly at the realization that this is all for me. Fuck, I've always been a slag for attention.

I follow the line of the soldiers to the right and down another corridor. I make a final right, then the guard at my back brings me to a stop in front of a substantial metal door that's standing wide open.

Inside, I'm led to a metal table and made to sit in the accompanying chair. It's a standard interrogation set-up, and I get comfortable knowing that I'll probably be here for a while. The guard secures the chain dangling between my bare feet to a bolt in the floor and the shackles between my wrists are secured to the top of the table.

When the soldier leaves, he shuts the door behind him with a *bang,* and I'm left here alone. There's no music in this room, and I breathe easily while I take in my surroundings.

The first thing I astutely realize is that I'm being watched. The red light on the camera in the upper left-hand corner of the room blinks at me. I wink in the direction of the silent witness. *Smile, little sis, you're on candy camera,* my brother teases me in my head, and I suppress the urge to laugh, the maniacal sound tingling on my tongue.

The second thing I notice is that the room is about five times larger than my living quarters, with three long shelves that line the expansive wall across from me. Tools of varying shapes, sizes, and types are displayed tauntingly. Next to the shelves is a floor-to-ceiling metal cabinet that looks more like a large locker. The doors are closed, so I have to use my imagination as to its contents. Unfortunately for me, I've always been too creative for my own good.

To my left, there's a door leading to God-knows-where. To my right, there's a metal table with hinges and levers placed strategically throughout, likely meant to transform the tabletop into whatever configuration the wielder has in mind.

I close my eyes for a moment and take a breath, the faint scent of disinfectant reaching me. Additionally, the air in this room is much drier, and I relax into the more temperate, hospitable conditions.

In the next blink, the door swings open violently. I don't flinch, despite being slightly startled by the abrupt noise. I was prepared to sit here alone for far longer, being made to "sweat it out."

I stare at the two brawny men consuming the doorway. Casually, as if I don't have a single care in the world—and in some ways, I don't—I smirk at them.

My eyes first meet those of my meal-time soldier boy, and I shoot him a playful wink.

He only huffs, but I still appreciate that he found me amusing, even if he won't admit it. He and his mate are clad in the same dusty, olive-colored mesh masks that are, apparently, standard-issue around here. In the full light of the room, I'm privy to his eyes the color of warm honey. I bet he has a nice smile, too, one that matches those pretty eyes, and I vow to make him pull that mask off and smile for me at some point.

The soldier to the right of Honey Eyes is dressed identically—in tan camo tactical trousers, a tight olive-green t-shirt, and army-issued camel-hued combat boots. They'd be hard to tell apart if it weren't for this guy's additional few inches of height and the fact that the skin around his eyes is a paler sandy color. A suntanned glow seems to have kissed his skin, which has me wondering if he got it wherever we are right now. I assumed we were somewhere warm and tropical based on the humidity and damp, moldy air in this place and his suntan confirms that.

When he narrows his gaze under my scrutiny, I notice that his are a silvery greyish-blue shade. The color of a thunderstorm rolling in, the color of the London sky in November, the color of a blade.

Despite wanting to, I can't seem to look away from this man as if something…otherworldly is forcing my gaze to remain fixed on him.

Like that feeling when you're pumping gas in the winter or brushing your hair and you know before it even happens that the thick static is going to shock you? That's what's happening. I can sense the electrical charge in the air, though I know that if I touch it, it'll sting.

He and Honey Eyes stalk farther into the room and shut the heavy door behind them, sealing the three of us in here together. A savage smile inches its way across my mouth at my realization that these two boys have no bloody idea who they locked themselves in a room with. Just because I don't plan on snuffing the light from their eyes today doesn't mean I couldn't if I wanted to, even chained to a chair.

Seemingly unphased, the two men drag the chairs back from the table across from me and take their seats.

Remembering what I overheard one of the men say in the transport van, I lean back in my uncomfortable chair, extending my arms before me fully.

I simper, addressing the one with silver eyes. "Pleasure to make your acquaintance, Digs."

The masked man cocks his head ever-so-slightly, but his steely eyes give away nothing, though there's a pregnant pause that hangs over the room before he speaks.

"Since you seem to be familiar with me already, why don't you introduce yourself?" His voice is low, smoky, with a slight huskiness that sounds as though it comes from his chest, not his throat. Much to my annoyance, the reverberation of his voice is something I feel between my legs, rather than between my ears.

I ignore his request for introductions, simply smiling at him instead. Silence decorates the room like nighttime snowfall. But I wait. This is a game and I play to win.

Eventually, Digs leans forward, resting his elbows on his knees. "You'll find that I don't give many chances for leniency."

He turns toward his mate when my muteness continues. His honey-eyed partner regards him, something akin to trepidation looming in his gaze, but Digs's frosty stare turns into one of fierce determination as he simply nods in response to the silent question. I admire resolution like that.

Without hesitation, Honey Eyes gets to his feet and rounds the table, wordlessly unlocking my cuffs. I look up into those golden eyes, trying to discern what's going through his mind, but his expression is indecipherable, any trace of apprehension gone. Even still, I can tell that he'll be the more readable of the two men.

With more force than is necessary, he yanks me to my feet and drags me over to the metal table to my right. He easily hauls me up onto the table and begins strapping me down. I don't bother fighting him. I've had enough training to know that I'm going to need to save every molecule of energy I can in preparation for whatever the hell is about to happen to me. My new amber-eyed friend disappears from view as I analyze my new position.

There are straps across my hips and forehead, above and below my breasts, two on each leg and each arm, securing me to the cold table. Suddenly, a motor beneath the table whirs to life and the entire contraption lowers two or three feet. The sound of metal grating against concrete—a piss-poor attempt to intimidate me—echoes through the room just as Digs appears behind the head of the table and stares down at me, his eyes flashing with excitement under the fluorescent bulbs. I wish I could see the accompanying grin on his face, despite the macabre situation. I bet it'd be gorgeous.

Underneath the gruesome excitement in his gaze, there's a darkness looming there, taunting me, warning me to tread carefully. My brother once told me that everyone shows you who they are; you only have to pay attention and believe what you see. That advice has never led me astray.

My gut tells me to take a deep breath, and I do. It's a good thing too, because a deluge of water engulfs my face. I sputter and cough, but recover faster than the average water-boarding victim. As I smile up into the face of Digs, his eyes narrow marginally in contemplation.

Honey Eyes stuffs a sopping wet rag in my mouth, then drops a cloth over my face, blinding me, and the table abruptly tilts backward as more water rushes over my head.

I once read that nearly fifty percent of people are afraid of drowning. It's a good thing I'm not one of them because the way my lungs are panicking at the lack of oxygen would be enough to send anyone with a phobia spiraling toward a permanent dirt nap. Additionally, the cloth over my face seems to add a layer of mild claustrophobia to the already dire situation. I don't miss the acute pain that oxygen deprivation provides, and I don't plan on experiencing it ever again.

Latching onto the miniscule amounts of air floating in my lungs, I resist the siren's dangerous call to take a breath until the spray of water ceases. Absently, I wonder if I've offended *Näkki*, the malevolent Finnish water goddess, because it sure feels like she's exacting her vengeance. It's as if she's squeezing life from my lungs, dragging me out to sea to drown me. If I could talk, I might be tempted to call her name and beg her forgiveness.

Gulping down watery oxygen filtering through the fabric over my face, I fill my seizing lungs as I prepare to hold my breath for longer than what's good for me.

There's no escaping this. There's no swimming to safety.

There's only endurance.

"Where's the next attack going to be?" Digs asks, his voice firm, yet melodic.

The cloth gag is removed as they wait, presumably for an answer, but I don't give them what they want. They replace the rag, rinsing and repeating.

Ten more times, the process is replicated as they make me feel like I'm being suffocated by water, followed by Digs asking the same question, then me meeting his inquiries with silence. This man must have shit for brains if he thinks I'll tell him anything. Or perhaps everyone else in here is simply weak.

Finally, the cloth over my face is torn away, and I cough around the soaking wet gag still in my mouth. When I've regained my composure for the most part, I smile around the muzzle. It's going to take *a lot* more than a little water boarding to get anything out of me.

Both sets of eyes gaze down into mine, blazing with determination.

Then, they begin again.

CHAPTER 5

Sean

This girl is a species entirely of her own. My unfortunate victims are usually begging for mercy and oxygen long before now, but Jace and I have been waterboarding her for more than two hours and she has yet to say one word since she name-dropped me, my damn nickname swathed in that charming English lilt.

I don't know how she learned that piece of information, which only makes more work for me. I'll have to question all the men in my unit to find out who opened their big, fat fucking mouth when they all know how I feel about passing out my name.

Not every inmate breaks through torture alone, which is why this place is designed for the prisoners' extreme discomfort, prodding them to the edge of sanity. From the lack of beds in the cells to the stale, shitty food and absence of sunlight.

It goes beyond that, though. If they have long hair and seem attached to it, I produce the razor. If they're concerned about their hygiene, they're forced to go months between bathing opportunities. If someone hates spiders, I'll lock them in a box with only a colony of Tarantulas for company. I pride myself on exploiting their weaknesses, digging into their souls and carving out their deepest fears and turning it against them for maximum discomfort.

That's why I don't share my name. If the other guards want to do that, that's their prerogative, but Jace and I prefer to keep the inmates at arm's length. Names are powerful, private even, and when you share that, you share an intimacy, whether intentional or not.

Besides, a win, however small, could keep a prisoner going for a month, negating weeks, months, or years of hard work I spent wearing them down.

"Who is your second-in-command?" I ask, as Jace opens another deluge over her face. I shifted the line of questioning, but that hasn't made any difference.

Again, my question is met with only sputters and silence.

I've been waterboarded once—just to see what it was really like—and to say that it was horrific would be putting it mildly. The feeling of suffocation is probably worse than the feeling of drowning this experience provides. I'm sure her lungs are burning and rioting. I really don't know how this woman is surviving this. I would've stopped half an hour ago with most of the other prisoners here, but she keeps holding out, and the compulsion to see how far I can take things is too strong for me to fight.

Absently, I wonder if I've finally met my match.

The way my dick is throbbing tells me that this girl is going to be a problem, for a host of reasons. Starting with the fact that she's incredibly beautiful, despite her dirty, disheveled appearance.

Pulling the gag out from between her pouty lips, I stare at the exotic features of her face, and rumble, "This is going to last as long as you keep your mouth shut."

Her dark brown irises glimmer with more than just glassy tears. She blinks rapidly for a moment, likely to clear the lingering pools of water from her eyes. Where I expect to find distress and maybe some anger in her gaze, I only see indifference and steadfastness.

Damn, I wish that wasn't hot.

"How did a pretty girl like you end up in a place like this?" I ask, so softly that I didn't realize I voiced that thought until a coy smile crosses her lips, her eyes dancing with amusement.

"Aw, you think I'm pretty?" she taunts, spewing excess water into the air like a fountain. "And to think that if I had known I'd have such handsome company today, I'd have tried a little harder with my appearance, though I seem to have misplaced my curling iron and I think I ran out of mascara."

Jace snorts from the other side of the table, and I shoot him a glare. He rolls his eyes, wordlessly telling me that I'm the one who started this.

"I'll see what I can do to remedy that," I deadpan. Her wet, short, matted onyx hair sticks to her wet face, but I find that I have the bizarre urge to brush it from her pale olive face. A notion I actively ignore.

Rising from my seat, I begin to unstrap her. It's clear I'm not getting anything out of this woman today. Jace helps me, and we get her up and off the table. When she doesn't fight us, I realize that I haven't seen her put up a fight whatsoever since she's been in here, which only baffles me further.

I open the door to the playpen and shove her into the grasp of two of my guys—Stuco and Martinez—and when they get halfway down the hallway, headed back to her cell, I murmur to Borman, "Blare the music as soon as she gets settled and come find me."

With a nod, he follows the guys down the hallway. When they're out of sight, I tug off my mask and turn to Jace, who's doing the same, and sigh. "I need a cigarette."

He chuckles as we head up to the ground level. When we finally get through the security measures and make contact with the bright tropical sunshine, we round the corner and lean against the exterior side wall of the building. I pull the pack of cigarettes from my back pocket and grab two, handing one to Jace. Jace offers me his lighter, and we both ignite the ends of our cigarettes. I wish it were a joint, but this will have to do.

We stand there in silence for a long moment before I finally ask, "Did you know she was a woman?"

"Yeah, her feminine face and voice kind of gave her away when I dropped her meal off. Did you really think a name like Louhi belonged to a guy?"

"I didn't think about her name one way or another. I made a bad assumption." I should've asked Jace for his assessment of our newest resident before barging into the playpen since he had already seen the tenant of Cell Eight.

He's the only one I feel comfortable admitting this to, and I catch his nod out of my periphery as he replies, "I thought it could go either way, like Ashley or Sam."

Chuckling, I exhale the smoke, the gray tendrils disappearing in the tree canopy shading us. "How many male Ashleys do you know?"

"Haven't you ever seen *Gone With The Wind*?" he adopts a falsetto voice, adding, *"Oh, Ashley, take me to Terra."*

A boisterous laugh thunders from my chest as I shove him. "You're a fucking loser."

Stumbling to the side, he laughs even louder. "Yeah, well, at least Louhi thinks I'm *handsome*."

"She thinks we're *both* handsome, you jackass."

He shrugs as he brings his cigarette to his lips. "Pretty sure she was only talking about me, but you tell yourself whatever you need to sleep tonight."

I roll my eyes at his ridiculousness, and eventually silence falls once again, both of us likely thinking about the same dark-haired girl who challenged the hell out of us a few minutes ago.

She's not only attractive because we haven't seen someone of the female variety in an absurd amount of time either. She's easily the most breathtaking creature I've ever laid eyes on, and that's an impressive feat, considering just how dirty and neglected she was. It stunned me when I first opened that door. After I got over my initial shock at her being a woman, I had to overcome the surprise of her being beautiful.

Fuck me.

"I've never tortured a woman before. Are we really going to do this?" I hate hearing the vulnerability in that admission, and I wouldn't have voiced it if I were speaking to anyone else. The army isn't the place for feelings. But Jace and I have been through a lot together over the last twelve years, and he won't give me shit for this.

He sighs heavily before replying, "Fuck, I don't know, man. What other choice do we have?" His question is rhetorical, but he has a point. It's not like we have an alternative option. He briefly pollutes the atmosphere with smoke before adding, "I've been trying to tell myself that I didn't bring her water after she asked for it simply because she's a beautiful woman. If I try harder, maybe I can convince myself that I did it because she amuses me and not because I'm a sexist bastard. She must've done some vagina voodoo on me."

I snort in affirmation, shaking my head to clear the hex. "Thompson told me that she was the most dangerous criminal here. You think that's true?" I ask, even though the answer already sits firmly in my gut.

"After what we just saw, I do. The smile she gave us when we sat at that table sent a damn chill down my spine. You think she'll break?"

"Everyone breaks eventually," I assert. "The question is, will she break before she dies?"

"How long does she have?"

It's not unusual for certain prisoners to have a finite amount of time locked in this shithole. Some are here indefinitely, to be abused and punished, for as long as we see fit. Others, like Louhi, are here only long enough to get answers and are subsequently terminated.

"Six months."

He scrubs a hand down his face. "Fuck."

It's not just about getting her to break. It's about getting the answers we need. Fine, it's a little bit about getting her to break. I want to see her shatter.

CHAPTER 6

Louhi

AFTER BEING UNCEREMONIOUSLY DUMPED BACK IN MY CELL, I spent the next several minutes puking up water into my toilet corner. It's anything but glamorous.

The second I was alone, I peeled off my wet black prison top and looped it around one of the horizontal bars of my cage door to dry. At least it got a good rinse. Some soap would be preferable next time it gets washed, though.

I don't think they were prepared to house a woman in this prison, considering I wasn't privileged enough to get a bra or panties. Not that I have a need for either of those here.

After resting for a while, I decide that I probably need to maintain my stamina if I'm going to be tortured every day. Getting to my feet, I assess my small space and determine that I have just enough room to work out.

I'm partially through my fifth set of push-ups—the metal music providing the perfect workout playlist—when Honey Eyes appears in front of my cell with my "dinner." I swear it looks less like food with each passing day.

Jumping to my feet, I move over to the barred door. I totally forgot that I didn't have a shirt on until those honey eyes on the other side of the cage drop to my full chest now glistening with sweat.

I've always found modesty to be overrated. I've had a "tits out" approach to life for as long as I can remember, and my philosophy hasn't changed, despite my new living arrangements. Or perhaps he's simply observing my ink.

"My shirt was a little damp," I offer by way of explanation.

I don't hide the way my eyes snake down his warrior's body and linger at his crotch that appears to be somewhat snug at the moment. I titter lightly, before adding, "I bet you request we have another day at the water park now."

He huffs behind his tight mask before shoving my food through the slot and sliding a cup of water in behind it.

Resting my forearms against the bars, I ask, "What's your name?"

"Don't worry about it." The liquid timbre of his voice is warm and has a note of friendliness, despite his gruff reply.

"A question for a question, then."

Widening his stance, he crosses his arms over his chest. He's not armed with a rifle like all the other soldiers I've encountered, but he's not unarmed either. His Glock practically glows like a beacon at his hip, and the smattering of tactical knives positioned on his body glint in the warm light from the hallway.

"Ladies first," I tease, waving a hand in the air, my arms still resting casually against the metal bars.

He chuckles, the sound low and somewhat muffled. "Why try to blow up the Federal Reserve?"

Masking my mild annoyance, I smile as I pull my hands back through the bars and examine my black painted fingernails that are starting to grow out. Of course he'd try to ask something serious. "Excitement is so hard to come by these days."

When he says nothing, I speak again, opting for something innocuous. "My turn. How old are you?"

"Thirty-one. How old are you?"

"Twenty-eight." My birthday is next month—October—but I don't feel the need to let him know that.

"Where are you from?"

"Here and there, but I suspect you know that." I wink at him as I say that last part and he lets out a puff of air—not quite an exhale, but not a laugh either.

"What does your mother think about you torturing men, women, and children?"

The hint of amusement in his gaze disappears in a flash and his stare goes cold. "You aren't a child, and I'm not even sure you're a woman."

My expression turns flirty. "I'd be happy to prove it to you further, in case my tits weren't enough."

With a huff, he turns and stalks away. I didn't miss the way he circumvented the comment about his mother altogether. I guess you can't be too careful in a place like this. I'm sure that's why they all cover their faces too. Although, I'll readily admit that the masks are doing it for me. *Mask kink unlocked.*

As he drifts down the hallway, my mind flutters over the content of his questions in combination with the repeated questions Digs hurled my way earlier.

What the hell has my brother gotten himself into?

I'm getting an early workout in when the green-eyed masked man from the last couple of days comes to collect me for, what I'm coming to realize, is my daily torture session. I was reacquainted with a few more rounds of waterboarding over the last few days—or weeks? Hard to tell—which I'm starting to get all too comfortable enduring.

After slipping my black uniform top back on, I'm led back to the same interrogation room, but this time, the only thing in the entire room is a single metal chair in the center of the space.

Oh, finally something new. That's exciting.

I'm roughly made to sit in the chair and the chain dangling from my cuffs is then connected to a bolt in the floor. Left alone, I stretch my neck from side to side as I close my eyes, settling into the silence of the room. I've nearly drifted to sleep when the metal door I came through earlier swings open. I internally roll my eyes at Digs's obvious flair for dramatics. It'd be cute, maybe even sexy, if I weren't on the receiving end of his unpleasant antics.

He saunters into the room alone, Honey Eyes nowhere in sight. I arch an eyebrow, waiting for him to start his barrage of questions I have no intention of answering. Circling my chair, he comes to a stop in front of me, leaning against the greyish concrete wall across from me that's tinged a blue-green color, likely from mold.

Folding his burly, well-muscled arms across his wide chest, he props a booted foot against the wall behind him as he addresses me with casual aloofness. "Feel like talking today, Lou?"

Lou. No one calls me Lou except my brother, and I find it irritating coming from this man.

"Depends on the subject."

He snorts with what I assume is laughter, but could be disappointment, but either way, it's amusing to me.

"Where is the next target?"

I answer him with silence.

"Figured."

New day, same shit. His line of questioning is not aging well, if I'm being honest. I'm already over it.

When I don't answer, he pulls a rag from his back pocket and approaches me. He leans down to tie the piece of fabric at the back of my head and covering my eyes. In the close proximity, I accidentally inhale him. He smells of hot testosterone, intense masculinity, and pure savagery. I wish I could bottle his scent and dab it on my wrists before charging into battle.

I wish I didn't like it.

When his seemingly powerful body abruptly disappears, I chastise myself for even appreciating his closeness.

Relying on my hearing, I catch the creak of a door opening, followed by shuffling, then the terse, shrill, distinct sound of a motor coming to life. I could recognize the humming sound made by a drill even in my sleep. I'm unable to contain the hearty laugh that bursts from me, my chest bouncing with the movement.

"You can't help yourself, can you?"

"Excuse me?" Digs asks, sounding puzzled.

"You live for the drama."

A chuckle sounds from somewhere else in the room, and I ask into the void, "That you, Honey Eyes?"

"Huh?" the man—not Digs—asks with confusion.

"Don't answer her. She's one brick short of a full load," I hear Digs say matter-of-factly.

"Ah, it *is* you, Honey Eyes. I knew I recognized you. He's just pissed that he didn't get a cool nickname."

I hear a dark chuckle, and I know, even without being able to see, that it came from Digs. The hypnotic sound sends a shiver through me, all the way down to my toes, and I feel like I'm wading into a lake in early spring, daring to submerge myself in what I know are sure to be dangerously cool waters.

"She's not wrong," Honey Eyes remarks.

"What kind of name is Digs anyway? Is it because you dig graves or something equally ridiculous?" When they give me the silent treatment, I add, "I already know your name, you sod."

Another beat of silence passes before he finally answers me. "Short for Diggory."

I'm gobsmacked that he answered me at all, let alone honestly. "So not even as cool as 'grave digger' then?"

I hear some low chuckles before Digs addresses me again, his tone all-business now. "As fun as this has been, it's time for *you* to start giving up some answers."

When I don't reply, my left foot is yanked into the air so my leg extends. Something cold and abrasive runs along the bridge of my bare foot. Bracing myself for whatever Satan—I mean Digs—can attack me with, I mentally take myself on a trip into one of my favorite memories.

The night air is crisp and cold. A veil of powdery snow resembling fluffy clouds blankets my surroundings, the radiant glow from the moon glittering against the white particles like reflective tape. I nestle into the little perch I made for myself on the rooftop of the building across from the nightclub.

Pulsing techno music escapes into the night every time the doors are opened—too often for my liking—but all has been quiet for the last hour. I know from the extensive reconnaissance I've done over the last few weeks that my target always exits through the front door and always at 3:27am.

Creatures of habit are easy, boring kills, but for once I'm grateful. I've been tracking this wanker for three weeks, ever since I found out he was still alive.

I glance down at my watch and see that it's 3:25 a.m. Flicking off the safety as I lean over the scope of my rifle, I peer through the viewfinder trained on the doors. Giddiness bubbles through me, and I take a calming breath to keep my emotions at bay. I can host a personal party later. Besides, there won't be anything to celebrate if I blow this because I got fucking excited.

Like clockwork, two minutes later, James Vungaärd walks through the double doors of his nightclub, flanked by two security guards. The driver of his waiting SUV rounds the front of the car to open the door to the backseat for him.

With the crosshairs trained on his head, I suck in air and hold it. Undiluted joy races through me as I exhale, pulling the trigger of the bolt action AR-15, the silencer muffling the sound of my shot.

I watch through the glass of the scope as he falls backwards, blood immediately pooling around his head, painting the pristine snow a beautiful shade of deep crimson. His security team scrambles around him, one of them pulling out his sidepiece, his eyes darting around frantically as he searches for the perpetrator. He'll never find me. No one ever does.

Retribution is a funny thing. It's like taking a hit of a drug that you know you'll only be able to savor once. It doesn't bring back those you've lost and you'll only be able to taste the intoxicating nectar of justice in your dreams, but it's electrifying, nonetheless.

Observing the chaos for another minute or two through my binoculars, I revel in the sight of my parents' murderer lying dead on the icy sidewalk that's now his tomb.

While elation and satisfaction gallop through me at top speed as I pack up my rifle, there's a thin membrane of disappointment that threatens to eclipse the delight that exacting my revenge brought me.

It's over—*in this lifetime, anyway.*

I'll pick up where I left off when I find him in Hell. Fortunately for my parents, but unfortunately for James Vungaärd, vengeance is something I think I might excel in.

Cracking through the flimsy crust of malcontent, a wicked, slaked smile stretches across my face as I sling my bag over my shoulder, disappearing into the night, knowing that this was the only acceptable version of justice.

When I come out of my dreamy memory, it's to my own agony. I bite down on my tongue to keep from screaming, but that doesn't stop the tears from wetting the rag covering my eyes and tracking down my dirty face. Blood fills my mouth, but I hardly notice it over the searing pain ricocheting through my body.

As my suffering continues, I pray to *Kiputyttö*, Pain Girl in Finnish mythology, to take my pain from me and hide it away in Pain Rock, so her snakes might eat my torment. I know she doesn't exist, but she's my best shot at easing my anguish.

Just then, Honey Eyes removes my blindfold, and I look down to find that I'm missing the second, third, and fourth toenails on my left foot, though I suppose that's better than the drill I thought they'd take to the ball of my foot. Deep crimson stains the floor and Digs's forearms where he's crouched before me. I'm sure my blood is on his massive hands as well, but his black gloves hide that.

"You really don't have anything to say?" Digs asks, locking his vast, oceanic gaze with mine as he stares up at me.

I say nothing. I don't have anything to say to him, but even if I did, I'm utterly incapable of speech at the moment.

"Maybe removing a few more will jog your memory."

I hiss out a breath, enough to form words and choke out, "Take them all."

His eyes widen a fraction at my brazen but honest statement. Sighing, he drops the metal pliers still in his hand, and they clatter to the floor, ringing out in the otherwise quiet room. The sound is still echoing in my mind as I close my eyes, willing myself to pass the fuck out. This pain is scorching, burning me from the inside out, and I have no idea how I'll be able to walk out of here. But I don't need to be able to walk and I certainly don't need toenails.

I simply need to be alive when my brother retrieves me.

CHAPTER 7

Sean

I'VE NEVER BEEN A SOFT OR GENTLE GUY, EVEN BEFORE THE army. I've never been the hold-your-hand, buy-you-flowers, cuddle-you-through-the-night, tell-you-all-my-warm, fuzzy-fucking-feelings guy. I'm all hard lines and sharp corners. A wolf, a predator, to my core.

According to the women I've dated relatively recently, I'm hard to love and even harder to put up with. I've been told I'm cold and detached. What they don't know is that I'm protecting them, shielding them from my inner darkness.

Even if I could tell a girlfriend about what I do for a living—which I can't—I could never truly be myself with her. I'd never feel comfortable enough to unlock the vault I keep the darkness locked inside.

There are guys here, guys like me and Jace, who hide the dark, depraved parts of themselves from their wives and girlfriends. I used to be one of them, shutting down my darker inclinations, pretending they don't exist. Not anymore. Now, I just fuck my fist.

I don't want to pretend I'm something I'm not in order to receive a woman's affection. I don't want to close my eyes at night knowing I'm a fraud. I respect myself too much to be inauthentic and I respect women too much to truly unleash myself on them.

So, imagine my shock to find myself standing in front of Lou's cell a few hours later, gauze and disinfectant in hand.

Looking into her cell in person for the first time, I'm glad I brought supplies. It's fucking filthy. Disgusting would be too benign of a word for this place. The foul smell that always permeates this hallway is somehow even worse as I stand in front of Cell Eight.

Louhi is sitting against the back wall, her head rolled to the side, eyes closed. The steady rise and fall of her chest tell me she's alive; though I'm not sure if she's conscious. She didn't lose enough blood to pass out, but I know the excruciating pain I must've caused her earlier, so I wouldn't be surprised to find that her body put itself to sleep to cope. Something foreign tugs inside my chest, squeezing tightly as if begging me to study the feeling, but I ignore it.

I fish the key from my pocket and use the retinal scanner to unlock the small cell. Careful to leave the barred door open, I take a step inside, resisting the urge to cover my nose or gag from the repulsive stench.

Telling myself that it's because I need to keep her alive until I have answers, I squat down in front of her and squeeze the bottle of disinfectant, sluicing it over her exposed and bleeding toes. Missing toenails won't kill her, but the infection she'll undoubtedly get in here certainly might.

She hisses even as her eyes remain shut. I'm not stupid enough to think that she didn't know I was here from the moment I approached her cell.

"I don't know whether to thank you or throat punch you for that." Her dulcet voice carries through the small space. Regardless of the content, her voice is what I imagine it would sound like to speak in cursive handwriting: formal, refined, and sophisticated.

I can't help the chuckle that snakes its way up my throat as I pour more of the runny liquid disinfectant over her feet, and she pops open her lids to level a glare at me. I smirk behind my mask as her attention remains narrowed on me. Averting my eyes, I pull the roll of gauze from my pants pocket and wrap it around her toes.

When I finish, I look up and meet her dark gaze, the color of strong coffee.

"You know that I'll keep having to hurt you until you tell me what I need to know."

Even in the low light, her eyes appear to soften marginally to a warm cocoa color. "I know."

I nod in understanding as I get to my feet and retreat from her cell, Major Thompson's dark warning replaying in my mind like an obnoxious pop song on the radio.

I'm rounding the corner as I leave the infirmary after returning the first aid supplies when I literally run into Borman. He mumbles an apology and starts to move past me when an idea sparks to life in my head, and I stop him. "Can you have the cells in Block One cleaned this week?"

His eyes nearly bug out of his head in surprise, but he doesn't speak, leaving me with a curt nod and heading down the corridor. The cells in Block One were cleaned three weeks ago and aren't due to be cleaned again for another two or three. I like to keep the accommodations in Block One less than ideal, but seeing Lou's cell this evening bothered me more than it should. The other assholes residing in that block will simply reap the benefits of my newfound generosity.

Back in the barracks, I sink onto the end of my bed, dropping my head into my hands as I lean forward. I tug my mask from my head aggressively and rub at the back of my neck, feeling weighed down from the day and the little terror living in Cell Eight. I toy with the mesh mask between my hands, spinning it around and around.

Jace and I were Special Forces when we were hand-picked for this assignment. Don't get me wrong, it's a nice change from the active combat we experienced, so I find it hard to complain. We've been at Exile Island for two years and there are some perks to being here, like the ability to explore this tropical paradise on occasion. Unbeknownst to the prisoners, we're located on a remote island three hundred miles off the coast of Hawai'i, but it's not part of that state. No one knows about this place since it's owned by the United States government, and it's not on any map I've ever seen.

To get here, you have to take a long-ass boat ride from Oahu or helicopter. If you're asking, I find the chopper method to be preferable, but I rarely leave, so it doesn't really matter. Jace and I both have three more years apiece in this tropical hellscape before we're granted the opportunity to bail or sign up for another round. Though, we're afforded more leave opportunities here than we were when we were Special Forces—even if I hardly take advantage of them. Jace has one coming up where he'll get a full week back on the mainland.

The man on my mind appears in front of me a moment later, raising the back of his hand to feel my forehead. I swat him away as he chuckles. "Are you sick? Borman said you asked him to have Block One cleaned."

He sinks to his bed next to mine, his honey fucking eyes—damn you, Lou—assessing me.

"Have you been down there lately?"

"Uh, yeah, I feed Louhi, Samuel, Kazi, Solomon, and Carlos every day. Why?"

"You haven't noticed how fucking inhumane those cells are becoming?" I ask, my brow furrowing. They're downright inhospitable, even by my standards.

"I have, but that's the point—for it to get so bad that they crack wide open and their secrets spill out."

I sigh. Yeah, that's the point. Or it *was* the point. I don't know if it was the sight of a beautiful woman slumped next to a pile of her vomit that changed things for me or if I'm going soft with age, but it suddenly feels wrong. Maybe Jace is right, maybe I *am* sick.

"They need to be cleaned," I remark sternly. That's all the

explanation Jace or anyone else is getting from me regarding the cleaning of Block One. Jace may be my best friend and second-in-command, but I still outrank him, and seeing as I'm in charge, what I say goes.

Not seeming to be offended by my tone, but sensing my tension, he asks, "Want a smoke?"

I nod, toss my mask into the bin at the foot of my bed, and follow after Jace.

I'm pissed the fuck off that Lou's cell is as fucking disgusting as it is. I'm a little annoyed that even Jace is breathing down my neck about cleaning the foul cell block. But most of all, I'm incensed with myself for caring about an inmate—even a little. I gave her my full fucking surname, for Christ's sake. I gave her a piece of myself, and I didn't even hesitate, like something other than my brain was controlling my mouth.

A smoke won't fix the angry storm swirling in my head, but it can't fucking hurt.

We go up to the roof this time, slumping down into a couple of the plastic chairs we keep up here for this purpose. The sun is bright overhead, a few wispy clouds dotting the horizon.

I take the zippo and unlit cigarette from his outstretched hand and light the end of the cigarette between my lips. Once I pass him the lighter, he does the same. We lounge in companionable silence for a bit before we start talking about Jace's upcoming leave and his trip home.

It's moments like this that make being here not so bad.

CHAPTER 8

Louhi

IT COULD BE TEN DAYS, OR IT COULD BE FORTY, THAT I'VE BEEN here. I have no idea. Either way, I'm not a fan. The conditions are…subpar, and I'd like to file a complaint. I'm not sure how long my brother plans to keep me in suspense before busting in here and sweeping me away. He's always been my hero—my steady ground, my protector, my best mate, my savior my entire life.

That's why when he asked for help, I jumped at the opportunity. He's never asked me for anything, and knowing I had the ability to repay some of his kindness from the last almost twenty years, I didn't hesitate. Even if that meant ending up in the armpit of a torture facility.

This isn't like a regular prison either. This is worse, more severe. Serial killers have it better. No one cares about you here. No one gives a shit if I die. For all I know, I'm already dead to the rest of the world. My name, my face, my identity are simply meaningless now. Obsolete.

I'd hate to have to get a new name when I bust out. I've always adored my name. In Finnish, it means "goddess of death" or "snake," both meanings I claim with equal fervor. It's what inspired my tattoo, but it's more than the meaning of my name to me; it's who I am. I'm the goddess of death to some, yet a snake to others.

Born in Finland, we lived there as a family until I was eleven and my parents were stolen from me. I haven't resided there since my parents' murder, but my brother and I meet at their grave on my mother's birthday every year. A piece of my soul seems to linger in Finland, which is probably why I spend so much of my free time studying Finnish mythology and my heritage.

I miss Finland: the culture, the people, the weather, the history, the landscape. I miss being *home*.

Pulling my knees to my chest, I inspect my feet. Too bad *Kiputyttö* never answered my silent summoning to erase my hurt. But what's life without a little pain?

I've had to adjust my workouts with my mangled toes. It's been aggravating, to say the least. At least Digs eliminated the need for me to clip my toenails. Silver lining?

My black fingernails have grown so long though that the black polish is nearly gone. It's been driving me bonkers, but I can't seem to chip off the last dregs of polish.

"Jeesus Kristus," I mutter in my native language, as I run a hand down my filthy hair next. I'm far too vain for this shit. I need a shower in the worst fucking way. The first thing I'll do when I'm free from this place is soak for *hours* in a steaming bubble bath with a fat glass of luxurious red wine.

I close my eyes now, attempting to transport myself to that blissful place in my massive washroom at home, but my eyelids fly open as I hear someone approach my cell. Things have been relatively quiet since breakfast, and I *almost* miss the barrage of noise that the metal music provides.

The guard I've heard referred to as Borman appears before my cell door a moment later, and he goes through the motions of unlocking my cage, giving the serpent within me a glimpse of freedom from confinement. I lull her back to her restful state. This is not the time. Not the way. I only need to wait. *Practice patience, little sister,* my brother would remind me.

Look, I *am* patient, but my patience has limits.

Never deviating from routine, he shackles me and leads me to the usual interrogation room, and I'm made to sit in a wooden chair this time. My arms are strapped to the armrests and my ankles remain chained.

Something new.

The different set-up tells me that Digs has something fresh up his sleeve. I have an appreciation for his artistic ability to inflict pain in imaginative ways. Digs isn't as sly as he thinks he is, though. I'm all too aware of his penchant for pain. I've caught the way his eyes glint with the hunger to hurt, the desire to see me bleed. I've also noticed how his cock thickens behind his zipper when he does something especially heinous.

He's a sadist, that much is obvious.

When the door eventually opens, Digs and Honey Eyes enter, the latter carrying a small cardboard box. *Oh, the intrigue.*

"Morning, Louhi," Honey Eyes chirps, like he's not about to do something grotesque to me. Both he and Digs have been growing more familiar over the last several sessions, and I can't help but think that they enjoy my company. Under a vastly different set of circumstances, I might enjoy hanging out with them too. They seem like blokes I'd meet for drinks at a pub to catch up. Okay, so I understand those would be called *friends*, but it feels odd to see my captors that way.

"Good morning," I parrot, as Honey Eyes leans against the wall in front of me, box still in hand.

"Feel like talking today?"

I only laugh in reply to Digs's inquiry. I've got to give him credit for asking. Although, I'm smart enough to know that he'd kill me the second he got what he thought he needed.

"That's what I thought." Resigned, he holds his hand out to Honey Eyes, who passes him the mystery box.

He takes a knee, his large frame now folding in half so that he's now eye-level with me. He carefully removes the lid to the small box, and I shift forward, peering inside. What I see has my internal excitement meter reaching new heights.

"Is that a yellow fattail scorpion?" I inquire, barely containing my awe. Those incredible, hearty little creatures are hard to come by, and I've never seen one in real life. They're magnificent, if you're into tiny venomous beings with impressive exoskeletons, which I am. Really, I'm into anything with venom and poison pumping through their veins. I feel as if I can relate to those buggers, you know?

Tamping down my buzzing sense of exhilaration, I question, "Can I pet it?"

Digs's head flies up, his blade-colored eyes widening briefly as they meet mine. Just as quickly, his gaze sharpens and narrows as he growls, "No, and if you don't tell me what I want to know, you won't get the antivenom if he stings you."

I roll my eyes dramatically as I sigh. "Of course it's a male. Did you know that female yellow fattails eat their male partners if they don't satisfy them during mateship?" I ask, waggling my eyebrows.

"Uh, no, I didn't know that."

"I do the same thing." I bare my teeth and clash my teeth together a few times in a mock display of biting.

Against the wall, Honey Eyes starts chuckling, his laughter growing louder, and I shoot him a wink. I think he presumes I'm kidding, but I'm sort of not. I really did kill a man once after failing to make me climax. In my defense, he was my target before I ever climbed into bed with him. But his lack of bedroom skills certainly made that elimination more satisfying.

"Lou," Digs chastises on an exhale.

"Yes?"

"Are you going to tell me what I want to know?"

"I think you should refresh my memory. I seem to have forgotten the question since yesterday and the day before that, and the day before that, and the day—"

"We get it," Digs says, cutting me off. "What's the next target?"

Wow, I can't believe the bellend fell for that. I say nothing, my face a mask of blandness.

He doesn't speak as he tilts the box so that the Androctonus shuffles out of his home, his tiny feet dancing across my exposed forearm. The hairs covering the scorpion's legs brush against my own pale olive skin.

Marveling at the little monster the size of my hand as he skitters across my arm, I smile down at him. As arguably the deadliest scorpion, surpassing the Deathstalker in terms of venom, he's a sight to behold.

I won't die today, at least this way. I know this for two reasons. The first being that Digs won't kill me until I tell him what he wants to know. Secondly, because I do not intend to make this little guy crawling around on my body feel threatened in the slightest. I maintain a steady rhythm of breathing, careful not to cause a spike in my heart rate. This scorpion poses no threat to me, and I would rather rip off more of my toenails than hurt him.

I'm not incapable of feeling fear, not by a long shot. I've been in terrifying situations before, but none of those have happened since I've been here. No, to get to me, you'd have to reach my heart, but I cut off all communication with that disastrous, wayward organ within my chest a long time ago. She's dead to me, entombed within its ivory coffin, at least where human beings are concerned. So, this scorpion isn't the danger that these men think he is.

All three of us watch the fattail scorpion fall from my arm to my thigh, thankfully landing on his feet. The room is silent as the miniscule beast pitter-patters over the curves of my thighs that I keep tightly jammed together.

Horror jolts my senses as Digs pulls a lighter from his trousers pocket and flicks it open.

No, no, no.

"Don't hurt him," I rush out to stop him, while feverishly attempting to keep my body's rhythms steady. No way am I going to sit by while I watch him light this little guy on fire. Keeping my gaze on the critter on my lap, I analyze the scorpion's body language, ensuring the hiccup in my pulse isn't setting him off.

Glancing up at Digs, while keeping one eye on the venomous creature, his masked head tilts to the side as he studies me, his expression curious and slightly dubious. I clarify by adding, "Don't hurt him. If you want to hurt me, burn me, watch my skin melt, cut me open and make me bleed, be my fucking guest, but put the scorpion away first."

His expression morphs into one of surprise and mild confusion. "Will you tell me what I want to know?"

I thought this might be a problem; nonetheless, I reply honestly. "Likely not, but that's still no reason to drag an innocent animal into our toxic dynamic."

His face gives nothing away as he stares at me for one, two, three beats. Eventually, he holds out his hand, and Honey Eyes pushes off the wall and once again places the box in Digs's waiting palm. I swear Honey Eyes smiles behind that mask of his, but even if I'm wrong, his eyes certainly beam sunshine. Well, until he winks at me. I don't respond—not with my eyes or otherwise—since I don't want to push my luck.

Digs gently coaxes the golden-colored scorpion back into the box, thank fuck, and shuts the lid, passing it back to Honey Eyes. My body sags, my lungs burning slightly as I release a full breath. Digs grows to his full height, which is mammoth tall, considering that I'm average height for a woman and he towers over me even when I'm on my feet.

His hulking frame marches over to the wall, and he snatches a blowtorch from the shelf. *Oh, fuck me, this is going to hurt like a right bitch.*

I was right. It hurt. Hurt like hell incarnate. I have a gash on the inside of my cheek and laceration on my lower lip to prove that I used and abused my own mouth like it was a leather bit. Leather would be preferable next time. I think I'll be tasting the metallic effects for weeks to come. *Good thing the food here is bland.*

I brought it on myself, though, and I still say it was worth it to save the scorpion.

Slouched on the floor of my newly cleaned cell, I attempt to breathe through my mouth so the smell of my burned flesh won't reach me.

My patience is beginning to fray with my brother and how long it's taking him to pull me out of this place. *"I'll come for you, little sister. Just hold on until I can get there. I'm proud of you, Lou."* My brother's parting words flit back to me as well as the memory of our foreheads pressed together as he held me to him.

Be patient, Louhi, I remind myself.

To pass the time, I close my eyes, filling my mind with pleasant thoughts of my closest friends: competing with—and beating—Viktor for the first time at his newly completed gun range and helping Conall track down a business adversary and eliminating them.

After an indeterminable amount of time lost in happier memories, I recognize the cadence of Digs's marching footfalls through the mostly silent cell block. He appears before my cell a moment later and unlocks my cage, allowing himself access inside. As he crouches before me, a tub of, what I guess, is burn cream is in his hand.

I watch him as he wordlessly grasps my left arm, turning it over gently to reveal the bubbling, angry skin just below my elbow. Wordlessly, he unscrews the lid to the salve and scoops some out with his fingers. His massive hand engulfs my elbow as he holds me firmly to apply the cream expertly.

This is beginning to feel like a bizarre form of aftercare. One I truly don't understand. Isn't the entire point of being imprisoned here to make me break? Why would he take the time to heal me at all? He'd likely be better off letting the infection set in and praying that I'll spill some beans in my delirium.

Not even gangrene could get me to talk, but Digs doesn't know that.

I hiss when he makes contact with my angry flesh, but the cool cream quickly goes to work soothing the irritated burns. After distributing the ointment thoroughly, he applies a dressing to the area, then he screws the lid back on the small tub.

Reaching into his pants pocket, he pulls out a small tube of ointment, dabbing some on the pad of his thumb. His hand moves toward my face and my breath catches in my throat as I realize his intention. I hold my breath as his thumb makes contact with my swollen lip, swiping gently across my split skin. My eyes are locked on his, tracking the way his gaze fastens on my mouth and doesn't let go, like a wolf with a prize in his sight.

The ointment is cool against my warm, irritated skin, soothing it instantly. Digs's touch lingers even after swiping on the balm, making my lip burn for an entirely different reason.

When his thumb releases my lip, I exhale, my breath whooshing out of me as it chases his retreating hand.

"Open," he orders next, his low, gruff voice bouncing off the walls.

"You'd like that, yeah?" I glance away with a snort, desperate for some distance from this man.

He doesn't speak until our eyes meet again, but when he does, his tone is softer, not quite tender, but close. "Come on, I know you ate your cheek for lunch. Let me look."

I wait for the *please,* but it never comes. *Figures.*

Still, there's something almost vulnerable swirling in his gaze, and it's that unguarded glint that has me parting my lips and showing him the inside of my mouth.

"Does it hurt?"

Why does it matter to him? My brow furrows, and I have the urge to scoff, because *obviously, it hurts.* Instead, I lie, shaking my head.

His gaze bores into me for so long that I wonder what he's seeing. With his eyes still on mine, he reaches into his back pocket, producing a small cloth like the gag I had in my mouth when I first woke here. He blinks a few times, like he's clearing his vision, as he shoves it into my hand before stretching to his full height.

Seeming to have eased his conscience enough for him to sleep—probably in a comfortable bed—tonight, he retreats down the hallway.

Digs is a hard guy to try to make sense of. He looks ready to eat me alive, his body nearly vibrating with anticipation and excitement every time he's about to inflict the maximum amount of pain and suffering to my body, yet he looks guilt-ridden and tormented every time he comes to care for my wounds afterward. I've been telling myself that he's been coming here to check on me because I'd be useless to him dead. But maybe that's not it. Maybe he *likes* me.

Sod off, Lou. He does not *like you.*

CHAPTER 9

Sean

Mining for the truth is what I love most about this job. Truth always prevails. Anyone can tell a lie—and most do—but truth is the ultimate hunter, always sniffing out and stalking his next target to take down. Truth is never the victim, never the prey—forever the predator.

That's what I'm thinking about as I grab Louhi's file folder and thumb through it on the rooftop as the sun descends below the horizon, painting the sky in a fiery color palette of burnished marigolds, bright yellows, and blazing reds. The automatic lights switch on as the light fades, flooding the rooftop in additional light.

I haven't read her file in depth yet—yeah, okay, I know I should've read it before now—but I like my subjects to open up to me first. I want to learn their personalities and see what makes them tick for myself. The in-person version always tells me more about someone than the on-paper explanation. That's true in every facet of life, though, not just this in this fucked-up torture prison environment.

As I flip through the contents of this folder, I get the notion that I really should've dug into her background before now. At just twenty-nine—I unknowingly treated her to a birthday gift of fire—this woman has already seen and done some shit.

Based on her reaction to the waterboarding I subjected her to the first time we met, I knew she had training. She was prepared.

In fact, she's seemed unfazed by almost everything I've done, except for my daring to harm the scorpion, which is still baffling to me. I've facilitated an inmate's execution via that yellow fattail before, so imagine my shock when I found myself maneuvering the scorpion back into the box. I never intended to burn the scorpion, but she didn't know that. Her brave, bold reaction to the pain she wrongly assumed I'd inflict on the scorpion only served to confuse me further.

I have no clue how she persuaded me to put the critter back in the box. Maybe it was the panic behind her words, or perhaps it was the way she literally *begged* me to hurt her instead. I'll be honest, I love it when a woman begs—preferably on her knees or on all fours, imploring me to *finally* fuck her—but I've never once been tempted by the pleas of an inmate. Not when they scream or cry, pleading with me to stop.

However, my cock has been warning me about this particular inmate for the last month. I haven't heeded those alarm bells, and now I'm worried I might pay the price.

Turning the page, I read down until I've got a better sense of the mysterious Finnish woman camped out in one of my cells. She's got a slew of crimes under her belt. To name a *few*: terrorism, murder, espionage, kidnapping, arson, destruction of government property via explosive device, cyber-crimes, and possession of biological weapons. *Damn, Lou, what* haven't *you done?*

Some of her crimes date back twelve years, which would mean that she's been a criminal longer than she's been a legal adult, which isn't all that surprising to me. What *is* somewhat unexpected is that she doesn't look anything like the leader of an international terrorist group. She looks like a woman you'd see on the cover of a magazine and think to yourself, *goddamn, she's fucking hot.* Even as dirty as she is right now, she's still a smokeshow. She's definitely got the looks to be a model with her light olive skin, high and defined cheekbones, straight teeth, slightly tilted almond-shaped dark eyes, hair blacker than the color of my assault rifle on the ground beside me, and those luscious, ample lips.

Damn, those perfect vermillion lips. They look so incredible every time they part to spew sass. Admittedly, they'd look better wrapped around my cock as I fuck her pretty face so hard she has tears clearing pathways through the filth covering her face. *Down, boy,* I mentally reprimand my wanting dick, trying to get a grip on myself.

I know next to nothing about Finns, but I know enough to know that Louhi doesn't look like what I assumed was typical of Finnish people, so I flip through the next few pages, scanning for more information on her background. All I find is a small paragraph informing me that she lived in Joensuu, Finland, with her Finnish father, Anton, British mother, Isla, and brother, Mercer, until she was eleven and her parents died in a car wreck. Her brother, who was eight years older than her, became Louhi's guardian and moved them both to the UK, where she lived until seven years ago. At that point, she moved to Boston, where she lived until she became my responsibility in this hellhole.

Unfortunately, this dossier doesn't provide much intelligence on her personal life, except for the tidbit about her having a brother. I wonder if I'll be able to use him to exploit information from her. I make a note to ask Jace about getting our hands on his file, assuming he has one.

Shutting the folder, I light a cigarette in an attempt to clear my head and stare up at the night sky, now sprinkled with bright stars, but I only find myself comparing the glossy shade of the inky night to the lustrous darkness of Louhi.

"I fold," Stuco mutters from beside me, gently laying his cards on the folding table before leaning back in his chair. He always folds. I don't even know why he plays.

Death, taxes, and bi-weekly poker games: the only sure things around here. With not much alternative for hobbies, the twelve of us sit around the table, shooting the shit and gambling away our salaries. The other two dozen men stationed here are on duty, which is why these stupid games are bi-weekly, so everyone gets a turn to lose their money.

"What's the deal with Koskinen?" Borman asks, failing to mask his dubious expression.

"What do you mean?" Jace parries.

"She giving you anything yet?"

"Only screams," I lie, my poker face securely fastened. She might not be screaming for me yet, but she will. One way or another, I'm determined to hear the delicious sound of her agony.

Borman snorts derisively, and I arch an eyebrow at his boldness. "Don't believe me? Ask Marshall," I tell him as I nod in the direction of my best friend.

Wisely choosing not to ask Jace to confirm my statement, he informs me. "Major Thompson is coming by tomorrow, and I'm sure he'll want some answers."

I grind my molars. Max fucking Borman has been an irritating menace since he was assigned here last year. His green eyes fix on me as he runs a hand through his shorn auburn hair.

"Okay," I reply, holding his gaze, not even blinking. He always withers, just like Stuco next to him, folding under the pressure. As I suspect, he looks down at his cards.

Thompson's arrival is less than ideal, but somewhat expected. I don't doubt he thinks that I'll have some information for him.

Although, everyone—including myself—has underestimated the vixen in Cell Eight.

I don't deign to know what would happen to me—or Jace—if we're unsuccessful in extracting information from Louhi, but I can't imagine that it'd be good. At best, it'd be worse than a simple dishonorable discharge. At worst, I'd find myself at the bottom of the Pacific. It's advantageous not to let it get it to that point.

After the game, I crawl into bed, grateful to finally get some sleep tonight. Sleep has always been one of my favorite things to do, though I don't get much of it. I love it. The peaceful world of slumber and dreams. My wicked shadows don't touch me here.

I've just shut my eyes when Jace whispers from the cot to my right, his voice so quiet that it barely reaches me. "Are you *actually* prepared for Thompson's visit tomorrow?"

I grumble an affirmative. I'm not even close to being prepared to tell him I have nothing, but no one needs to know that, even if Jace likely smells my bullshit.

CHAPTER 10

Sean

"You working out with us today?" Jace asks from behind me as I stare at the monitor in front of me, displaying all the cameras in Block One. "It's leg day," he adds.

"I'll join you when I'm done. I've got something to do here," I tell him. Glancing over my shoulder, I find we're still alone in the barracks.

Cocking his head to the side, his dark eyebrows crinkle. "Need help?"

"Just reviewing some footage before Thompson gets here."

He snorts, bending to lace up his sneakers. "More like deleting evidence that you've been taking care of an inmate."

I say nothing, turning back to the cameras. Jace is the only other soldier here with access to the footage, but Thompson would have access here, too, and if he asked to see something, I wouldn't be able to refuse him. While he's never asked to see footage before, I don't want to risk being unprepared.

I'd much rather face the consequences of showing him a tape of deleted footage than the punishment that would come with presenting evidence that I've been tending to the wounds of a prisoner.

Without asking, I know he'd tell me to let the gangrene or infection set in. If it were any other inmate, I'd have no problem with that, but something about Louhi is *different,* which is why I'm skipping the mandatory gym time—yet another thing I could get in trouble for; add it to my tab—to erase the proof of my questionable actions.

"Hey, no shade, man," Jace comments, and I sigh, dropping my forehead into my palms as I lean forward on my elbows.

"She's fucking with me," I grumble.

He huffs, the sound full of mirth. "I think that's just who she is."

Therein lies my problem.

Navigating to yesterday's footage, I scroll through the list of cameras until I find the one that reads: CELL EIGHT. Even if Thompson wasn't coming here today, I'd only have forty-eight hours to erase the footage before it'd get stored on the government's server somewhere.

"I'll meet you in the gym when I finish this."

"You know I'm going to force you into doing an extra set of squats for every one you miss just for making me put up with Borman and Stuco."

I chuckle. "That's fair. Just toss on some Knocked Loose to drown out the sounds of them metaphorically sucking each other's dicks."

He grunts, and I know if I turned around, I'd find a grimace on his face at the prospect of subjecting himself to Knocked Loose. Instead, I keep my eyes fixed on the screen as I appear, opening Louhi's cell.

A second later, the door to the barracks opens, then closes, leaving me with only the past for company. Less than a minute later, the sound of a true throwback seeps under the crack at the bottom of the door as "Monster" by Skillet serenades me from where he blasts it from the gym.

Knocked Loose would be a better choice.

After isolating the time slot where I tend to Lou, I delete the ten-minute chunk of footage, praying that no one will ask about it. It's not the first time I've deleted myself caring for her and, unfortunately, it probably won't be the last—even if I want it to be.

With the weight of that footage lifted from my shoulders, I jump to the active feed, planning to check on all the fuckers in Block One before joining Jace. God knows I don't want to have to do more than one or two extra sets of squats.

Where I expect to see Lou working out, I find her leaning against the back wall of her cell, staring directly into the camera. It feels like she's looking at me, her face cast in shadow, her dark irises seeming to stare into my soul. I can't tell if she's blinking at this distance, but I wouldn't be surprised to learn that the little witch wasn't.

The way she's staring at me is unnerving, sending a chill down my spine, the room suddenly feeling icy.

Moving my curser to the top corner, I'm about to exit out of the feed entirely when Louhi smiles, the expression unlike any I've seen from her before. No, the smile she wears now bleeds seduction, tempting me to watch what she does next.

And I do.

On screen, Lou's hand leisurely glides up her torso, her graceful fingers slipping around the column of her neck. Her touches appear gentle as she caresses her skin, skating down to trace her exposed collarbone with the backs of her fingers.

What the fuck does she think she's doing?

My dick lengthens inside my boxer-briefs as I lean forward on the squeaky swivel chair, swallowing thickly as her other hand comes up to squeeze her breast through her uniform top.

Oh, fuck.

Rubbing at my jaw, I tell myself that I shouldn't be watching this. Anyone could walk in and catch me.

She likes to fuck with me, and Jace was spot on when he said that's just who she is, so is that what's going on here?

Or is she just horny and bored?

Like I'm the King Cobra and she the snake charmer, I watch, transfixed, as she slips her hand into the waistband of her black uniform pants. I suck in a breath and hold it when she promptly removes her hand, sucking her middle finger into her mouth.

My cock jumps, and I grit my teeth to mute my groan, begging myself to shut this down, to turn off the monitor and walk the fuck away from this woman. Nothing—*absolutely nothing*—good can come of this.

Her lips part, her eyes still fixed on the camera as she swirls her tongue around the digit, sliding the pad of her finger deeper into her mouth.

My balls begin to throb as she clamps her mouth down again before releasing her finger with what's surely an audible *pop*, and I'm suddenly wishing that these damn cameras captured audio.

I'd do anything to hear the sounds she makes. Is she a moaner? Or does she save her sounds for herself, bottling them up for her own pleasure?

As elegantly as moving water, her hands float to her waist, hooking her fingers into the elastic of her pants, shedding them. She tosses the black fabric at the bars, as if someone were there to catch them, but there's no one—only the camera. *Only me.*

Then, like a spring flower opening up after a long winter, she spreads her legs.

I'm surely looking at the devil, the serpent offering me the forbidden apple in the form of her ripe, juicy cunt on display.

Even in the dim, minimal light, her pussy glistens like a shiny diamond in the depths of a mine.

Glancing at the door, ensuring I'm still alone, I palm myself over the outside of my pants. I was hoping it'd alleviate some of the discomfort, but I only seem to be making it worse as my dick spasms. It doesn't help that Lou slips in her middle finger, slowly beginning to fuck herself on the screen.

A groan climbs up my throat, but I trap it in my mouth before it can escape.

This woman is wrecking me.

Her finger disappears inside of her as her movements grow in tempo and depth with each passing moment, shifting from languid and teasing to wild, more frantic thrusts as she fucks herself in earnest. Her free hand seems to squeeze her neck gently before moving down between her legs, circling her clit.

And here I thought this place was Hell. Turns out, Louhi is the personification, and I seem to have booked a one-way ticket.

Hurtling toward release, frenzied and feverish, her back bows against the concrete. I'm in fucking agony by the time her feet arch, toes scrunching as she scrambles for purchase on the smooth, dirty floor of her cell. The sound of my own ragged breaths fills the barracks as her sexy lips part, her mouth dropping open.

Is she crying out? Making noise?

The moment that thought zips through my mind, Louhi's mouth curls around a word, forming an obvious sound.

Not a sound.

A name.

My name.

Stunned, my hand squeezing the hard bulge at my crotch, I hit rewind, watching her cry out my name again. Then again. Exhausting the rewind button before she licks her fingers clean and shoots a wink at the camera.

After quickly erasing the performance she just put on, my heart pounding in my ears, I grab a clean uniform and storm out of the barracks. Resigning myself to a heinous make-up workout, I bypass the gym and head straight for a shower, where I can replay everything in my mind's eye with my hand wrapped tightly around my cock.

"What have you got for me, Diggory?" Major Thompson asks as I stand before him in the small, pathetic office, my arms clasped behind my back with my mask bunched in my fist.

Louhi's earlier cameo as a cam-girl still spins like a vinyl record in my brain. I can't, for the life of me, figure out what her game was with that. What I do know is that I want to see that cunt again. I want to hear her say my name. I want to take a bite of that apple she tempted me with.

With a confidence I don't possess at the moment, I reply, "She's going to break for me, sir."

"But she hasn't yet?" His eyes narrow, the lines around them crinkling like old wax paper.

"Not yet, sir." I keep my face a stoic mask of impassivity, unperturbed on my face.

"How long until you can get some answers for me?"

"Do I still have another four months?" I skirt around his question delicately, because if there's one thing I've learned about Lou, it's that she's unpredictable—as evidenced by the private show she put on for me earlier. *But did she know it was me watching? Or did she think someone else would see her?*

I've never seen her get off before while reviewing the footage, but what if I missed something?

No, no, that can't be right. I'm confident I didn't miss anything. This had to have been the first time she's done that.

My thoughts are a mess as I try to sort out what I saw on the camera today, but I need to pull my shit together. Louhi's hourglass is running out…and so is mine.

There's no telling when I'll get answers from her—could be tomorrow—but it's looking more and more like *never* is more realistic.

"Yes, but the sooner the better. We *need* the intel."

"I'm on it, sir," I assure him.

"You better be. It won't be good for *anyone* if we don't get what we need from her. Do you understand?"

Loud and clear.

"Yes, sir," I reply succinctly. It's abundantly clear by the way he says the word "anyone," that *I'm* the one who will suffer the consequences should I fail.

It's time to take things up a notch, Lou.

CHAPTER 11

Sean

"BATH TIME," I GRUNT FROM THE OTHER SIDE OF LOUHI'S cage door. She shoves off the back wall of her cell and shuffles toward the barred entrance just as I swing open her door. Coming to a stop before me, she folds her arms below her plump breasts, jutting them upward. Her eyes trace my body as she looks me up and down before arching an eyebrow at my masked face. I'm certain she's just taken stock of the absence of my rifle, but the presence of my Glock and tactical knives still strapped to me. She never seems to miss a damn thing.

"Does this bath happen to include a clawfoot tub, an endless supply of hot water, loads of foaming bubbles, and maybe a bath bomb? Oh, and wine, please tell me there's wine."

A snort threatens to escape, but I glare at her instead, locking onto her eyes the color of the bark on a pine tree. I jerk my head in the direction of the mouth of the cell block where Jace and Stuco wait for us. Her keen gaze slides in their direction, assessing the situation.

I've been waiting for the moment when she untethers her self-restraint, but that's yet to happen. If Thompson's warning is to be believed, this woman could take me on without a problem. *So, what's stopping her?*

Most inmates thrash and fight like hell is nipping at their heels—in a way, it is—when they arrive here, pitching all manners of fits, but not Lou. Lou's maintained a surprising level of decorum and restraint, and I wonder what it'll take for her to show her teeth.

Stepping into the hallway, she glances back at me. "Just so I'm aware going forward, what *is* the bath schedule? I didn't see it mentioned in the welcome packet."

Again, I stifle the huff of laughter, but I don't bother to stop the roll of my eyes since she's now walking in front of me.

As we pass Samuel's cell, he leers at her, and my fists clench at my sides. He's in here for being one of the most prolific cyber terrorists the western world has seen. Like Louhi, he's given us a few answers, but I still like to torture him for the hell of it sometimes. Louhi sticks her tongue out at him, and I mentally admonish her for it. It's not a good idea to get on Samuel's radar, but it's still not as bad as ending up on Kazi's. That fucker is the one most likely to find a way to break out of his steel-enforced cell like a starving animal and rape her. Planning ahead, I had Borman take Kazi to the playpen for a session before I collected Lou.

When we reach my counterparts, the two men lead us down the hallway and toward the shower room. The inmates don't get showers very often here, but when they do, they all have to be escorted and monitored the entire time. Fucking tedious.

As we reach our destination, Stuco and Jace take up their posts outside the door, and I usher Louhi inside, shutting the thick metal door behind us.

I had the shower room prepped for her ahead of time so that a fresh uniform waits for her on a bench next to a clean, but dingy towel. The shower stalls in here aren't enclosed, so I watch as she reaches inside and flips on the water, letting it heat up. She's lucky I'm not feeling like being a complete dickwad today and allowed her the use of the hot water. Alright, it's not *hot*, per se, but it's not cold. I'm rarely this generous, and I curse myself for going soft.

Leaning against the wall, I survey the scene before me. Louhi wastes no time stripping out of her dirty clothes, tossing them in a pile on the floor, and in the light of day, she's even sexier than she was on screen. When she's bared before me, she tosses me a coquettish wink, her expression dripping in sin. *Fuck me.*

She steps into the stall, the spray from the showerhead drenching her instantly. Her head tilts back and her eyes close as the meager spray cascades down her body. She has a lone tattoo: a delicate black snake that slithers and winds itself along her left side. Halfway up her ribcage, the serpent coils around her breast, its head placed just over her heart, baring its fangs in a clear attack. I have a hard time pulling my eyes from the mesmerizing artwork. It looks so incredibly lifelike.

Eventually, she begins soaping herself down. My eyes are glued to that tiny bar of soap as it glides over her skin, leaving a trail of sudsy bubbles behind that the water whisks away. *What I would give to be that bar of soap.*

The soap skims over her calves, ankles, then feet. "Do you wash your legs and feet?" she asks, never glancing in my direction.

"What?" I grunt, confused as all fuck.

"You know, do you *actually* wash your lower body, or are you one of those heathens who lets the soap just slide down your torso as you rinse?"

"Who the fuck does that?" I reply, keeping my gaze hard and cool, like granite. *Of course I wash my goddamn body.*

She shrugs, the bone in her shoulder moving, my eyes tracking the movement as I resist the urge to run my tongue along the osseous matter hidden beneath her skin. "I should've known that would never be you. I bet you wash every inch of yourself...thoroughly, not leaving a single speck of your skin untouched."

She is *not* working to alleviate my raging erection whatsoever, and I have to assume that's intentional. Fuck, this woman is a handful.

An incredibly hot handful, my brain supplies rather unhelpfully.

I stay rooted to the spot, my arms crossed over my chest, my jaw ticking behind my mask. Fuck, she really is beautiful. Her proud nipples stand at attention as she runs the soap over them. She glances my way as she gives them a little squeeze, nibbling on her full bottom lip. Holding my gaze, she slides the fucking soap lower, lower, lower through the smattering of bald skin, and settles the soap between her legs. I kind of want to ask how she's managed not to grow any hair, but I don't. It's none of my business and *I don't care.* Instead, I grind my teeth and attempt to tether myself to this spot against the wall. *Do. Not. Move,* I tell myself.

"I'd say that you can look, but not touch, but we seem to be past that now that you have my toenails in your possession," she taunts, wiggling her toes dramatically.

Her tantalization is all it takes to snap my weak, pathetic tether in half, and I launch myself at her. Grabbing her by the throat, I shove her against the tiled shower wall, ignoring the way the water soaks my clothes.

She can't see through my mask, but I'm snarling as I growl, "That's where you're wrong, Lou. This place is mine, and I do what I want within these walls. If I want to touch, I will."

Her pulse spikes beneath my thumb, and I tighten my grip as I cup her sex with my free hand. Before she can see it coming, I pull my hand back and slap her pussy. *Hard.*

She gasps, but her mouth quickly spreads into a wide, feral grin. It's a smile that *begs* me to kiss it, fill it with my cock, and fuck it.

She's still grinning when I release her and march back to my post against the wall, not caring about the water falling from my clothes in fat drops and pooling on the floor beneath me.

My eyes narrow on her still standing where I shoved her against the wall as I bite out a command. "Hurry up."

Louhi bites her lower lip again, slowly moving back

underneath the spray. I'm halfway surprised that she hasn't complained about the lack of amenities, but she hasn't said a word. She works the bar of soap into a lather and attempts to wash her jet-black hair. Seeing as she's the first female prisoner we've had here, it's not as if we have girl shit—not that we'd let her use it if we had it.

Thinking about 'girl shit' leads me to making a mental note to talk to Jace later about the fact that she's been here a whole month and, to my knowledge, hasn't bled. I have a sister, so I know that should've happened already. *Right?* I swear to heaven and hell that she better not be pregnant. I don't know much about menstruation, but she's too young to have already gone through menopause, so what's the alternative?

Zeroing in on her stomach, she doesn't *look* pregnant, the skin and muscle toned and taut, her abs on display as she moves the soap over herself.

Maybe she's on some kind of birth control or something? That's probably the more logical explanation. I could call Callie and ask her about this. Ah, fuck that, I'd rather just search online. I am *not* talking to my sister about birth control methods.

She rinses her hair free of the suds and shuts off the water before dragging the towel over her body, drying off and wrapping her shoulder-length hair into the towel. After donning the clean clothes, she looks at me and audaciously snaps, "What about brushing my teeth?"

I pull a brand-new pre-pasted toothbrush from my pocket and pass it to her. I'm not a *total* Neanderthal—I am, but that's not the point. Of course, I planned to let her brush her teeth. It's been nearly six weeks since she got here and this is the first time she's been to use the washroom, so letting her brush her teeth seemed like the half-decent thing to do.

When she's finished, I hold my hand out for both the trash and the toothbrush. No way am I letting her leave with that. Just because she hasn't tried anything yet, doesn't mean I don't think she will.

She slaps the toothbrush into my palm as she asks, "Have you got a comb?"

I show no emotion as I pull the comb I spent far too long digging around for this afternoon from my pocket and pass it to her.

Taking it from me, she unwraps the towel from around her head, moving to stand in front of the lone mirror on the adjacent wall. I watch her make a face as she takes in her appearance in the mirror. I wonder what she sees, what she's thinking, but her expression quickly morphs back into one that's inscrutable and emotionless.

Thankfully, she makes hasty work of combing out her hair. Something tells me that this woman would take *forever* to get ready for a night out, though.

Once again, she smacks the comb back into my hand at the same time that her lips quirk into a smile drenched in impertinence. My patience wanes. *Does she have no regard for her own life?*

I've never been particularly tolerant of disrespect, but even less so now. The men in my unit know better than to talk back to me or question my authority. My word is law, with no one daring to push me. But this girl? She's done nothing but crawl beneath my skin like an incurable rash, festering and itching, persisting no matter how hard I try to throw her from my mind.

"Time to go," I grumble as I reach for the door, but Lou slides past me, brushing her long, slender fingers over my crotch—which has been harder than the concrete walls of this prison since we walked in the washroom. Halting her movements, I grab her delicate wrist, my fist swallowing it entirely.

I glare down at her, but she purrs, "It turns out that camouflage can't hide a hard-on."

The only thing worse than what she told me was the way her delicate fingers felt grazing the fabric of my pants.

Fuck me. This woman is going to be the death of me.

She swings open the door before I can reply and struts back down the hallway, Stuco hastening to catch up to her. Jace's eyes track down my entire body, and when they reach my face, he states the obvious. "You're wet."

"No shit," I mutter before stalking after Stuco and Louhi, Jace on my heels.

CHAPTER 12

Louhi

As soon as I arrive back at my cell, I notice how clean it is. Okay, *clean* isn't the right word. I should say it's *less disgusting*. The waste has been removed, and it appears that some kind of disinfectant has been haphazardly splashed around the space.

Once I'm locked inside the cage, I brace my forearms on the cold metal bars and stare at the three men, my lips tipping up into a smile. It's not the same smile I gave Digs earlier, but it still reeks of danger…and other fun things.

Like that shower.

Taunting and teasing Digs is quickly becoming my favorite sport: pushing him to the brink so that his control is stretched so thin that it could snap at any moment.

I suppose that's the reason I spread my legs for the camera, too. Well, that was a bit for me as well, though an exhibitionism kink would be new. I can add it to the list behind my new mask and fuck-with-Digs kinks.

I also admit that there's an element or two of Digs's cracked restraint that I didn't anticipate being quite so fond of, like the way his large hand wrapped around the column of my throat. And the way his dirty words hit me squarely between the legs.

"Do you think I could request a turndown service? It'd be lovely to have those little chocolates placed on my pillow in the evenings."

No one responds, and the shortest of the three men turns and leaves me alone with Honey Eyes and Digs. A minute later, black metal with a wicked bass blares through the cell's speakers. Yesterday, they played only death metal, so I appreciate the slight variation today. Fuck, I hope I'm still a fan of metal when this is all over. *That'd be a crushing blow.*

A smile inches over my face as I ask the two remaining men, "Are you taking song requests? Because I'd love to hear anything by Insomnium or Wolves In The Throne Room. I wouldn't mind some Slaughter to Prevail either. *Ooh,* I could even go for something by Orbit Culture. I bloody love those guys."

Digs glares daggers at me, not the least bit entertained by my antics. Huffing, he turns on his booted heel and stomps away. My smile grows when I see that I've gotten to him, even if I was serious. It's not as if I don't have the cash to throw at the juke box in this hellhole.

Honey Eyes shakes his masked head, and I swear he's trying not to laugh at my antics. "I think the poor sod likes me," I inform him, to which he only snorts in response, but hey, he still acknowledged me.

After Honey Eyes leaves, I retreat to my usual corner and sink to the floor, my knees pulled to my chest. At least my cell and I are both clean. That's something. I didn't think I'd get a bath at all, so I'll count this as a win.

I let my head fall back against the wall behind me and close my eyes, but as soon as I do, Digs's behavior from the washroom floods back into my mind. The primal look in his eyes spoke to my own inner animal, and the serpent living within me preened in response. She's been *dying* to be released from captivity, and it appears that Diggory's inner beast is rattling his cage door as well.

There's a piercing shrill scream from down the hall, and I can tell it's coming from one of the other cells in this block. Unfortunately for me, the inmate's screams are the only source of music this evening, and I'm starting to get more than a little irritated.

By the time Honey Eyes brings me my breakfast the following morning, my inner predator is rattling the bars of her enclosure, anxious for release. She's hungry, and I want to let her feed. The bellend down the hall spent all bloody night bellowing, and I'm primed to commit murder this fine day. *Patience be damned.*

"Want me to shut him up?" I drawl lazily when the soldier slides my food tray through the slot, just as there's another scream from down the hallway.

He only inclines his head in question, so I elaborate in a sugary sing-song voice, "We both know you want to."

The inmate wails again, and I roll my eyes, knowing I won't be able to get my hands dirty. Annoyance isn't enough to break me, not by a long shot, but it's been *so* long since I felt the sticky warmth of blood between my fingers, and I'm dying to treat myself. I miss seeing the light fade from the eyes of my marks. I miss the smug satisfaction that roils through me at knowing I'm the one who stole their life.

Honey Eyes just shakes his head in defeat, but changes the subject, saying, "Eat fast. You've got somewhere to be."

Interesting. Just as I'm about to ask some questions, he stalks away, but down the hallway, I hear him growl, "Shut the fuck up, Carlos, or I'll do it for you."

I smile proudly to myself as I dig into my meal of mush with my hands. No matter how many times I do this, I never seem to stop *loathing* eating with my hands.

After I'm done, I shove the tray back out to the middle of the hallway, watching the resident rodents pick at my leftovers, as is my routine, and a few minutes later, Honey Eyes returns with two more men—the one called Davis, I think, and the short guard from yesterday.

They usher me down the hall, but instead of turning right at the mouth of the cell block, we go left. I follow them past the entrance to two more cell blocks and another few doors on the right side of the concrete passageway. We come to a stop before a metal door on the right, halfway down the long corridor.

Davis opens the door to reveal an infirmary. My hackles rise, and I hesitate for a moment at the door when Honey Eyes comes up behind me and gives me a gentle push. It's not a violent shove, but it's enough to remind me that I don't really have a choice about whether I want to enter. My mood shifts from the annoyance I experienced earlier to something far darker and more menacing.

I haven't been inside this room, yet I already hate it with its sterile white walls and antiseptic smell. Three metal cots on wheels line the wall to my left. There's a long counter stretching the entire length of the wall across from the beds, with cabinets above and below. Jars of who-bloody-knows-what line part of the counter next to a sink.

Suddenly, Digs and another tall, slender man in military uniform step through the double doors on the opposite wall from me. A white lab coat covers much of the masked newcomer's uniform. But his brown eyes shine with something harrowing and cold, making my spine prickle.

As the men approach me, I grit my teeth, willing myself not to retreat. Focusing on my breathing, I attempt to maintain my composure so that they don't discover just how uncomfortable I am. Inside, my panic threatens to bust open at the poorly sewn seams, and I know I'm only moments away from losing the control I wield over it.

Digs jerks his head toward the double doors, and I assume he thinks I'll follow him willingly, like the demure little puppy dog I've—somewhat—pretended to be thus far, but not this time. No fucking way. Not with the *pilu* standing beside him with icy danger lurking in the shallow depths of his gaze.

When I don't make a move, my bare feet staying cemented to this spot, Digs turns around and glares at me. When I return the look, he narrows his eyes further and marches right up to me, wrapping his fist around my forearm to tug me along. I wrench my arm from his grip brutally as I stand my ground.

His blue-grey eyes turn to thunderclouds, promising me a violent storm, but my resolution knows no bounds. I will *not* be poked and prodded like a lab rat. I will *not* become a specimen. It's not the drugs they will undoubtedly pump me full of that I'm wary of, it's the idea of this cruel-looking wanker putting his fingers on my skin. It's this room. It's the reminders of less savory moments from my past. It's the memory of how I became the dangerous nightmare lurking in the dark.

Digs nods at the short guard to my right and the gormless berk attempts to put me in a headlock. Seriously? *A headlock?* His lack of decent judgment is my gain, though. I tilt my head down and bite on the soft skin of the underside of his beefy forearm. He howls, but I bite until I taste his blood and sink my teeth in deeper; his skin and the muscle beneath giving way, and I smile to myself. The guard's shrieks are a song I'll be dancing to long after this is over.

Another set of hands is on me—probably Honey Eyes's—but I ignore them as I release the soldier's arm. Looking directly at Digs, I smile broadly, my mouth dripping with blood and pure savagery. Before I can catch his reaction, the shorter soldier, still gripping his arm, steps in front of me with a look of vengeance in his eyes. *Don't do it.*

He doesn't heed my silent warning and lunges at me. This seems like a good time to show them exactly what I'm capable of.

Sorry, Mercer, I couldn't behave. I tried, sort of.

When he gets close enough, I reach out my shackled wrists

and swiftly slide his tactical knife from its holster at his hip. It's no surprise that he doesn't feel me remove it in his revenge-filled haze.

He just keeps coming, and I pull my hands up at the same time he wraps a hand around my throat, but it's too late. I've already buried the knife in his chest. Right into the soft, fist-sized organ that distributes his lifeblood. His eyes go wide as he stares into my face. I watch as the spark of life dims and extinguishes altogether. Then, I twist the knife before pulling it out of his chest.

What happens next is a blur. He falls to the ground, the knife wrenched from my beautifully scarlet-painted hands, and an onslaught of foreign hands are all over me. Digs's masked face is the last thing I see before a needle pierces the muscle of my shoulder, sending me into black nothingness.

CHAPTER 13

Louhi

When I come to, I'm strapped to a metal medical table. Out of my periphery, I can see Honey Eyes and Digs murmuring against the wall to my left. I hear the clanking sound of metal on metal, and I try to lift my head to see where it's coming from and, more importantly, *who* is making the sound, but I can't move. When I make another attempt, I'm met with the same inability. I can't even wiggle my fingers. I'm paralyzed. Despite whatever drug is flowing through my blood, I can still feel straps digging into my skin, securing me to the table. *Vittu. Fuck.*

Suddenly, cool metal skitters across my shin and ascends higher and higher, gliding up toward my thigh. Cool air kisses my skin, and I realize with horror that my clothes are being removed. Curses in both English and Finnish—even some in Irish—spew from my lips. I try to buck and thrash, but my body won't cooperate.

The scraps of my trousers are pulled from me and the metal scissors remove my top and bare me to the room. A second later, the doctor from earlier enters my periphery and places the bell of a stethoscope on my chest. I hope he can *hear* the ire and barbaric rage being pumped out of my heart and into my veins. I hope he can *hear* the sound of his impending death, because I *will* kill him. *He's a walking dead man.*

I won't deny it to myself anymore: I'm scared—bloody terrified. Being in the infirmary with this strange man's hands on me, I'm flooded with the feeling. I've never liked hospitals, and I like doctors even less. I didn't like them when they came out and told Mercer and I that our parents were dead. I didn't care for them when they told me at seventeen that I'd never be able to have children, and I bloody well hated them when I underwent that surgery from hell.

Mercer, you're getting the arse-kicking of the century when I see you. He'd have to swoop in on a white horse *right now* to save me from this, and that's not happening. I'm on my own, but I can do this. I can handle this. This will not destroy me.

Another curse leaps from my lips in a feeble attempt to revolt despite not being able to move as gloved hands roam over my exposed body, squeezing and kneading as he examines and scrutinizes me.

I will live through this. I am strong. I've survived worse. I don't know how many times I repeat this mantra to myself, but the affirmations aren't working the way they normally do. Something cold and hard prods at my entrance and horror surges through me as I identify the telltale feeling of a speculum sliding between my spread legs.

I'm not able to fixate on that, though, when there's a sudden pinch at my cervix. My breaths are coming shorter and more forcefully now. I need to calm down.

Silencing my muttered curses, I mentally take myself somewhere I rarely go before the panic gripping me roots itself.

The heavenly scent of freshly baked bread permeates the kitchen of our cozy home. I flounce around the space, getting underfoot, as soft music plays.

My mother bends as she pulls the loaf from her opulent navy-blue and gold oven and wipes her hands on her apron before she reaches around and unties the bow at the small of her back. She folds the cotton apron and places it on the counter before turning in my direction. Her long dark blonde hair swishes around her face and she tosses it over a shoulder as he squats down to my seven-year-old level, the skirt of her brown and white dress pooling around her ankles.

"Can we dance, Äiti?"

She smiles, the gesture softening her already delicate features. She rights herself and turns up the music, the vintage love ballad now filling the space. Her smile is bright as she takes my hands and dances with me to the beat. I mirror her grin and giggle as she spins me out and back. I bounce on the balls of my small feet as we both laugh and belt out the words to Frank Sinatra's "The Way You Look Tonight."

Since my mother is a fan, I've grown up listening to all the Big Band classics. The Frank Sinatra dance parties we have are easily my favorite way I spend time with her. She beams down at me now, her brown eyes shining brightly.

"You look happy, Äiti."

Her nose crinkles and the lines around her eyes become more prominent as her refulgent smile somehow glows more radiantly. Her English accent is thick as she replies, "I am, my love. You make me happy."

She spins me again and my feet pitter across the wooden floor. When I whirl back into her lithe, slender body, I ask, "Does Mercer make you happy too?"

"Of course, he does."

"What about Isä?"

"Daddy makes me very happy too, Louhi."

We belt out the remainder of the song together, and when it's over, she tells me, "Loving your dad feels like the sun shining on the coldest day of the year. This world is a cold, dark place, and he makes it warm and light for me." She crouches down, the flecks of gold in her brown eyes glinting in the late afternoon sunlight that peeks through the window above the sink. Her gaze is intense, but full of affection as she continues. "Someday, I pray you find your own warmth in a man—or woman, whatever you prefer, my love—and I hope they love you the way I love your father."

My brow furrows as concern ripples through me. "What if I don't?"

She swipes a rogue strand of my black hair from my face and tucks it behind my ear as she responds, "You are strong, Louhi. Always find solace, power, and love within yourself. You need no one but yourself. You are a treasure. Recognize that within yourself and the world will see it too. You don't need a man for any of that; he's only a bonus. But if you find him, he'll simply enhance your shine. The love he has for you should be so brilliant that when you see it reflected back, you're nearly blinded by it. Every day should end brighter than it started with a man that loves you."

She scoops me up then, setting me on the countertop, my bare feet dangling off the edge as she slices into the warm bread.

When I come out of the haze of the memory, my cheeks are wet from crying, and I'm sprawled out on the floor of my cell. I look down and see that I'm wearing a new black prison uniform, and it's then that I notice that I've regained movement. I test things by making a fist. It's weak, but the ability to move is there. *Thank fuck.*

I don't immerse myself in that memory often since the feelings of sadness and grief are so powerful, they border on overwhelming. However, I needed it today. I needed to reach back and hold on to the joy and love I felt back then.

Gingerly, I wipe at my damp face and internally cringe at the knowledge that those men saw me cry. I'm not a big crier, but thinking of that day I spent with my mum prompted the action.

I miss her. I miss my dad too. And fuck it, I miss Mercer, despite him being the arsehole that sent me here in the first place. He rescued me when my parents were taken from us, and if torture is the price of that, I'll willingly pay.

Slowly sitting, I lift the hem of my shirt over my head. When I'm naked from the waist up, I inspect my skin for evidence of what was done to me. A voice in the back of my mind reminds me that I should've been cognizant of what was happening to me while I was on that table, but I couldn't do it. It was too much.

I find affirmation of needle pricks in the crook of both elbows, but nothing else. I already feel mild cramping in my lower abdomen from that harrowing gynecological exam, and I pull my trousers down to see if I can find anything else. I don't.

When I'm fully dressed again, I slump against the wall and allow one more tear to escape. An impending sense of despair knocks on the door of my mind, begging to creep inside, but I lock away those thoughts, manning my mental fortress once again. The tear tracking down my face is the last one I'll let fall.

I followed my mother's instructions to the letter. I learned to love myself, found my power and recognized myself for the treasure that I am, then became more than just a treasure. I became a treasured weapon.

CHAPTER 14

Sean

"SHE DOESN'T HAVE A UTERUS."

I narrow my eyes on Jones as he explains his findings from the exam he performed. "What do you mean, 'she doesn't have a uterus?'"

He stares at me flatly as he answers, "Exactly what I said. There's no uterus. It's gone."

"Why?"

"I can't answer that, but I suspect that the likely explanation was removed, along with her uterus. You'd have to ask her about it."

Jace scoffs from where he's stationed next to me in the infirmary. He knows as well as I do that Louhi won't tell us shit.

"Did you find—or not find—anything else?"

He shakes his head. "She's healthy, all things considered."

I mutter a thanks, and he leaves us alone. Jace tugs off his mask, and I replicate the action. My friend leans against the metal table that Louhi was strapped to just a few minutes ago, crossing his brawny arms over his chest.

"So, what are we going to do about the hellcat in Eight?"

I blow out a heavy breath. There's no denying that Lou's been a problem today. A huge fucking problem, to be precise.

She killed Stuco. She stabbed him in the chest as if that meant nothing to her. But that's not what sent a chill down my spine. No, it was the minacious smile she gave me when our eyes locked. Her expression told me that she'd love to do it again.

The look on her face as she woke up on the table is haunting me. Sure, I was across the room, but the room is small, and I could easily make out the violence and terror swirling in her dark eyes as she attempted to combat the drugs in her system. She was afraid. I hadn't seen that look on her face before. There wasn't a trace of it when I practically drowned her. It wasn't there when the scorpion tiptoed over her. It was even absent when I torched her alabaster skin.

But there was something about this experience that frightened her, and I'm determined to learn what it was. Was it the fact that she was naked and exposed? Or maybe it was the fact that she was restrained and paralyzed, even temporarily? Or was it Jones and his examination?

"We're going to experiment, Jace."

I'm bent over the computer with headphones in as I watch Louhi on the monitor. I've gotten in this disgusting habit of watching her whenever I can. I can't resist the temptation to see what she's up to. Mostly, it's boring. She's either working out, reciting song lyrics, or talking through the process of baking fucking bread. Today is different, though.

I rewound the tape to see what she's been up to since Jace and Vincent took her catatonic body back to her cell. She was still unreachable in the same way she was when I removed her toenails. I've never seen a prisoner check out for that long before, and I find that fascinating.

She swipes at her face. Fuck, is she *crying*? Why? Did Jones hurt her? I'm still attempting to decipher the meaning of her tears when she begins to undress and inspect her body. Does she truly not know what was done to her? Damn, she must've *really* gone elsewhere in her mind.

Something bumps my shoulder, and I turn to find Jace. Pulling the headphones off, I look up at him from where I'm sitting.

"Chopper is five minutes out. You sure you don't want me to stay?"

"Nah, man. You should take your leave."

He nods, and I give him a note to pass to my mother, when he inevitably sees her. There's nothing but the usual shit in the letter, but it will make her happy and that's all I ever want for my mom. She deserves a better son than me. At least she has Callie.

Jace nods and stalks out the door, leaving me alone in the barracks. I'm about to resume the video, when a loud crash from down the hall echoes against the concrete. Quickly, I exit out of the camera feed and rush toward the sound.

The first thing I notice is the overturned folding table in the middle of the room, a toppled chair adjacent and Borman towering over it, his breathing heavy and his fists clenched at his sides. Jones and Davis stand across from him.

Dammit, they must've told him about Stuco.

"I'm going to *kill* her," Borman snarls as he picks up a chair to hurl at what, I don't know.

Stuco and Borman were tight. Probably as close as me and Jace. I'd be rioting if something happened to Jace and certainly something as violent and senseless as the way Stuco died. But he was foolish, reckless. Louhi became a caged animal the second she stepped into the infirmary. I should've done a better job of securing her the moment I noticed that something was off. That's on me. His death is on my shoulders, and that's a burden I'll carry with me every day. I've already added it to the invisible pack strapped to my back, weighing me down.

I step in front of the snarling soldier, getting in his face. "Stand the fuck down, Borman."

The vein in his neck protrudes, pulsing in time with his ire, and his chest heaves with uneven, ragged breaths as his body practically vibrates. His eyes flare with enmity, and while I fucking get it, destroying government property isn't going to help anyone. He must come to that conclusion too, because he tosses the chair aside and marches from the room, with Jones following him. Better him than me. I'm not good with feelings.

"What the hell happened? I told you to wait for me and that I'd tell him," I gripe at Davis.

He wears a hangdog expression, knowing he and Jones went against my order. I wait far longer than I should to receive an answer, but eventually, Davis utters, "He knew something was up when Stuco didn't come back with us, and he asked us point blank. We couldn't lie to him."

"You should've had him come to me." I stretch my neck from side to side, attempting to quell my ever-mounting stress, before sighing. "I'll deal with you three later. For now, go get Peter from Block Three and take him to the playpen."

He nods and scurries away to obey my order—this time. Peter is one of my favorite prisoners to toy with. He's a pedophile and trafficker. I've already gleaned all the information I can from him, but he always screams so pleasantly, and I'm in the mood to wreak some havoc.

I didn't kill Peter; however, I thought about it. I thought about it the entire time I was strategically breaking the various bones in his hands. I thought about it while he screamed for mercy. I thought about it when he pissed himself. In fact, I'm still thinking about it, even now, as I lie in bed. The only thing that stopped me was the knowledge that I wouldn't be able to fuck him up again. Playtime with Peter would be over. I'd end his suffering. I'd complete his life cycle. I'm not ready for that.

Unlike what was evidenced on Lou's face this morning, I don't enjoy killing anyone, only inflicting the maximum amount of pain and torture. I live for the sound of my victim's screams, the way it fills the time and space around me. Like a vacuum, I'm sucked into their anguish. But I don't share in their agony, nor do I feel an ounce of remorse. Yeah, I know that's fucked up. *I'm* fucked up. Some might even call me a sadist, and those people would be one hundred and ten percent correct. I more than enjoy my job. I derive pleasure from knowing someone is suffering by my hand. I *like* hurting people. Their terror, unwillingness, and hurt excite me.

The second I step foot in the playpen, I shred all traces of empathy, like removing a heavy coat in a warm room. I can still empathize with others when I'm not in *that* headspace, although I typically have to work a little harder to get in touch with the more *human* side of myself. But it's there. The dark part is always easier to tap into. It's almost like a split personality, except that it isn't. I've had that checked with a non-army therapist.

When Jace and I were still Special Forces, our unit was deployed on a mission that went south and tragically ended with three guys in boxes draped with American flags. As a result, the army ordered the rest of us to see a shrink. It was in one of those sessions that the therapist stumbled upon my darker desires—desires I'd never breathed to life before, no matter how much I wanted to—and she's the one who threw out the "sadist" label. After that, I stopped sharing my thoughts with her and she never learned another goddamn thing about me, but the damage had been done.

I think I knew I was a sadist before she ever tossed out the term. How else do you explain that I got harder than concrete any time I'd pinch a woman's nipple a little too hard, causing her to yelp in pain? Or the fact that nearly every fantasy I'd ever had consisted of me hurting a woman…and *liking* it?

However, once that damned word was swimming in my brain, it became difficult to pretend that regular, plain sex would do it for me anymore. As the impulse to hurt the women I was fucking became all-consuming, the frequency with which I got laid slowed significantly. Now, I only have sporadic sex, and when I do, I exhaust myself trying to shut down my dark urges.

The scariest part is that it went beyond sex. I wanted to hurt people, see how far I could push them before they cried, begging me to stop.

I mentally fought that diagnosis for a long time, denying the sadist part of myself. After all, I'd never once acted on those impulses, and I was surviving just fine. *Right?*

I wasn't a bad guy, and I never wanted to become someone's worst nightmare. Shit, I was Special Forces, defending America against Her enemies.

At least that was the case until the army saw my file and sent me here. The only silver lining is that Jace got sent here, too. I suppose there was a reason Jace and I struck up an immediate friendship all those years ago, like our brains sensed that we had an undivulged darkness in common.

Jace and I realized that telling the shrink our truths and letting her inside our brains was a mistake. One that cost us both.

They began training us, and while having Jace around as the dark parts of ourselves were released from the cages of our minds made things easier, shit was *hard*. I didn't want to be the fucked-up guy the army was having me become. I wanted to keep the darkness at bay; I didn't want to lean into that part of me. I tried to fight it. I didn't want it, but once I tasted the ecstasy of torture, I knew there was no locking that beast away again.

If someone had done tests on my brain while I learned how to torture people, they would've seen the joy and pleasure sensors lighting up like fucking fireworks. I swear I've never jacked off more in my entire life than in those eight months—until Lou had the audacity to show the hell up here, anyway.

Rolling onto my side, I wrestle with my pillow to get comfortable enough to sleep, though I'm sure that it's going to be a long night. I wish my deep appreciation for sleep was enough to lull me into unconsciousness. I've been sleeping less since *she* arrived, just as I've been fisting my cock more.

Motherfuck me, I need to pull my shit together.

CHAPTER 15

Louhi

I'M BEING PUNISHED. IT STARTED WHEN I JOLTED AWAKE, covered in sweat, with the nightmare of regaining consciousness on that metal table. The cosmos must be out to get me, because then, Honey Eyes never appeared with my breakfast—dinner? No idea what meal I should be eating at this point. I haven't eaten since before Doctor Doom's exam, and I'm more than a little put out. It's not that I'm hungry, though I am, it's that I'm being penalized for simply trying to survive.

I don't feel a skosh of guilt or regret about taking that guard's life. He touched me without my permission and in a way I didn't appreciate. Absolutely *no one* gets away with that. While I'm a tolerant woman—okay, I'm not, but I like to delude myself into *thinking* I am—some things just can't be forgiven. I certainly don't plan to let the doctor off the hook. I need to kill him for the sake of my sanity.

Now that I've been reacquainted with what it feels like to end a life—God, it'd been too long—I need another hit. I'm dying for another mark. I miss my life outside of these walls, where I walked with a sense of freedom, doing *whatever* I pleased without consequences. I know I'd never have been caught if Mercer hadn't asked me to be.

I'm leaning against the back wall of my cell, with my arms folded under my breasts, waiting. My gut churns with the awareness that someone will come for me today. At some point, I hear the stomping of footsteps from down the hallway. Things have been relatively quiet, with only Carlos making his usual racket. I haven't figured out which cell noisy Carlos is housed in yet, but he's officially made my kill list too, simply by being too loud.

I'm not *good*. I have no moral compass. The only guide I follow is the one I've created, which consists of two self-imposed rules: children and animals are off-limits, and I never kill if I don't want to. That's it. There's no level of depravity I won't stoop to.

Digs, along with four other guards, appear before my cell. I don't attempt to stop the amused snort I emit. *Of course he brought back-up.*

My captor unlocks the cell and swings the door open, filling the doorway with his large frame. He's got to be around six-foot-four, maybe six-foot-five. His wide, muscular shoulders fill the space and the tight army-green T-shirt he has on does nothing to hide those mouthwatering biceps or forearms. I'm abso-bloody-lutely an arm woman and all I want to do right now is sink my teeth and nails into his hard muscles. I bet he tastes the same way he smells: like pure masculinity.

I don't allow my thoughts to show on my face, maintaining the same cocky smirk I've worn since Digs and his posse arrived. He steps inside my space, his attention wholly on me, and I resist the urge to clench my thighs together. I can confirm that the mask is still doing it for me. He tilts his head to the side slightly, scrutinizing me, as his intense gaze continues to pour over my body before settling on my face. I wonder what he sees.

The dense air in the cell seems to thicken to the point where it's hard to draw a breath. It feels as if the predators residing within each of us are warring over the limited oxygen. My snake uncoils herself, fixating on her prey, baring her venomous fangs, hungry to strike. His inner-wolf snarls, peeling back his lips to display his razor-sharp canines, his hackles raised for attack.

Several beats pass before Digs asks, "Are you going to behave today, or do I need to have one of my friends here secure you with a straitjacket?"

My eyes dart around the sliver of space next to Digs's body and find a guard holding the aforementioned restraint, and that's going to be a *fuck no* from me.

Instead of telling Digs that, though, I reply casually, "I suppose that depends."

"On?"

As I toy with him, my playful smile grows. "On second thought, I prefer to operate on a moment-by-moment basis."

I don't miss the roll of his eyes before he turns, retreating toward the hallway. He pauses at the opening to my cage, where he glances at me before ordering me to follow him.

"Oh my God, are we going somewhere?" I feign delighted surprise, staying rooted to my spot in my cell. Flirting with his patience is becoming quite the pastime.

"Let's go, Lou."

Lou. I loathe that my exasperation with him calling me that is waning. Outside of my brother's use of the moniker, people only ever refer to me by my full name, until fucking *Diggory.* Unlike when it comes from my brother in a playful, loving way, it sounds like a dark, sinful promise every time it leaves Digs's lips.

"Where are we going?" I inquire in vain. As expected, no one answers me, but curiosity gets the better of me, and I start for the hallway, my bare feet following behind Digs.

I saunter past the guard holding the straitjacket, then two more I don't recognize, and the other guard who came to collect me yesterday. As we turn down the next hallway, Digs finally deigns to answer my question. "We're going to have a little chat."

My lips twist into something wild and grotesque, and I use it to mask my relief. Torture, I can handle.

"Don't tease me like that, Digs."

I'm spread eagle on an X-cross similar to a St. Andrew's cross, with my wrists and ankles secured to the four corners. Digs disappeared after strapping me to this wooden contraption, and I haven't seen any of the guards since they shoved me into our usual room.

Having been left in the center of the space, I'm able to take stock of my surroundings, but I don't find anything out of the ordinary: the light from the camera in the corner still blinks at me, tools still line the shelves, the metal cabinet still looms large in the corner.

The irritating thing about this cross is that there's nowhere for your head to go. Far too much energy is expended simply to hold it up, and it's uncomfortable as hell for it to loll backwards; it's worse when your head slumps forward. They're obviously designed that way—along with immobilization—but it's aggravating, nonetheless. I've never been attached to one of these crosses before, but I have secured someone else to one to play with. The memory makes my lips tip up into a smile.

Digs reappears after fuck knows how long, dragging a metal chair behind him, the sound scraping down my body like nails on a chalkboard. He shuts himself inside the room and positions the chair against the wall directly across from me. Taking a seat, he rests his boot-clad ankle over his utility trousers and plucks his combat knife from its slot at his waist.

My eyes scan his masked face, searching for a change in his demeanor, but I don't find anything out of the usual. Of course, there is the glaring fact that Honey Eyes—nor anyone else, for that matter—doesn't appear to be joining us today. I wonder what that's about.

I'm not so obtuse as to think that Honey Eyes keeps Digs in check, considering the icy coldness that frosts over his golden eyes when I'm pushed past the point of agony, but something about having him here is moderately reassuring. As if his mere presence keeps things from spiraling out of control. It's been clear from the start that Digs runs this entire show, but the ease with which he and Honey Eyes interact indicates that they have a relationship that goes beyond that of a commander and subordinate.

Digs begins to pick at the callouses on the palm of his massive, veiny hands with the tip of the menacing blade before asking casually, "You won't be answering any of my questions today, will you?"

The corner of my lips quirk. "Perhaps if you asked better questions, you'd receive more satisfactory answers."

His eyes flash with something inscrutable, but it's gone before I have time to decipher its meaning. The blade in Digs's hand catches the light as he climbs to his feet, evaporating the distance between us, his hulking body now towering before me.

Neither of us so much as glance down as he slices my black uniform shirt in half down the middle. Cool air swats my skin as I hold Digs's stare, mesmerized. Dark, tenebrous shadows swirl in his stormy gaze, and it's a look I've seen countless times in the mirror. I guess it takes a monster to recognize one.

The ominous thunderstorm within him is heavy, threatening to rain down hellfire, and fuck if I don't want that. I'm hungry, *starving*, craving the taste of what he's truly capable of.

He flays the shirt, cutting through the short sleeves and tugging the scraps of fabric free, exposing my torso completely.

Outside of being strapped to an exam table, being naked has never bothered me. I own my beauty. In my line of work, being physically fit is a matter of survival—*fine,* I like feeling and looking hot, too—and I work hard to maintain my toned physique. I'm proud of my body and the power it wields.

Unfailingly, I handsomely reward my body for its strength, fierceness, and stamina that I brandish like a superpower. I've been with countless men and women alike, but I've never felt more desired in my entire life than when Digs's silvery-blue eyes observe my naked form, blazing with unfettered heat. The sultry flames of his gaze lapped at my skin in the shower, and that fire's intensity doesn't appear to have abated in the slightest. A primal hunger has leaked into the swirling cyclone of his gaze, and unbridled satisfaction surges through me. I'm affecting him, and I rather like that.

A mild twisting sensation flashes through my breasts, and I know without looking that my nipples are tightening. Chancing a look down, I find that he's tenting the front of his trousers, which has my lips tweaking into a smirk. When my eyes meet Digs's once again, the lusty look that was just there is nearly eclipsed by the shadowy imperilment.

I fight a shiver as his eyes narrow in warning, but the bulging vein in his neck that slithers out from beneath the bottom of his mask like a hungry snake already told me that his grip on control is quickly slipping. My heart rate spikes as my tantalizing smile broadens.

He's making me nervous, but in an anticipatory, yet pleasant way. Right now, his darkness is a mirror that I'm more than comfortable gazing into. For the first time, I don't necessarily feel in danger—not yet. I'm not complacent, though. I know things could change. Should that happen, I'm prepared to allow the bomb inside me to detonate, raining down shrapnel on everything standing in my way.

My breath hitches as the sharp scratch of the spine of the steel blade lazily trails up my abdomen and between my breasts. We both slant our heads, my chest expanding with each breath, as we observe the weapon ascending my body unhurriedly, leaving behind bright pink tracks that look more like poisonous vines.

Suddenly, he deviates from his path, gingerly dragging the blade over my left breast, then the snake's head tattooed over my callous heart. He moves to my right breast, repeating the process before flicking my nipple with the tip of the knife, blood bubbling to the surface and seeping from the wound.

A venomous look slashes across my face as the sight of my

own spilled blood spikes my adrenaline, and I chastise, "You fucking nicked me. I've killed men for less, you know."

He tilts his head to the side, his eyes still unlit. "You want to kill me for scratching you?"

"Maybe."

"I've done worse to you, yet a little scratch is what will be my downfall?"

Amused, I snort, my lips spreading into a daring, seductive grin. "That was simply a little foreplay, Digs."

His eyes go from dark to a shade so black that it reminds me of a moonless night sky in the Finnish countryside. His wrist flicks as he swirls his knife over my left nipple, taunting me. "And what would you call what we're doing right now, Lou?"

"I suppose that all depends on your end game."

Consider me gobsmacked because his free hand moves to lift the bottom of his mask up over his mouth, revealing a small glimpse of the sharp jawline and perfectly masculine, rosy lips that have remained hidden beneath mesh.

Bloody hell.

My tongue practically wags in the confines of my mouth with the desire to lick along the smooth, squared-off, tanned skin I'm able to see before he dips his head, sucking my blood-tinged nipple into his hot mouth. His lips tug hard, his tongue swirling around the bud, exploring, and a low growl rumbles from his chest, making my pussy flutter.

Closing my eyes, I focus on the sensation, my head growing lighter than it's been in weeks—months?—with the glimmer of pleasure. Digs sucks harder, and a breathy moan slips past my lips as my chest rises and falls rapidly. I'm nearly panting by the time he pulls back.

If I were to list all the ways I thought this torture session might go today, this wouldn't have been in the top million, maybe billion.

He rights his mask before facing me again, his eyes dancing

with aphotic amusement. As he sinks to one knee in front of me, my stomach drops along with his movement, his masked face level with the apex of my thighs. Lifting the knife, he wordlessly drags the sharp edge of the blade through the waistband of my trousers and down my leg, slicing the fabric as he goes. He cuts me out of my other pant leg and yanks the scraps from my body.

My core squeezes and my chest tightens as my mind begins to whirl, tripping over itself in an attempt to understand what's happening. *Is this some kind of test? What the living fuck is he planning to do? Why can't I make sense of this situation?*

Two sets of heavy breaths are the only sounds that can be heard within this concrete room. Daring to look down, I find him analyzing my body. And while I know I have nothing to be ashamed of, I can't help but ponder the fact that I'm not clean, not having bathed since that day in the washroom with Digs.

A few years ago, I lost interest in the upkeep of shaving and waxing and chose to have electrolysis nearly *everywhere,* removing every scrap of unwanted hair. Thanking my lucky stars I had that done, I make a mental note to send my electrologist a second tip when I get out of here. Who knew that would come in handy, but the fact that I'm not clean still irks me. Then, I remember that Digs is the one who's responsible for that, so he can deal with those consequences.

Refocusing my attention on maintaining even breaths, I attempt to ignore the way my skin prickles as he glides his free hand up the inside of my pale olive-hued skin, his tan complexion a stark contrast with my own. After his manual exploration of my smooth legs, he flips the knife in his hand, sliding the spine of the blade up the inside of my left leg, beginning at my ankle, painting my skin with more of those noxious vines. By the time he reaches my inner thigh, my shoulders and chest heave with unsteady breaths.

He looks up at me as he demands, "Be a good little convict and tell me what I want to know."

That gets my attention, but the knife's blunt side is now

perilously close to my cunt, so I try to remain calm as I reply breathlessly. "Not…a convict."

The chuckle that reverberates from him can only be described as sinister. "No?"

My voice is firmer this time as I grind out, "No. To call me a convict would imply that I've been convicted of my crimes. I've not had a trial; therefore, I'm not a convict."

The bastard halts the knife just above my clit, looking up at me now. "Are you saying that you didn't commit the crimes you've been accused of?"

A smile dripping with the threat of blood and violence crawls across my face. That's all the answer he's getting, especially considering I haven't heard a single person tell me what crimes I've been accused of committing, not that it necessarily matters.

"You're saying that you aren't guilty of terrorism, murder, kidnapping, possession of biological weapons, destruction of government property, at least ten different cyber-crimes, espionage, and arson?"

Jeesus Kristus. With my face a mask of cool aloofness, I briefly sort through what he's said. Murder and possession of more than a couple of biological weapons over the years are a definite check. The various cybercrimes and espionage are also a yes. What *isn't* a yes is terrorism, arson, kidnapping, or the destruction of government property. I did none of those things. It's not my style.

My brother, on the other hand? Yeah, he's guilty of all of that.

CHAPTER 16

Sean

I'VE BEEN UNPACKING AND ANALYZING MY ENCOUNTER WITH Lou since we parted ways, but the thing I keep coming back to is the look she gave me when tied to that cross. Her eyes challenged me to do my worst, and although I resisted the temptation—barely—I *wanted* to do all kinds of fucked-up things to her. I craved her screams, her body writhing beneath my cruel touch. I wanted to see if she'd succumb to pleasure or feel only pain.

I'd never played with an inmate like that before, and I swear it started out innocently. An experiment, if you will. I wanted to see if it was being naked against her will that upset her in the infirmary, but once I got my answer, I couldn't stop. I couldn't resist tasting her bloody skin. The reality was even better than anything I could imagine, too.

Alone on the roof, I pull the cigarettes from my pants pocket, having come straight here after storming out of the playpen: irritated, unsatisfied, frustrated, and harder than the rocks on the steep, stony cliff far below me. Yanking my mask off my head, I stare at the fabric in my hand, still pissed at myself for lifting my mask in front of Lou. I've never done that in front of a detainee, ever. I can simply add it to the ever-growing list of shit I've done with her that I shouldn't have.

What is it about this inmate that has me tossing all my rules out the goddamn window? I'm not this reckless guy, that's not me.

Risky madness aside, I don't know why I'm worried, considering she, nor any of the other prisoners, will be walking out the front door again. Once you come to Ex-I, you don't have the privilege of leaving. This is home until you find yourself with a dirt dwelling six feet underground. They're all "lifers" here, the only variable being how long that life in question lasts.

Lighting the cigarette, I inhale, slumping down in the chair so that my head rests against the back. The sun is high in the sky, relentlessly beating down on the rooftop, but I make no effort to shield my face. I hate being cooped up in the concrete prison, so I soak up every ounce of sunshine I can. Besides, it seems to be the only source of true light in my life these days.

Lou's distracting me. She's pulling my attention away from what's important and that's getting the information we need to protect our national security and innocent citizens. I need to recenter my focus. But the dark part of me wonders why I can't have my cake and eat it too. *Why can't I siphon information from her by poking the naked beast?*

Luckily, I caught the surprise that bolted through her dark chocolate irises like lightning when she learned of her various charges. I don't know what to make of that yet, but it was there. Maybe I can capitalize on that.

Like a rubber band snapping against my skin, my slice of isolated bliss is cut short when Davis swings open the door. "You have a video call. Computer's been flashing with that annoying-ass notification chirp for a while."

Cursing, I get to my feet, putting out the cigarette. I forgot all about the call I had scheduled with my mom for this afternoon, and I'm sure she's panicking now that I've missed it.

My mask dangling from my fingertips, I follow Davis back down to the barracks. He disappears, probably to get ready for the poker game we've got in a few hours, but I've still got half a day's worth of work before then, which is why I wanted to sneak in a few minutes of solitude.

I sink down in front of the computer and wait as the chat connects. Taking a sip of my water, I wonder if she'll be able to smell the cigarette smoke on my breath through the computer. She's got one of those *mom intuitions* that seems to go off when I'm hiding something. You'd think I would've aged out of that by my early thirties, but no such luck. She'll kick my ass if she discovers I was smoking "cancer in a cardboard package," as she refers to them. Logically, I know she's right, but there's not much to take the edge off around here. I only smoked on the rare occasion before Lou blew into my life like a summer tempest, sudden and destructive.

"Hi, honey," my mother says with a warm smile when it finally somewhat connects. Service on this damn island sucks and the barracks are the only place you can get a spotty internet connection. The guys on patrol still communicate through old school walkie-talkies.

"Hey, Mom. Sorry I missed you earlier." I swallow past the dryness clogging my throat and plaster a fake-as-fuck smile on my face that hopefully conveys that everything is fine. Though, that couldn't be further from the truth. At this point, I'd be lucky if she learned I was smoking a cigarette. That's the least of my indiscretions.

I haven't even stopped to let myself think about Stuco's death. It's going to hit me at some point, though. He was one of the newer guys here, but I liked him, and we got along. His death has everyone on edge. As a result, I've tightened security, doubled down on protocol, and requested additional manpower, which, I'm sure, will get denied.

Maybe this place has graduated from the first circle of hell to the second.

I must not excel in selling the expression I wear because my mom's brow furrows as she asks, "What's wrong?"

"Nothing, Mom. I'm just...busy. How are things at home?"

She hesitates at my obvious deflection, but answers me anyway. "Things are great. Callie and her kids will be here for Christmas in a few weeks. What about you?"

"I don't think I'll get the time off, but I'll let you know." I hate disappointing her and that's the only reason I left that thread of hope hanging loose. I know I won't be at Christmas. Even if I did find a way to go, I'm not going to sit around that table while everyone talks about the past year and whatever they're grateful for. What would I even say other than *I'm grateful for a family that loves me*? It wouldn't even be true since they don't even know that I'm undeserving of that love, and if they did discover the inner workings of my mind, they'd stop loving me.

I ask her some questions about what desserts she plans to make for Christmas dinner and whether Jace's mom will join them—she is—and I'm about to jump off the call when she asks softly, "Sean, will you tell me what's wrong? Talk to me, *please,* honey."

My mom is a good mom, and I'm damn lucky she's mine, but that luck only goes one way. Something must've gone wrong in my brain at some point. It's not her fault I'm this way. My sister is proof of that. She's everything good and pure, everything I'm not.

Feeling unworthy of the depths of my mother's kindness and love, I close my eyes for a beat. I can't tell her the truth, even if I wanted to. I can't tell my mom about my job, about the death on my hands, or the woman who's weaseled her way into my bloodstream like an infectious disease.

Part of me thinks there's no point in even telling my mother about Lou. Especially since I've made an effort to convince myself that my fixation is simply due to the fact that Lou's an anomaly. I'm sure I'd be equally as wound up about any other seemingly shatter-proof inmate.

The more logical part of me has me internally rolling my eyes at my own ignorance. Lou's becoming more than just another inmate, no matter how much I try to persuade myself otherwise. At best, she's a curiosity, a toy I enjoy playing with. At worst, she's an incurable, all-consuming obsession I'll be reluctant to let go of.

Sick of all the deceptions I end up throwing at my mom on a regular basis, I decide to tell her the truth for once, at least the part of the truth I can.

Alone, I glance at the door to the barracks to make sure it's still closed and locked, and when I see that it is, I admit, "I can't tell you much, Mom, but my head's not right."

Concern etches her features, and even my sick, twisted heart lurches at the sight. "You're not thinking of doing something reckless, are you?"

My stomach churns like I've consumed sour milk as guilt swirls until I think I may be sick. I want to assuage her concern, though, so I clarify, "It's…a girl."

Her eyebrows raise, and a knowing smile creeps over her face, but before she can ask questions, I explain, "It's complicated."

"Considering the fact that I don't know anything about the situation, the only advice I can give you is that you can always trust your heart, even when you can't trust your head."

My mother's words swim in the murky depths of my mind for the next several hours as I get a debriefing from the perimeter unit, walk through safety protocol with Davis, discuss the transportation of Stuco's body with Jones, and sit down to play poker.

Rubbing at the back of my neck, I attempt to loosen the tension I'm holding there.

"I'm out," Davis mutters, and Vincent echoes the sentiment, leaving me, Martinez, Borman, and Jones still in the game.

I'm still mulling over my mom's advice when I lose that round of poker and win the next. We're halfway through the third game when I decide that following my heart has never led me…well, anywhere. Besides, her advice can't mean jack shit if she doesn't know any of the facts, right?

Until recently, you could've easily convinced me that I didn't even have a heart, maybe just a skeleton of the organ that distributes my blood. Although, now I have to admit—even if only to myself—that assessment might have been wrong. How else do I explain the tight, stretching sensation within my chest that feels an awful lot like a predator waking from a long, peaceful slumber?

What if the obstinate organ was simply lying dormant? Waiting for a reason to wake.

Shit, that would be *bad*.

"What are you planning to do to punish Koskinen?" Borman grinds out from across the table, tugging me out of my musing.

Glancing up, I pin him with my heavy glare, and he shrinks down into his seat, averting his eyes back to his cards.

I grind my molars when Davis gripes, "Yeah, what's going to happen with her? We can't let her get away with killing Stuco."

"She won't. She has an expiration date," I remind them through clenched teeth.

"She needs to suffer before then," Borman seethes, apparently locating his backbone.

I arch an eyebrow, keeping my voice even as I ask, "Is torture not enough?"

"Not the way you've been doing it," Borman mumbles almost unintelligibly, but I heard it. That little shit knows next to nothing about what Louhi has endured at my hand, only gleaning the vague, abstract basics in my reports.

"Say that again," I dare him, my lip peeling back. Borman's balls must be cosplaying as the magic beans in 'Jack and the Beanstalk' because there's no other explanation for why this fucker is choosing to go up against me. Well, I suppose he could just be a fucking idiot. There's always that.

With his gaze fixed on mine, he pushes, "Jones told us how

you've been raiding the infirmary, taking shit to tend to her wounds." My attention slices toward Jones, who is shrinking in his seat, clearly uncomfortable with being dragged into this conversation. He clearly doesn't know when to quit because Borman goes on, "I think we deserve to see the footage from her cell. Who knows what else—"

"*Enough,*" I roar. Shooting to my feet, my body vibrates as my palms slam against the tabletop, my cards forgotten. My patience has snapped in half. I'm in charge of this slice of hell, and he's under my command. I won't be spoken to that way, even in light of his grief. Being upset over the loss of your best friend doesn't give you permission to act like an insubordinate prick. And *nothing* gives him the authority to question me.

Except for the whirring of the fan in the corner, the room is as silent as the dead. Every set of eyes are on me with varying degrees of fear or detestation etched onto their accompanying faces. I typically have a decent handle on my anger, rarely losing my cool, but I'm *done* with this guy. My blood is still a rolling boil when I spit, "That's the last time you treat me with disrespect. I've been lenient with you. I could've sanctioned you for losing your shit earlier this week, but I didn't. That courtesy just ended."

He scowls at me, the stupid asshole unable to help himself. His lip curls and he snarls, "She should've been terminated on the spot for what she did."

I bolt to my feet and thunder, "Get the fuck out of my sight, Borman. *Now.*"

Borman shoves to his feet and tosses his chair across the room before storming out. He's always been a hothead, but I've never seen him like this. Davis acts like he's going to follow him, but I pin him with a warning that promises retribution if his ass leaves that chair.

My chest is still heaving when Martinez reaches over and picks up Borman's cards. "He was going to lose anyway," he mutters.

Low, uncomfortable chuckles spread over the room. Slowly, I

sink back into my seat, picking up my cards as a sign that we're going to finish this damn game if it's the last thing we do.

I begrudgingly took Borman's hissy fit to heart and decided that he's probably right to some extent, though I loathe to admit it. I *have* been going easy on Lou. She should be a shell of herself by now and the fact that she's not is a problem.

Needing an edge with her, I sent Jace an encrypted email asking him to get me the file on Lou's brother. I asked Thompson about it when he was here last, but I haven't heard anything from him since, and I know Jace has a contact in the records department, so maybe he'll have better luck.

I take things up a notch over the next couple of days. I *need* her to talk to me, to give me something. *I need her to break.*

In one session, I subjected Lou to more fire. In another, I broke her fingers, not just hearing her bones snap, but feeling them as I cracked her left pinky and ring finger with my own two hands.

As the bones in her pinky fractured and splintered, she had looked me squarely in the eye, her vision a mixture of pain and defiance, hardly blinking as I moved to the next finger.

While her brazen recalcitrance turned me on, it's also why I stopped at two fingers. The torture I'm forcing her to endure isn't garnering any results. Not the waterboarding, not the bubbling of her flesh as I subject her to burning, not the physical breaking of bones.

Creativity where torture is concerned isn't something I'm typically short on, but something tells me that subjecting her to claustrophobia by locking her in the tiny box I've often forced inmates into wouldn't get her to crack either. Neither would forcing her to stand for days on end until she collapses.

I've never encountered someone with a will as strong and

unwavering as hers. I admire that, even if it never ceases to frustrate the fuck out of me.

She's fighting me at every turn, and it's undeniably attractive. I like my victims unenthusiastic, to say the least, and the fact that she doesn't fall apart as I push her only makes me hard. No matter how many times I tell my dick to calm the fuck down, he doesn't get the message.

After Davis and Vincent dragged her from the room yesterday, I marched straight to the shower and tugged on my cock with Lou's defiant expression in my mind's eye and the smell of her burning flesh sticking to my skin like perfume. I came to the image of her bubbling skin rioting beneath the glow of my torch.

Lou is destroying me.

I need to break her before I lose myself completely.

CHAPTER 17

Louhi

I MISS MY FLAT AND MY COZY BED WITH ALL THE BLANKETS AND my favorite pillow. I pout as I think about that bloody pillow. It took me years to find that perfect pillow, but when I finally found it, it was *game over*. I never slept anywhere without it. The damp concrete floor of this inhospitable cell is a far cry from that plush bed in Boston.

Thoughts of Boston remind me of Martin, the owner of the upscale, exotic wine market down the street from me. I'd buy a bottle a week from him, sometimes two or three, just because I loved listening to him talk about the grapes. I smile to myself as I meditate on if Martin wonders what happened to me. Did the older sommelier notice when I stopped showing up, pestering him with questions?

Outside of my brother, Martin is probably the only person I'd consider an actual mate. There's still Viktor and Conall, but can you really refer to the heads of the Bratva and the Irish mafia as *friends*? Well, perhaps.

Actually, I know for a fact that you can.

I've known Viktor for as long as I can remember, our thirteen-year age difference meaning nothing to each other. While Viktor likely would've had more in common with my brother, it was me who he spent his time with, choosing to play with me while our fathers and his grandfather worked.

While we don't see each other as often as I see Conall, due to proximity, we'll pick up wherever we leave off. *Will Conall reach out to Viktor about my whereabouts now that I seem to have dropped off the map?*

I wince as I move. Everything hurts. My fingers need to be splinted and the smell of my burned flesh reaches my nose when I breathe too deeply. I was a little surprised when Digs never showed up to administer a dose of his aftercare. I'm still not sure what's behind the bizarre form of treatment Digs provides either. Is it because he feels guilty about what he's done? Or is it because he wants to check on me out of concern? Why would he care what happens to me? And why did he stop?

Hunger scrapes its talons along the inside of my stomach, and I've been dreaming of my first real meal when I escape this place. The contents of that meal change on a daily basis, but today, it's a fat glass of dry red wine paired with a prime, medium-rare steak with a fresh chimichurri sauce and something bright green on the side, because I would *kill* for a vegetable.

I'm itching to get out of here. I've cursed myself a thousand times for not demanding a more certain timeline from Mercer other than his cryptic *"before the anniversary,"* for precisely how long I'd be stuck here. Instead, I simply vowed that I'd *try* to behave. I've kept that promise, generally, so I give myself pats on the back for that.

Groaning, I shift, and though I'm not freely swinging from the eyebolt in the ceiling, it's no less uncomfortable. My wrists chafe, the noisy iron chain digging into my skin hard enough to bruise, as I push higher on my tiptoes to relieve some of the pressure placed on my joints. I've long since given up forecasting what fresh hell each new position I'm left in will bring, so I haven't bothered analyzing my current predicament.

My shoulders scream in pain by the time Digs saunters into the torture room, dragging a chair noisily behind him. Positioning the chair against the wall that faces me, he begins to pick at his *un*broken fingers with his knife as I contemplate how good it would feel to slice him open with it. I'd be willing to bet that his blood would spill prettily.

"Get on with it, then," I huff impatiently. I'd rather skip to the end of this bullshit. I'm losing patience with *everything* these days. I want my damn pillow and my decadent wine. I want to slip my feet back into my black stilettos, or combat boots, depending on my mood. I want to tug on my leather jacket and slide onto my bike, sans helmet, letting the night wind dance wildly through my hair as I pick up speed.

Most of all, I crave to get back to work. It keeps me sane. The bloodletting of that guard has hardly soothed my fraying nerves, but it's been enough to keep me somewhat tame…for now. How long that will last is anyone's guess, and Mercer should know better than to leave me here for an extended period of time. I'm patient, but there are limits.

"Get on with what, exactly?" Digs questions without even glancing up.

"Whatever it is you've planned for today."

"What is it that you think I have planned?" *Lovely, he wants to play games.*

Just then, the lightbulb above my head flickers, casting the room in an eerie ambiance that makes me roll my eyes. He probably loosened it before I arrived.

"I won't presume to understand the mind of a sadist."

His head snaps up, shock momentarily turning those watery blue eyes to icicles, and I grin. *Nailed that diagnosis, not that it'd take a genius.*

"A sadist, hmm?"

"No need to feign ignorance with me. I've seen the way my pain makes your cock grow."

Not responding, he pushes to his feet and crosses the room, only stopping a hair's breadth from me. He leans forward until his masked mouth is next to my ear, and I inhale his musky, masculine scent. *He smells amazing. Clean.*

"Would you like to see that now, Lou?"

His words send a shiver down my spine that I don't suppress, wishing I could have felt the way his breath would have breezed over the shell of my ear when he spoke.

When I don't answer, he pulls back, scantily cocking his head to the side as he demands, "I asked you a question. I want an answer."

"We can't always get what we want, can we, *Diggory*?"

A rippling sound is all the answer I get as he cuts through the entirety of my clothing with his knife, leaving me with an obvious sense of déjà vu. "You should really stop doing that."

His head tilts and his eyes widen a fraction in an expression that wordlessly asks, *why's that?*

"I'd hate to get spoiled with all these new clothes you'll inevitably provide."

In answer, he brings the blade up to my face, spinning it around in a failed attempt at intimidation. My eyes track his as the cheek of the blade skates across my bottom lip before pressing the tip into the tender flesh, pricking the skin. Blood bubbles and my tongue darts out to catch it, capturing his attention.

"I had something else planned for you today, but now I want to test a theory."

What theory?

He disappears through the door opposite the one he came through as I realize that I've never seen him access that door before. When he returns, he's carrying a small black box that he places on his chair. Through his T-shirt, the muscles in his back pop and strain as he digs around in that mystery container. When he spins around to face me, he's holding a needle. *Bloody great.*

He prowls forward like a single-minded predator, my breath

catching as his hand darts out to pinch my right nipple forcefully between his thumb and forefinger before he plunges the needle into the sensitive nerves. *What the fuck?*

I hiss, pulling my open-mouthed gawp from the scene unfolding at my chest to Digs's masked face. There's something swimming in his intense gaze now that wasn't there earlier: something both icy and hot; hungry yet sated.

He repeats the process on my other nipple before taking half a step back and his mask pulls slightly as his obscured face stretches into what I can only presume is a smile. What I would give to see the deranged madness on display right now.

I have no idea what I've been injected with, why he had to depress the needle into my center of my nipples, or what this wanker has planned for me, and I'm most interested in checking out his *smile. Jeesus Kristus,* I'm fucked in the head. If I could send an SOS signal, I would.

Packing the needle back into its box, he vanishes behind that secret door again, where he's gone for several minutes. He must not have been lying about having pivoted from his original plan for this torture session, because this time he comes back with a mid-sized bin that he positions on his chair.

My nipples are beginning to tingle as I survey him removing the lid and pulling out…an ice cube? *Bloody hell?*

He saunters forward, the ice in hand, and grazes my distended nipple with the small frosty block. I gasp, holding my breath. When I finally let it out, a moan escapes with it.

What the hell did he inject me with? *Shit, fuck.*

The pain is excruciating, but there's a faint thrum of delicious pleasure that filters through periodically, like swimming in a warm lake and encountering a pocket of cooler water that's drifted up from the bottom. The sensation is nearly overwhelming.

I've experimented with temperature play before, but not like this. Whatever he shot into me has the stimulating thrill sparking to life as if it's an all-consuming fire feeding on whatever he injected into me like its oxygen.

Right now, I'm cursing my already sensitive breasts. He glides the cube over both and the searing, painful pleasure is somehow worse than the blowtorch. The sensation shooting through me with every pass of the ice is nearly indescribable. I can *feel* the hardness and unbelievable responsiveness of my nipples like I'm having an out-of-body experience that only seems to be connected to my breasts.

Panting, my chest expands haphazardly as I study his face. Nothing about his shadowy blue eyes has changed, but his attention hasn't deviated from his task. I whimper on his next pass over my nipples just as wetness pools between my spread legs.

The stinging, white-hot pain shouldn't be doing this to me, should it?

After what feels like forever, the ice has mostly melted. With the drops of water trailing down my exposed skin, he shoves the cold remnants between my parted lips, his fingers slipping into my mouth as well. I close my lips over his three fingers and swirl my tongue around the oral invaders. When his eyes flash, I suck harder. He spreads his fingers apart inside my mouth and then pulls them out a fraction before thrusting them back in more forcefully. He does this a few more times, and when I think he's grown comfortable, I smile around his fingers and bite down, hard. He hisses as he yanks his fingers free. Attempting to conceal my obvious arousal, I wink at him before he retreats to the bin on the chair.

This time, he returns to me with clamps, and I know before the metal ever bites into my skin that this is going to be severely unpleasant. He attaches them both and I seethe, muttering curses, but he only chuckles. In an effort to combat the agony of my chest, I grit my teeth so hard I wonder if I'll crack a tooth.

Äiti kusipää. Mother arsehole, it hurts.

Next, he stuns me by unclipping the chain around my wrists

from the ceiling, bringing my bound wrists down in front of me and detaching my spread legs from their captivity completely. As I'm jostled, the chain connecting the nipple clamps swings gently with my movements, reminding me of its growing presence.

Does he realize how dangerous this is?

I gain my bearings enough to mask my shellshock of being released as Digs towers over me and threads his massive hand through my dirty hair, tugging my head back to look up at him. As I stare up into his dark and dangerous blues, it hits me between the eyes like a gunshot.

I fucking like *Digs*. Fuck, when did that happen?

It's why I haven't really fought him, I realize. It's why I haven't allowed myself to consider what will happen to him when I escape. It explains why I find myself looking forward to my sessions with him, however unpleasant. My inner beast calls to his. It's why I'm not afraid of him, despite our dynamic.

Don't get me wrong, I'd still like to get a couple—*fine,* more than a couple—hits in, and I want to cut him open and watch him bleed a little. Yet I don't want to kill him, and that tells me everything I need to know regarding my mental state where this guy is concerned.

I could fight him now. I could likely even kill him and end his life right here, but I don't. Instead, I allow him to explore my face with his hand, relishing the feeling of his warm, rough skin against my cheek as he brushes the pad of his thumb along the bone. He brushes over my still-angry bottom lip as I blink up at him.

"Let's talk, Lou."

I focus my attention on my breathing, and when I don't reply, he tugs on the chain attached to the clamps, making me squeak. "When is the next attack?"

When I don't respond, he yanks harder on the chain, spearing me with pain, and I grit my teeth to prevent another yelp from escaping. Whatever he injected me with is exacerbating the agony, and all I want to do is scream or rip my breasts from my body with my bare hands, probably both. Somehow, I manage to hold it inside.

"Where is the next target?"

I lose track of how long we do this song and dance for, and my nipples are stark raving mad by the time he chooses to change tactics.

Digs points to the floor before him, indicating that I should kneel, and I haven't a clue why I do it without question. Curiosity, perhaps? *We'll go with that.*

Kneeling before him, my breaths are ragged, and I can nearly taste the tension emanating from him. I didn't notice it earlier, lost in my own chaotic mind and the pain lancing through me, but now that I'm opening myself up to the moment, it's obvious.

There's something deeply formidable about being on your knees before a man. It may seem like he's the one in charge, but I can assure you that I'm the one with the power in the palm of my hand. In spite of my discomfort, I smile up at him, daring him to follow through with whatever he has planned. The fitted mask allows me to make out the flutter in his tight jaw, and I feel nothing but satisfaction.

"Take off my belt," he commands, his voice gruff.

I don't move. I'm not remotely compliant by nature, but I have a feeling that he doesn't want me to be docile or amenable, not that I'd even know how. He grips the back of my hair and yanks my head back roughly, this time growling, "I said, *Take. Off. My. Belt.*"

Again, I make no move. His hold on my hair tightens, and I swear he rips some out, which makes me smile a little.

I'm not a true masochist. I don't derive pleasure from pain. What I *do* derive pleasure from, however, is seeing Digs's wild side come out to play. I'm getting off on watching him become someone else entirely. A lowering man capable of making the darkest fantasies a reality. And that's something I'm *very* interested in seeing more of. There's something hypnotic about watching him transform.

"Now, Lou," he commands, his eyes hyper-fixated on me.

Deciding that I've pushed far enough for now, I reach up and unfasten his belt, keeping my attention locked on his masked face.

"Unzip me," he orders, as if I were some bimbo oblivious to what's clearly on the agenda here.

My eyes are halfway through their dramatic roll when, lightning fast, he clenches my jaw tightly and squeezes. Holding my gaze, his voice is lethally calm as he states simply, "I will crush you. I will crumble your soul, your spirit, your body. Do not underestimate me and absolutely never disrespect me. Unzip me."

I narrow my eyes into slits as he releases my chin with a jerk, and I nearly fall back, but he tugs on the chain attached to the clamps. Squawking in pain, I pin him with a nasty scowl. My nipples are screeching, but considering the little speech he just gave, I opt to play it safe and unbutton his trousers, freeing him.

I tug his cock loose from the confines of his boxer briefs and sigh. A micro-penis would make this whole *I'm attracted to him* thing I'm currently wrestling with much easier to squash. Alas, I'm not that lucky. His massive cock matches his powerful body, and it's nothing short of glorious.

My mouth waters as I stare down the first real piece of this man I've been privy to, and I can only hope that the rest of him looks as incredible as his dick.

Subconsciously, I think I knew the moment Digs brandished the needles that this *session* was going to be new territory for us. I want to be mad, furious that he's taking advantage of a prisoner in this way, and while I'm mildly put out by the situation, a peculiar curiosity mixed with a startling amount of arousal—that I'm blaming on the bloody drugs—keeps the flame of anger at bay, preventing it from taking on a life of its own. Still, how far is he willing to take this?

The iron chains binding my wrists clank softly like violent wind chimes as I bring my joined hands up to coast a fingertip down the soft skin sheathing his solid erection. Jerking me back by my hair, he stops me. "Your mouth. Only your mouth. If you aren't going to open your mouth to talk, I'm going to fill it."

My eyebrow arches and my lips curl into a sneer, but I lean forward nonetheless. It's not as if I'm not dying to get my mouth on him. He sucks in a sharp breath as I wrap my lips around his thick head, swirling my tongue. I flick my eyes up to meet his, and he stares down at me with an unreadable flicker in his eye as he shoves my head down, clearly impatient.

Calm down, mate, I'm getting there. Instead of saying that, though, I follow his silent instruction and swallow more of him, sucking his cock into my mouth until he hits the back of my throat. Without warning, he thrusts, ramming himself past the point of comfort, making me gag as I sputter. Breathing through my nose, I attempt to acclimate so that I might take more of him. A bright burst of surprise bubbles through me when he allows me to pull all the way back, but the feeling is short-lived when he slams my mouth back onto his cock roughly and begins to fuck my face.

If I was able to use my hands, I'd drag a finger over his balls before cupping him, interested in learning all the little things that might make this man tick.

When he tugs my head back again, tendrils of saliva drip down my chin onto my bare chest, and I nearly gag again as he slams back into my mouth, battering against the back of my throat like a loose shutter in a windstorm. Tears track down my face as I choke on his cock for what feels like hours. He tastes like a delicious poison, one that I can't seem to stop guzzling down, but that I know might kill me. When I finally glance up through watery lashes, I find him glowering at me.

What could you possibly have to be sullen about, Digs?

He's getting his dick hoovered, and based on the fierce grip he has on my hair and the erratic cadence of his chest, his heavy breaths filling the air like a chorus of wordless praise, I'm doing a damn good job.

Digs's body locks up, his posture going rigid, and I know he's about to come. For the briefest of moments, I contemplate clamping my teeth down around his flesh, taking a bite of him like a delicious snack, but decide against it as the urge to taste his cum overwhelms me.

"Swallow, Lou."

My vision narrows in defiance as his body vibrates slightly with mirth. "Do as you're told. Swallow."

Hot streams spill down my throat, and I swallow greedily. I would've swallowed, regardless of what he demanded of me. I've never been a spitter—at least not in this capacity—so when he slides from my mouth, I lick my lips, savoring the way he tastes. *Like salty, powerful masculinity.*

"This is where you say, 'thank you, Louhi, for blowing my mind,'" I taunt him with a smirk while I stagger to my feet as he tucks himself away. His gaze flicks to mine and the stoniness there tells me that any gratitude is out of the question.

Reaching up, I move to unlatch the alligator clamps assaulting my precious nipples, when he catches my wrists. I eye where he's gripping me, then drag my eyes up achingly slowly to meet his and tilt my head, my expression both a warning—or a dare—and a query.

The sharpness of his gaze never dulls as he simply grunts, "Don't touch those."

He quickly snatches the chain dangling from the ceiling, restraining me. *Back to square one.*

CHAPTER 18

Sean

Slipping into the storage closet, I gather a few more items. Though mostly, I escaped to this room in a feeble attempt to regain my composure. It's splitting like a glacial crevasse. I'm completely and thoroughly *fucked*.

Leaning against the wall, I knock the back of my head lightly into the concrete. I shouldn't have let her wrap those pouty, supple lips around my cock. I shouldn't have fucking done it—but I did—and now I'll never be able to erase the memory of the way she looked on her knees.

As incredible as it was to see her choke on my cock with tears streaming down her cheeks, I couldn't help but imagine what she'd look like all done up with pretty crimson-painted lips wrapped around me. I want to see that solely for the opportunity to mess it all up, smearing her lipstick and mascara while she sputters as I fuck her face. I want to cut off her air and have those dark-rimmed eyes pleading with me to let her breathe, but I won't acquiesce. I'll hold out until she's on the verge of passing out, and only after I come down her hot throat will she be allowed the oxygen she'll crave.

Yeah, I'm totally fucked.

There's no future for the two of us. There's no version where she's choking on my cock of her own free will in my fucking house, even if I, selfishly, want that. Nothing good can come of these thoughts.

I really shouldn't be doing this, and I shouldn't be imagining her outside of these walls.

I scrub a hand over my masked face. I'm not naïve to the fact that there are prisoners here who get assaulted and raped, despite my zero-tolerance policy regarding my guys poking their dicks anywhere near the prisoners. Unfortunately, I'm not omniscient and can't be everywhere, monitoring everyone at all times. It goes without saying that what I'm doing here is against the unwritten rules, not to mention my *own* rules. I've never forced a prisoner to suck my dick. That's not me, but fuck, it *is* me where Lou is concerned. I'm becoming unrecognizable to myself.

Now that I've come, I've calmed down a notch. Not much, but a little. Enough to keep the darkness at bay…for now. Shoving off the wall, I reach for a uniform from the stack on the shelf and stalk back to the beauty waiting for me in the next room.

She's like a damn magnet; I can't stay away. Like a mythical siren, she calls to me, luring me closer, and I'm powerless to stop that inevitable draw, so my only choice is to lean into it.

Her nipples must be in agony by now, and after tossing the uniform on the lid of the bin, I eat up the short distance between us and tug on the chain between them. She growls, the sound low and feminine, shooting straight to my hardening cock. Smirking behind my mask, I circle her like the prey she is right now.

I like having her tied up for me like this. It's superior to the cross in many ways, but I mostly appreciate the completely unobstructed access to her body.

Behind her, I trail a hand over the velvety soft skin of her shoulders and down her spine. Brushing her short sable hair to the side, I dip my head into the space where her neck meets her shoulder before skating both hands over the globes of her perfect ass and around to the front of her thighs. I inhale her sultry, brisk scent, breathing deeply, the smell reminding me of a snowy winter's day. Even through the grime and sweat tacked to her skin, she smells so fucking good. I'd maim and kill to be able to lick a stripe up the column of her delicate throat to see if she tasted like that too.

She hisses a breath as I continue my in-depth inspection. Walking around the side opposite her snake tattoo, I find an ancient scar between two of her ribs about the dimensions of a knife, and I bark, "Who stabbed you?"

"A bloody prat."

When I don't respond, she clarifies, "A moron."

I snort, knowing better than to think she'd have given me a name. There's another faint scar several inches below the knife wound, this one longer, slithering around her side. It looks as though it might've been left by a whip, and I'm not sure how I haven't noticed it until now. I gingerly run a finger over the mystery scar, as I inquire, "What happened here?"

"Something best forgotten," she muses. It's perhaps the most honest thing she's said and something about that hits me like a bullet to the chest. It's clear that whatever—whoever—is responsible for leaving this scar is a part of her past that she's not willing to revisit. For some bizarre reason that I choose not to analyze, I don't push it.

Standing in front of her again, I trace the intricate lines of her tattoo twisting up her torso. When the ink disappears beneath her breast, I cup her, squeezing as she fills my palm. With my other hand, I unclamp the clip and she cries out, a tear sliding out from the corner of her eye. I grow harder at the sight.

As I roll her abused nipple between my fingers, she lets out a prolonged, shrill whine. The enhancement drug I gave her must be working in overdrive because another tear spills down her cheek just before she throws her head back. I knew it'd hurt more for the clamps to come off than when I put them on, with all the blood rushing to the over-sensitized region, but her reaction is far more intoxicating than I could've imagined.

She's sobbing after I repeat the entire process on her right nipple, her cries filling the room, her tears giving me a raging hard-on.

She doesn't appear to be in quite the agony I expected, though. Her eyes are cloudy, her gaze distant. She looks like she's floating through space, and I wonder if she's *enjoying* this. If that's the case, I'm pretty sure that'll *ruin* me.

I'm desperate to see if I'm right, though, and if I am, well, I'm going to stand amid the storm that's sure to rain down around me.

"You're such a little deviant, aren't you, Lou? You like what I'm doing to you."

Her head has lolled to the side, resting against the inside of her upper arm, but she glares at me as she bites out, "No."

My head tilts, a hidden smirk creeping over my mouth, and I'd be willing to bet that she can see my mask tugging with the movement. Pulling on both of her nipples, I question, "You *don't* like it?"

She groans before clenching her teeth. "No, I don't."

Lou, you beautiful, enchanting liar.

I wonder if she can smell her wet cunt because I can, like a decadent wine I want to indulge in…to excess. Darting my hand out, I slide two fingers through her entrance, coating my fingers in her slickness. She inhales sharply, and I weave my hand up between our bodies, twisting my fingers in front of her face as the evidence of her arousal glitters in the warm fluorescent light.

My voice is low and smoky as I explain, "Lou, baby, your pussy's weeping. You pretend not to like this, but your leaking cunt tells me otherwise."

If I thought I wanted to lick her neck, it has nothing on my desire to feast between her legs. I try to resist my next move, I really do, but the damn siren can't be ignored.

I tug my mask up from the bottom just enough to shove those two fingers into my mouth. A taste that can only be described as so very Lou settles on my tongue as I find myself licking off every drop. Lou's eyes are glued to my mouth as a moan vibrates in her throat. I'm not even sure she realizes the sound left her, but I revel in it, dying to hear it again.

Reluctantly, I remove my fingers from my mouth, righting my mask again before dipping a finger back inside her sopping cunt. Her brow creases and something akin to pain lances across her face as I pump my finger in and out slowly as her tight body bucks against the restraints. I add a second finger and continue my assault, then a third. She's quaking now, but her body jolts violently as I brush up against her sweet spot. I do it again, eliciting the same gratifying response.

What the fuck am I doing? Why can't I stop? More importantly, why don't I want to?

If Louhi were a drug, I'd be deep into my addiction by now. Every part of her body simply seems to entrance me further, and now that I'm fucking her thoroughly with my fingers, I can't seem to stop, no matter how bad this idea is.

"Digs," she mewls.

"Yes, Lou?"

"Wh—what was the theory?"

The smile I crack beneath my mask is pure sin as I answer her honestly, "That I'd enjoy this more than making you bleed."

"I…hate you," she breathes, making me chuckle.

"I don't care for you much either, but you can hate me while you come, can't you?"

When the deviant minx doesn't respond, I brush a thumb over her clit.

"Jeesus Kristus."

"There's no God here, only me," I tell her, blindly stabbing at the translation of what she said despite the fact that I don't speak Finnish or whatever language that was.

She's writhing in her restraints as I continue to stroke that spot inside her. When I brush her clit again, it's like getting a front-row seat to watching a bomb detonate: her deep brown eyes roll back into her head and violent tremors wrack her body. She gasps for breath, her slender, elegant fingers—at least the unbroken ones—wrapping around the rope binding her wrists. She screams through her climax, sounding like a dark angel in worship.

It's nothing short of stunning to see her unravel, especially knowing I'm the one responsible for getting her there. *I'm the one she's worshiping.*

Her legs are still quivering as she comes down from her high, but she lifts her head enough to look me square in the eye as she pants. Where I assumed I'd see pleasure, or confusion, perhaps even a sliver of hostility, there's nothing. Her expression is downright enigmatic and that stings a little.

I'm not sure what I expected or wanted to see, but it wasn't… nothing. It's not like anyone else is bringing her this level of ecstasy.

That thought prompts another, and I find myself wondering when someone else last got her off. Was it the day before she arrived? Two days? Six months? Five years? And who got her there? Was it another man? Maybe a woman? *Fuck*, why do I even care about any of this, and why do I suddenly want to be the only one ever bringing her pain or pleasure again?

I will be, since she's expected to die in less than four months. That thought sobers me up faster than a drunk driver being pulled over by the cops, and I step back from her lithe form. She blinks at me a few times as I retreat and rub a hand down my masked face, still able to smell her on my fingers, even through the fabric of my mask.

Snatching the fresh uniform, medical tape, and nail clippers from the bin, I carry them over to her, freeing her ankles from the restraints. I help her don the black pants before freeing her wrists from the chains.

Aware of the danger I'm creating by freeing her hands and feet, but for some reason, I'm not concerned. I probably should be, but if she wanted to slip my Glock free and land a round to my chest, she would've done so already. She sure had the opportunity to maim me when my dick was out, yet she didn't take it. *Why?*

I tug the uniform top over her head, and once she's redressed, I reach for her hand, her gaze wary as I tear off a long piece of medical tape, attempting to rudimentarily splint her broken fingers. I could spend hours, days, *years* analyzing the care I provide her, but I don't know if I'd like the answer, so I don't.

Daring to sink to my knees before her, I tap her ankle twice in a silent directive for her to lift it. Glancing up at her, I find her staring down at me before slowly lifting her left foot.

I've never been a foot guy—and I'm still not—but there's something I deeply appreciate about Louhi's delicate bone structure. Cupping her arched foot in my hands reminds me just how feminine she is.

Lifting the nail clippers, I begin trimming her toenails—at least the ones that are still attached. I didn't anticipate doing this, but something about seeing her once black-painted toenails so long and unruly irked me.

When something grazes the top of my head, I bristle. My whole-body freezes, going rigid as I hold my breath, anticipating her next move. Though I'm still wearing the fitted mask, I can practically feel her nails gently scraping through my short, cropped hair, and I wish, not for the first time, that the stupid fucking barrier wasn't between us. Although, neither of us makes a move to remove it, and I'm grateful for that. Fuck knows, I've had enough intimacy for one day.

Her hand remains on my head as I finish grooming her. When I finally tilt my head back, our eyes clash, and the intensity in her burning gaze tugs the tension between us taut.

Several beats pass and neither of us moves. Eventually, Lou slides her hand from my crown down my face, exploring my features with the gentle pads of her fingers, as if she were blind and aching to discover what I looked like. In some ways, she is.

The oxygen in the room seems to evaporate, and I hold my breath as she cautiously runs her fingers over the bridge of my nose—can she tell it's been broken a few times?—and over the hollows of my cheeks before brushing her fingertips along my jawline. Her index finger trails over the seam of my mouth, and I glue my eyes to her, yearning to read her inner thoughts. The invisible mask she wears so well is firmly in place, so I don't find what I'm looking for within those dark brown eyes of hers.

When her hand slithers back to her side, I ask hesitantly, "Will you answer some of my questions?"

I don't know why I even tried, but I obviously just hacked into our bubble with a hatchet. Regret fills me as her face hardens to stone. "No."

Sighing, I sit back on my haunches, holding her attention. "Lou, you have to work with me so I can help you."

She laughs, a hearty real one. I know because the lines at the corners of her eyes crinkle, the sound filled with authentic amusement. Feeling the need to be on an even playing field with her, I climb to my feet. A foot and some loose change shorter than me, she tilts her head back as she smiles, the expression dripping with danger and something else. *Regret? Wistfulness?*

Her English accent sounds slightly more pronounced as she explains, "The list of people who could help me is very, *very* short, and I hate to be the bearer of bad news, but you're not on it."

The sincerity within her words doesn't do anything to lessen the bruising blow. Of course, what she's saying is nothing but the truth. Why *would* I be on that list? Despite my offer, I'm not entirely sure what I'd do to "help" her either. Probably just give her a swift death, instead of drawing it out the way I usually would.

In light of the fact that I'm not on her *short list,* I have a suspicion I might know who is, and to verify that, I need Jace to come through with that file.

CHAPTER 19

Sean

THE MINUTE THE CHOPPER LANDED THIS AFTERNOON, I MET Jace at the helipad on the other end of the island and brought him back in the ancient utility vehicle. We went straight to the rooftop, sinking into the two chairs next to each other. The roof and playpen are the only places in this dimension of hell where cameras aren't found. The camera in the playpen doesn't even work, despite the fake recorder I've got set up in the corner. Major Thompson insisted we disable it so there's no proof of the depravity that exists here, though I elected not to tell any of the guys on base that it doesn't work outside of Jace.

Sounds of the violent, angry waves crashing against the cliffs below us and seagulls cawing in the distance mostly drown out our voices, but we keep them low, nonetheless.

"Have you looked at it?" I ask him, flipping through the file in my hands.

"I skimmed a few parts, but it doesn't seem like much is there. Mercer Koskinen is your run-of-the-mill assassin. Nothing special."

Five years ago, I would've scoffed at how casually he talks about an assassin. "What are the odds that both brother and sister are international criminals?"

He shrugs. "I'd say pretty good, considering how high up their father was in the Bratva."

I arch an eyebrow. "The Russian mafia?"

"One and the same. Makes you wonder what their family dinners were like. Seems like Lou and Mercer kept the family business alive after their parents died." He touches his cigarette to his lips, taking a long drag and letting it out as gray smoke clouds the space between us.

"The family business of *murder*?"

"Yup."

This is getting too sticky for my taste, but as I turn the next page, I ask, "What's his kill count?"

Tipping his head back, he closes his eyes as he soaks up the rays of the late afternoon sun. "The file says 108, but I'm not sure I believe that."

"You think it's less?"

He lifts his head and stares at me flatly, as if I might be the stupidest fucker on planet earth. "No, shithead, I think it's way, way more."

"Why?"

"Flip to page eight," he instructs before settling back into his previous position to stare at the cloudless sky.

I'm beginning to think he did more reading than *skimming*, but I follow his instructions. The second I turn to the aforementioned page, I'm hit with a list of photos of various victims, as well as a list of *some* of his reported methods of execution that range from basic stabbings to poison and *everything* in between.

There's a photo of a middle-aged woman clad in red lingerie, whose skin has a bluish tint to it and vomit pooling around her mouth. The caption below the picture names her as Judy Calperson, a Congresswoman from Pennsylvania, found dead from tetrodotoxin poisoning.

At the bottom of the page, there's yet another image depicting a man lying in the snow, a hole in the center of his forehead. The description names him as James Vungaärd, a businessman with ties to the Bratva, found with a .223 round embedded in his brain.

The next page boasts a picture of a dead man in his mid-thirties, naked and bound on a bed, covered in blood with his dick grotesquely cut off and lying next to him. *I DON'T KNOW HOW TO USE THIS* is printed on a piece of paper and stapled to his detached member.

Mercer has one hell of a dark sense of humor. That must run in the family, too.

The pages of victims go on and on, but I don't need to see them all to understand the depravity that Mercer obviously possesses. There's seemingly no rhyme or reason to his kills and no job he won't accept.

"Do you think he knows anything about his sister's little act of terrorism?" I voice aloud.

"I have no idea, but according to that file, he lives in London and wasn't in Boston when Lou planted or attempted to detonate those explosives. Did we ever learn why she chose the Federal Reserve?"

"They were moving a large sum of money that day—we're talking *billions* of dollars—but robbery doesn't seem to fit with her modus operandi."

Jace chuckles. "I love it when you talk fancy to me, Digs."

I snort, rolling my eyes, though he's still not looking at me as he adds, "Sounds like we may need to get to know Lou a little better."

"Uh, about that..." My throat feels tight as I force myself to breathe through the apprehension of my impeding confession.

Eyebrows raised, he rolls his head toward me then, waiting for me to continue, but I avert my gaze, staring out at the vast blue ocean.

"She sort of sucked my dick yesterday."

He laughs out loud, a full belly laugh. I'm glaring at him by the time he regains his composure, and I snap, "Why is that funny?"

Of all the reactions I thought I'd get from Jace—censure, disappointment, disgust—amusement didn't make the list. If I'm honest with myself, I'm not nearly as ashamed as I probably should be, and I'm not the least bit remorseful. If anything, I'm tempted to do it again.

I know it was wrong, but that didn't diminish how good it felt.

"It's not, but I definitely saw that coming. I'm jealous. Lou's fucking hot and I bet she sucks cock like a pro."

She does, but for some reason, I don't want to affirm that fact. Jace and I have shared women before—more than a few times—and we work well together since we understand each other's preferences and less-than-savory *tastes*. But when it comes to Lou, I want to keep her to myself.

Louhi

Hours later, I'm still struggling to comprehend what-the-bloody-fuck happened with Digs. He's a puzzle I can't assemble, the shapes of the pieces constantly evolving and morphing into an entirely different picture. I locked down my feelings the second I came, throwing up that external mask so that I could sort through my own thoughts. The last thing I need is to be vulnerable.

After I sucked him off, his demeanor seemed to shapeshift into something…softer, dancing on the line of reverence. Sure, he was rough and dirty—he is who he is—but his touch was full of admiration. No one's ever touched me that way before. I felt *appreciated*.

The skill with which he set my body alight was unmatched by any of my previous partners, even those who left me thoroughly and sufficiently satisfied. Those who didn't aren't around to disappoint anyone else.

I was wholly enjoying our session until he ruined it with more of his questions. When is the tosser going to learn to stop asking such stupid questions? I'm growing bored with his games. *Fine, maybe not* all *of his games.*

I told him the truth. He's not on my list of people who could even begin to get me out of this situation. He can't *help* me, and just because I think he's hot and enjoy his company to some degree, doesn't mean I want his assistance. But, fuck, is he attractive. I could feel the hard lines and planes of his face through his mask, and I'm certain he wouldn't be disappointing to feast my eyes upon.

Like a cat, I stretch out on the floor of my damp, dark cell, planning to nap before they blast more music in a lame attempt to keep me awake. I'm just about to doze off when Digs's words flit back on a mental cloud: *I will crush you. I will crumble your soul, your spirit, your body. Do not underestimate me and absolutely never disrespect me.* I scoff out loud before settling back in and closing my eyes.

Too bad for him that I will not bend; I will not break. I will not surrender; I will not shatter. Not for him. Not for anyone.

"Let's fucking go, Koskinen," the guard commands, jolting me from my peaceful slumber. I didn't even hear him approach, but now that I'm conscious, the heavy bass of the music explains that.

At some point, exhaustion took over. I've adapted to falling asleep in defiance of the hammering metal music that's blaring more often than not. It's just like these arseholes to wake me when I was resting, and irritation has my lips twisting into a snarl as I glare at the wanker who dared to wake me, refusing to make any move to follow him. *How long have I been asleep?*

As he stands in the doorway of my cell, I recognize his eyes and build as one of the usual guards, but he's different from the others. It's nothing short of obvious that he carries a deep-seated hatred for me, but he wouldn't be the first. I won't pretend that I have a healthy outlet for dealing with those that aren't fans of mine, but they usually fuck off before I'm forced to resort to more extreme measures.

Taking a steadying breath in order to tamp down the more appealing violent option of murdering him, I get to my feet, pinning him with a warning.

I saunter past him as I'm led down the hall to the usual torture spot. Damn, I must've really been out of it if I was able to sleep all night. It was probably the orgasm that Digs left me with that did the trick.

I'm made to stand in a similar position as last time, with my legs spread and restrained to the bolts in the floor. However, this time, my wrists are crossed behind my back and bound with rope.

After waiting for what feels like ages, eventually the door swings open, revealing Digs and… "Honey Eyes," I exclaim, a bright smile popping onto my lips.

I'm choosing to believe that he smiles behind his mask and, even if he doesn't, his voice is kind as he greets me in return. "Miss me, Lou?"

"You know I did," I reply with a wink.

"Quit your fucking flirting," the other man gripes, and I turn my attention to his formidable presence and say sweetly, "Aw, don't be jealous, Digs."

He rolls those pretty blue eyes of his before disappearing into what I'm starting to think is a storage closet when he reappears alone. I don't know what happened to Honey Eyes, but he's gone. Digs is only holding a folded uniform and a small bag of something else I can't make out.

No toys? My mental state must be deteriorating because I think I might be a tad *disappointed.* Mercer needs to launch his rescue mission before I lose the plot entirely.

At least Digs has silently indicated that I'll end up naked again, so I'm not surprised when he sets the uniform on the shelves with the tools. Pulling out his tactical knife, he proceeds to expose me completely to the room.

Does he truly think that getting me naked is the best way to get me to talk? Or is he simply looking to play? *Why don't I care?*

Never one for embarrassment or shame, I'm not a blusher—I'm *far* more likely to make someone else blush—but the way he makes sheep's eyes at me has my nipples tightening.

Digs stands before me, running a hand up my torso, over my tattoo, and palms my breast. I glance down, absorbing the alluring sight of his tanned hand exploring my body. When he flicks a thumb over the hardened point, I suck in a breath. He seems to study my reaction before circling me until his front is flush with my backside, gripping my hip with one hand and cupping my sex with the other. As I let out a soft moan, my eyelids flutter.

I don't know what his goal is here, but what he's doing feels *good,* even if I know that things are about to get painful, given Digs's proclivities. My pussy clenches around air at the prospect. Why am I not more put off by his brand of pain?

Without warning, he slips a finger into me. A gratified groan floats in my mouth as my head falls back into his chest, and he stiffens before settling into my touch. Wanting to even the playing field, I run a palm over his crotch, feeling the swell of his hard length trapped beneath his trousers. I'm rewarded when his chest vibrates against my back, egging me on. My wrists may be bound, but I still have use of my hands to some extent, so I cup him this time, tugging on his balls.

A sound between a hum and a giggle rattles in my mouth before I quip, "Someone's eager."

"Since you're in such a teasing mood, Lou, why don't we play a little game, yeah?"

CHAPTER 20

Sean

DAMMIT.

Like most things where this woman is concerned, I shouldn't be doing this. I didn't mean to, but *fuck, I want to.*

Today was never supposed to go like this. Truthfully, I had something else in mind. I had planned to leave her bound with a hood over her head for at least the next twelve hours, maybe longer, subjecting her to auditory torture by filling the room with the sound of loud sirens. I was even prepared to inflict some extreme temperature torture, by tossing buckets of ice water over her and cranking up heat, so she'd feel like the humidity threatened to melt her insides.

I've seen prisoners go crazy after simply being hooded for days at a time. I didn't want her to have a psychotic break, just shaky enough to tell me what I need to know.

But all that changed the moment I saw her bound and waiting for me. I need to remember that having her bound, legs spread for me, is now a weakness of mine.

It's why I told Jace to get lost when we were in the storeroom. He simply rolled his eyes and said, "Don't do anything I wouldn't do." Luckily for me, that leaves damn near *everything* on the table.

With my heart jackhammering in my chest, I flick my middle

finger over her clit, making her jolt against me. "I asked you a question. Answer me," I order her.

"Yes, sir." *Oh, fuck me straight to Hell.* My dick kicks in my pants, and I nearly come right there, a single word practically undoing me.

"Sir, huh?" I murmur into her ear mirthlessly, lazily dragging my hand up from her breast to the front of her throat. I don't squeeze, just linger there threateningly.

"Isn't that what you army blokes like to be called?" she replies, her voice vibrating against my palm.

"I think I like that. Keep doing it."

"No," she snaps. Regaining her composure, her body stiffens in my arms.

"I don't think you're in a position to negotiate here, Lou," I admonish.

"Neither are you."

I smirk beneath my mask. This is the side of Lou that I never tire of seeing come out to play.

"No?"

"I'm the one with the answers you seek."

"Ah, but I'm the one with my hands on your hot little body," I say as I tweak her clit, reminding her who's in charge. "Since you're all tied up with nowhere to go, it seems to me that you're not in a position to be making demands."

I can't see her face, but the way she sucks in a breath tells me that she's gearing up to launch into a tirade, so I cut her off, pinching her clit hard as I cut in, "Now that we've gotten that out of the way, let's play a game." Moving my hand from her throat back down to her breasts, I roll her nipple between my fingers. "You know, since you like playing those so much."

Clarifying, I explain, "I watched that little porno you made. You like being a tease, don't you, putting yourself on display like that for me, dipping your fingers into your soaking pussy until you come with my name on your lips?"

She laughs then, the sensuous noise fizzing through the room like effervescence rising to the surface of bubbly wine. "Would you like a repeat performance? I'm on again at eight."

Ignoring her retort, I pinch her nipple until her amusement disappears, replaced by a squeak of discomfort. *Good, I hope it hurts.*

"You're going to answer my questions."

"That's not going to happen."

"Then you don't get to come today, but I'll still allow you to scream my name."

While this wasn't how I anticipated today's session to go, I'm chomping at the bit to see if I might get some answers this way, after all. Now that I'm here, her incredible body naked and at my mercy, I can't stop, can't shut my inner sadist down.

Lou and I are both doomed now that the darkness has been unleashed, but if anyone can find a way to develop night-vision, it's this woman. So far, she appears to be able to see me through the pitch dark, but I wonder if that'll still be true if I push her harder than I have before.

"Do you want to admit how wet you are right now, or should I be the one to tell you?" I ask into her ear, and she squirms against me. She's wetter than the Pacific, but I suppose that Hell will have to freeze over before she'll admit that. My chest vibrates with an amused hum as I answer my own question. "You're wet, Lou, but I think you could be wetter."

I dip my fingers inside her once again, slowly pumping in and out of her hot, sopping cunt before inquiring, "How many people work for you?"

When she says nothing, I try again, "Who is your second-in-command?"

Still, silence, only the sound of her pussy feasting on my fingers filling the room.

"What about the next attack? Where is the location of that?"

Her mouth remains closed, and I bend down to rest my masked

cheek against hers as I withdraw from her desperate sex. Crushing her clit between my fingers, she squeaks as my gravelly voice reappears in her ear. "You're not starting off very well. I think you need an incentive," I offer, stepping away from her body, taking a moment to *try* to pull myself together.

I want to break her, reduce her to a withering mess, I think to myself, determined to get what I want.

Right now, all I want is her: her body, her mind, her goddamn soul. I want her to languish in the pain I inflict, suffering as I dole out unspeakable things.

I want to hurt her.

Breathing through those savage thoughts, I squat down, unstrapping her ankles, leaving her wrists restrained at her back, before stepping in front of her. My voice is hoarse, full of thick, tenebrous desire as I order her. "Get on your knees."

She says nothing, her chin lifted in defiance, making the sick-and-twisted thing inside of me smile. When she doesn't sink to her knees, I tuck a lock of her hair behind her ear as I command, "On your knees, sweet Lou."

That gets her attention, her eyes snapping to mine as she stares at her devil. She scoffs incredulously, sneering in disgust. "Are you mental? I'm not sweet."

I smirk, sure that no one, and I mean *no one,* has ever described Louhi as sweet.

"Oh, you're anything but sweet, but you're going to be sweet for me right now, aren't you?"

She sneers, refusing my order, which forces my wicked smile to grow in size, surely stretching the mesh fabric, as I give her my back, reaching for the black opaque bag I brought with me from the storeroom. Pouring the contents on the ground in front of her, I litter the floor with tiny white grains of uncooked rice. Her milk chocolate gaze widens, nearly bugging out of her head, as my intention clicks inside her brain.

Her face quickly contorts into a scowl as she obviously prepares to spew poison from her pouty lips. Seizing her by the throat once more, I squeeze, cutting off her air supply as I spit, "This is the last time I ask nicely. Now, be a sweet girl and *get on your knees.*"

Darkness rapidly sweeps across my gaze, threatening to consume me, and the woman must have a painful death wish as she pushes me, clearly desperate to see the blackness that lives inside me.

She smirks, even as I grip her neck tighter, hoarsely replying, "No."

"Have it your way then."

She shouldn't be testing, pushing me this way. I can't re-cage this beast once unleashed and the grasp I have on him right now is weak, at best.

Releasing her throat, I attempt to shove her to her knees by the shoulders. She struggles to jerk out of my firm hold, but no matter how strong this woman is, she doesn't have the muscle mass I do. I wrestle her down to the ground, the beautiful, naughty woman combating me every step of the way.

Her chest heaves, and while she looks like she might begin to breathe fire, there's something else gleaming in her eye, something akin to lust, hunger, and arousal.

But that's not the only thing that gives away her desire, and as she continues to fight me, I tell her, "I can smell your wet cunt. You like this, don't you?"

Her nostrils flare, and in a last-ditch effort to avoid the impending discomfort, she brings her knee up to try to nail me, but I block her with a muscled thigh. A claggy, amused chuckle tumbles from my lips at her pitiful attempt at stopping me.

When her bare knees eventually make contact with the painful grains of rice scattered across the concrete floor, she snarls up at me, her chest expanding as she breathes heavily. Her knees must be screaming as the rice digs into her skin like shrapnel. With a boot to her inner thigh, I kick her legs open wider so that she's resting on the inside of her knees, and her face contorts, giving away the moment the pain becomes excruciating.

"Open. Tongue out."

As expected, she doesn't do as I command, and my boots crunch over the rice as I step up to her, gripping the sides of her mouth, squeezing hard. Clenching her teeth, her jaw flexes, fluttering against the pads of my fingers.

Every time she defies me, fueling my depravity, my hold on my darkness strains further. "Open your mouth or I'll do it for you."

Without warning, her jaw unlocks, lips barely parting. *Is she scared of what I'd do to her if she refused me? Or is she simply interested in complying to get off the rice faster?*

"So she *can* follow orders...to an extent," I muse, as Lou's eyes narrow into thin slits.

When I chuckle at the sight, an honest to God *growl* leaves her throat in response, but I simply snatch a fistful of her dirty hair, yanking her head back so that she glares up at me.

"Tongue out, Lou."

I tighten my grip on her hair in a clear warning, daring her to disobey me. Slowly, tentatively, her tongue peeks out, and I reach into my pocket and pull out the clothespin I stuffed there in the storeroom as Jace closed his eyes, smiling as he shook his head at me.

"Since you don't feel like talking, I'll make sure you can't." Clamping the clothespin around the tip of her tongue, Louhi spears me with a look that promises retribution.

Her breathing is ragged as she attempts to remain completely still, so as not to ignite more suffering. But that's okay, the agony I can inflict on her is not in short supply.

Crouching down behind her, I slip my hand into my pocket again, removing another clothespin. Cupping her sex, I slide my fingers through the wetness gathered there, tendrils of her arousal snake around my digits before I clamp the clothespin around her clit.

She shrieks, and the sound has pre-cum dampening my boxer-briefs, my stiff dick fighting for release.

"All you have to do is tell me what I want to know and this can end," I whisper into her ear, flicking the end of the pin clamped around her tongue. "Oh, wait," I say, snapping my fingers. "You can't talk, can you?"

She squawks, her body jolting as if she's going to fight me, but I simply laugh, shoving her into the rice harder. When she groans low and deep around the wooden clothespin filling her mouth, I thump on the end of the pin around her clit, likely sending spirals of pain through her.

"You like it when I play with you like this."

She growls in response, practically snorting smoke, but I simply swipe my fingers through her soaked pussy, gathering her wetness and smearing it over her lips.

"Your cunt says you do."

A whimper falls from her open mouth, telling me she does, in fact, like this. I tap the end of the clothespin at her pussy once more, adding, "Let's find out what else you're into. How about a little breath play?"

The words are barely out of my mouth before I wrap my hand around her throat, applying enough pressure to severely constrict her air. Clearly no longer bothering to pretend that she's not into this, she shines.

"I think that's a yes." I grip her neck even tighter, cutting off her oxygen entirely as she wheezes. Thrusting two fingers into her eager cunt, it takes a concerted effort to stifle the groan in my throat at the addictive sounds she's making as she gasps for air.

The hypnotic sound of my digits pumping in and out of her easily fills the air, mingling with her futile gasps, as I remark, "I knew you were deviant, Lou. Fortunately for you, so am I."

With that, I squeeze her throat tightly, choking her out until she leans into the sensation like I knew she would. If there's one thing

I know about Lou, it's that she's got a darkness swimming within her, too. It's not of the same variety as mine, but she's not innocent or meek, as evidenced by the way her cunt begs for my touch.

My fingers continue to fuck her, teasing the nerves within her cunt, periodically toying with the clothespin over her clit. The moment her body goes rigid in my arms, I release her, completely removing my hands.

Her body betrays her, coming apart with a guttural groan as her climax rocks her so hard she nearly topples over, but I catch her before she can fall. I snigger as I right her onto her knees, making her whimper as she's set back onto the rice shards.

Unclamping the clothespins from her clit and tongue, I click my tongue. "What am I going to do with you, Lou? You couldn't follow the rule of the game."

Her mind must be fuzzy with the aftermath of her ecstasy, as she manages a labored and bewildered, "Huh?"

"The rule of the game was that you don't get to come if you don't answer the question. But since I'm feeling generous, I'll give you a choice: answer the question or learn what happens to disobedient convicts."

"Option two," she croaks, her tongue clearly still not quite functioning correctly.

I chuckle behind her, signaling that I was *hoping* she'd choose that.

Abandoning her to her lethargy and exhaustion, I leave her curled on the floor as shivers wrack her body despite the thick, warm air in the room. Moving to the storeroom, I roll the metal table into the room, along with the few items I'll need, flicking the brakes on the wheels once I position it the way I want.

By the time I'm ready for her, she's folded herself into the fetal position, her teeth chattering noisily. I slant my head as I take in her form, small and vulnerable, and the sight makes my chest twist in a way that I actively choose to ignore.

When I scoop her into my arms, she curls into me on instinct, and I want to rage at her that she's not safe with me, that she's not safe here. But I don't.

Instead, I savor the brief, fleeting moment of this woman in my arms, clinging to me as if I'm her savior. For a few seconds, I pretend that I'm not hurting her or *enjoying* that I'm hurting her.

Setting her on the table, I spread her out like a starfish, restraining her as I explain, "Since you like coming so much, I think we should make sure you get to do that."

Clearly teetering on the edge of overstimulation, I plan to take advantage of the situation, metaphorically flinging her off that cliff. Too much pleasure leads to pain, and I want to send her hurtling down that path.

Reaching for the syringe I brought with me, I swab the crook of her elbow with alcohol before plunging the needle into her vein, injecting her with a dose of adrenaline. Sweat breaks out over her skin as a result, shifting into full-body tremors. With two fingers over her pulse point in her neck, I find her heart participating in a high-speed race.

Good. Her eyes are wild and frantic as I snap the small rubber band I have around her nipple. She cranes her neck, trying to assess the situation as I repeat the process on her other nipple.

Resigned, her head drops back on the table with an audible *thud*, making me chuckle to myself. I notice her breathing regulating, and I suspect that she's attempting to focus on her breaths and not the pinching in her nipples.

When she attempts to lift her head again, I fist her hair, forcing her head back down. Her eyes glisten with a mixture of unshed tears and resolution that I shutter by wrapping a cloth around her head, blinding her.

Moving back between her legs, she moans, attempting to squirm as my fingers slip inside of her, the wet, seductive sound feeling more like a blaring alarm as it weaves between the atoms and particles in the space surrounding us. My other hand begins alternating between her breasts as I knead them, Louhi whining as she strains against her binds.

Once she's worked into a frenzy of panted breaths, soft moans, and writhing limbs, I yank off the bands. She screams, her toes curling at the same time my cock becomes painful within my pants.

The gray cloth over her eyes grows darker as her tears soak the fabric. I knew she was already sensitive, *too sensitive,* when I placed her on this table, but the wails slipping from between her swollen lips as I begin to play with her engorged nipples, tugging and pinching them, make me think that this has ventured into the territory of pain.

Surprise billows through me when my name slips from her lips like a prayer—or maybe a hex—and I command, "That's it. Scream my name, Lou."

Swiping my thumb over her clit, I continue to finger-fuck her, drawing small circles as she cries my name. Her fingers curl around the edge of the table while her body shakes, and I back off slightly as she comes.

I find myself wishing I could only torture her with orgasms for the rest of her tenure here. She's fucked me up, made me hooked on the sight of her coming undone beneath my hands.

Once she's marginally recovered, I shove her back to the brink of rapture once more.

"Again," I order, forcing her to endure the continual bliss that will eventually turn only to pain. Alternating between pinching and stroking her clit languidly, she comes again, just as I've instructed, crying out as a river of colorful curses flows from her mouth.

Only a few heartbeats later, I play with her breasts again, and where my touch was firm earlier, I ensure that it's agonizingly soft this time—*too soft.* Between her legs, I'm now fucking her with two fingers and brushing over her clit just often enough to keep her from free falling from that precipice. A smile blooms behind my mask when her body bucks as I remove my hand from her wet cunt, slipping between her cheeks, and prodding her back entrance. She tenses, attempting to wriggle away, and I wonder if she's ever had something—someone—back here before.

"Relax or you'll hurt yourself."

"You'd like that," she snaps through heavy, panted breaths, and I snigger.

"I would, but you wouldn't."

She must realize that I'm right as she *tries* to relax a fraction, but the adrenaline pumping through her is probably making that difficult. Abandoning her breasts, I swirl my fingers around her clit, pushing one all the way into her ass, slowly thrusting in and out. Shoving two fingers back into her pussy, I match the tempos as I wage war on her body.

Husky, grating screams erupt as I scrape against the overly sensitive balls of nerves both inside and out of her. She unspools like a ball of yarn, thrashing against the table so hard that when her head comes up and slams back down, she goes limp.

No, no. Shit, no.

Panic seizes me, and I tear the cloth from her eyes, tapping her cheek, begging her to wake up, but she doesn't.

She doesn't so much as stir.

What have I done?

CHAPTER 21

Louhi

When my eyes flutter open, I'm met with a bright white tiled ceiling. I study more of my surroundings without moving my head, realizing I'm in the infirmary.

Fuck, shit, no.

Panic seizes my chest, and my breaths become shallow and ragged as I consider my limited options to flee. A scream is snaking up my throat when a hand slams over my mouth, muffling any sound I might make. I'm about to bite that hand when Digs's masked face comes into view, his gaze gentle as he stares down at me.

"Shh, you're okay. You're safe, Lou." His deep, husky voice is softer than I've ever heard it before.

I'm safe with him. Digs might want to hurt me, but he won't crack me open.

He repeats those words a few times until my respirations begin to even out and he slowly removes his hand from my mouth. It's then that I realize I'm not on the metal table I was strapped to the last time I was in here. I'm on an actual cot with a real cushion and a pillow. Don't get me wrong, it's still not my perfect pillow or my fluffy bed in Boston, but it's the closest I've been to comfortable since I got here.

Digs moves to sit on a chair next to my bed, but he's close

enough now that I can see him in my periphery. I tilt my head down when I notice the black uniform back on my body and a blanket covering my legs and stomach.

My voice is hoarse as I rasp, "What happened?"

He leans forward and slides a hand onto my upper arm, brushing his thumb over the delicate skin of my inner bicep.

Why the bloody hell is he touching me like that?

I want to snap at him and tell him to remove his hands from my person, but nothing comes out when I open my mouth to gripe.

"You hit your head so hard on that table that you gave yourself a concussion. You blacked out."

With a groan, I start to reach up and touch the back of my head, but handcuffs bite into my wrist, making me grind my teeth in irritation. *Of course, he kept me cuffed.*

I roll my head toward Digs and wince. My movements are sluggish and drowsiness edges in, but I push past that and clear my throat before asking, "How did we get here?"

He shifts in his seat, his eyes darting around, and he appears uncomfortable. After a beat, he answers, "I cleaned you up as best I could and redressed you before hauling ass down here." He coughs awkwardly before asking, "Are you okay?"

My eyebrows nearly hit my hairline, ignoring the throb that beats against the inside of my skull like a hammer. *Is he* worried *about me?* Does he feel guilty for sending me to Heaven—or Hell—and back? Why does he care?

I have an intimate relationship with a darkness that matches his, and I've never once felt remorse for that. I live in the dark, relishing the inky blackness that surrounds me, leaning into its shadowy embrace as if it were a lover. The more I'm around Digs, the more I wonder if he can say the same about the darkness living inside him.

"I'm fine," I reply, staring back up at the ceiling. I close my eyes before they blast back open wide. I can't go to sleep. I'm not safe in this room. I have to stay awake. I couldn't help it when I was unconscious, but I can help it now, and I blink hard against weariness tugging at me.

Digs scoots closer as he sweeps a hand over my forehead, pushing some of my hair back. The gesture is achingly tender and something peculiar flickers in my chest as if a candle's been lit, but I snuff it out. "I promise you're safe. No one knows you're here. I haven't left you since bringing you in here and Ja—Honey Eyes is outside the room. Nothing bad will happen to you while you sleep."

How can I trust the man responsible for so much of my suffering? I *want* to believe him, and the veracity shining in his luminous silvery-blue eyes is so bright that I don't doubt their sincerity. I've always made it a habit to rely on the steadfastness of my gut feelings, and that's never led me astray before, so I shouldn't question my instincts now.

Besides, I'd be stupid to pass up the opportunity to sleep on a bed.

There's something I've been wanting to know for the last several days, though, and considering the pleasant mood Digs appears to be in, I decide to explore that trust a little more—however reckless that may be—I murmur, "What month is it?"

"December."

My eyelids slam shut then, blotting out the anguish now pricking the backs of my eyes at hearing that single word.

Sean

I sat at Louhi's bedside all night, watching the steady rise and fall of her chest. Beautiful is too slight a word to describe this woman, and I couldn't resist the temptation to touch her, telling myself that tending to her wounds and checking on her broken fingers wasn't *really* touching her.

With an impressive display of self-restraint, I managed to hold off until she was awake before putting my hands on her in any meaningful way, but I didn't stop after she fell back asleep. Keeping her small hand in mine, feeling her pulse thrum against my middle finger, I held her hand until she regained consciousness once again.

When she woke back up, I mentally slapped myself for going so fucking soft as Jace and I took her back to her cell, leaving her with some food and water.

I should be getting answers for Thompson, not ensuring her comfort and safety.

I'm not sure if it's the lack of sleep or the fact that this woman is upending my entire life, but after Jace and I both showered and changed, I grumbled at him to meet me on the roof.

Before heading up there, I made a detour to snatch Mercer's and Lou's files from the locked cabinet in the office, where I've kept them since only Jace and I have the combination.

Jace is smoking a cigarette when I get to the rooftop, and he offers me a smoke that I greedily accept, considering what a long-ass night it's been.

Slumping in the chair next to him, I sigh. He mutters an amused affirmation, adding, "Fucking Lou."

I grunt in response and take a drag of the cancer stick before bringing life to the thought that's been lurking in the darkest corners of my mind. "What if she didn't do it?"

"Do what?"

"What if she didn't attempt to set those bombs off? What if she didn't even plant them in the first place? What if she isn't the terrorist responsible for that?"

Jace scoffs as he tips his head back up at the morning sky. "You're delusional. Of course, she did it. She wouldn't be here unless she was guilty."

I face him, despite his eyes being closed as he soaks up the sun's rays. "Hear me out. I think we have it wrong. I don't think she did it."

He lifts his head then, eyeing me with both confusion and concern.

"Sean," he starts. People *rarely* use my first name, so I know he's serious when he continues. "The government doesn't fuck up when they send people here. If you're at Exile Island, you did what you're accused of, you're a problem that needs to be solved. You know this."

"But what if the government fucked up *this time*?"

I'm not a conspiracy theorist; I believe facts. And I've been fitting together facts like a ten-thousand-piece puzzle when it comes to Lou. The image isn't revealing itself to be anything like the one I've been told to see.

Jace shakes his head before arguing, "Command doesn't make mistakes like that. I think you're seeing what you *want* to see."

He might be right. I don't want Lou to be responsible for such heinous acts and, more importantly, I don't want to have to put her to death. However, there's a piece of me that truly doubts she did the things she's being accused of. If there's a chance—even a small, miniscule chance—that she's innocent of those crimes, I want to give her the opportunity to keep breathing, to keep living.

Pushing further, I retort, "Seriously, what if they did?"

Jace sighs before taking another drag and relenting. "*Fine,* I'll bite. Why do you think that?"

"What if she hasn't been answering our questions because she doesn't know? She has no idea where the next attack will be. She doesn't know why the Fed was targeted. She doesn't have anyone working for her. What if it's all because she isn't the terrorist the damn government claims? She said once that I needed to ask better questions and what if that's because she can't answer these?"

He appears to ponder that deeply for a moment before declaring, "She's still clearly some kind of criminal, though. She killed Stuco in cold blood."

"I haven't worked out that part yet, but I don't disagree."

After a beat of silence, he admits, "If you are right, and I'm not saying you are, what does that mean for her?"

"I don't know, but I'd think we need to report the mistake before it's too late."

Neither of us speaks for what feels like hours as we both lose ourselves in our thoughts. I don't know what crimes she's committed, or how the hell she got here if she didn't do what she's being accused of. But I'm not stupid enough to think she's innocent. She showed up prepared to endure extreme torture and that can only mean she's wrapped up in something shady.

I'm not sure what any of that means for her or her future. However, I *am* certain that I'm attached. I'm hooked on Lou, and I don't know what the fuck I'm going to do about that.

CHAPTER 22

Louhi

ON THE FLOOR OF MY CELL, I CAN FEEL MYSELF BREAKING. Shattering within. I told myself I'd never splinter or collapse, but the price I'm paying is too steep, the burden too heavy.

It's *December,* for fuck's sake, and while I'd like to think that Mercer wouldn't abandon me, reality is settling in. It doesn't even matter what day it is in December, considering that my parents passed on the last day of November. *"Before the anniversary,"* he'd said.

It's impossible to imagine that Mercer would intentionally doom me to death like this, so I have to surmise that he's either dead or locked in a similar prison himself. *Is he here?*

Either way, I'm on my own now. He's not coming, and there's a crushing finality to the knowledge that I'm going to die here. Whether that's today or six years from now is anyone's guess.

I'll never drive a car again, get on a flight, boil water to make pasta, paint my nails, or apply my makeup. Damn, I'll even miss my next round of Botox. All the seemingly mundane, inconsequential things you do in a day that you never think twice about. I'll never again do any of them. Fuck, I'll never have the opportunity to breathe in the scent of fresh flowers or eucalyptus again. I only have my memory of those things, and I know that will eventually fade.

I'll never relive the feeling of slipping on my favorite pair of jeans or tasting the sparkly bubbles of crisp champagne buzzing along my tongue at a cocktail party while I prance around in a slinky dress and flirt with attractive strangers. I'll never dance my heart out in the middle of my living room while I sip a glass of wine, or head-bang in the mosh pit of a metal concert. I'll never skip among autumn leaves or feel the frigid winter air against my cheeks as I walk down the street.

I'll never see Finland again.

At this point, I'm standing at the mouth of Hell, banging on the doors, begging to be let inside. *Fucking take me already.* Anywhere, even Hell's inferno, is better than being here.

I'm crying, full-blown weeping as I sort through the things I'll never experience again. My silent sobs are wracking my body as I hear footsteps approaching. Why couldn't this be one of those moments when they choose to leave me alone in this cell to rot in peace?

Dipping my face inside the collar of my shirt, I wipe at my face, and for once I'm grateful for the dim lighting in this tiny rectangular concrete box.

Unyielding music masks the sound of footsteps until they're standing before my door. When I lift my head, Digs is the one that appears through the bars, holding a tray of more foul food, cocking his head to the side as if he's trying to discern what might be upsetting me, but I remain silent.

Instead of sliding the food through the slot, he opens the door to my cage and steps inside. I push to a sitting position as he squats down in front of me, setting the tray to the side. His eyes narrow as he studies my face, his expression clouding with something indecipherable, but for a split second, I wonder if that might've been concern.

Seizing me by the jaw, his strong, deft fingers dig into the hollows of my cheeks. His voice is low and gruff, all traces of his earlier gentleness gone as he asserts, "Fight, Lou. If you have to, make me your villain, your personal demon, the enemy of your state. Go to war with me if you must, but you will not break like this. This is not how you fall apart." As he tightens his grip, pain shoots through my mandible as I fight to clear my blurring vision. "I will be the only one to break you, and when I do, I promise to put you back together."

He releases me and stalks from my cell, slamming the door shut behind him. I sit there for a moment, soaking up his words, and for the first time since my parents' death, my heart begins to yawn open like a bear emerging from hibernation.

I don't know how many days pass, but I've had enough time to attempt to climb out of the black hole I spiraled down. Hell obviously rejected the idea of accepting me—for now—and I've found myself again.

I need to fight for myself. I have to find freedom however I can. I can't have done my skincare routine for the last time or had my final manicure. I haven't had my last glass of Bordeaux or slice of truffle pizza. And I certainly haven't killed my last victim. My time in this realm isn't over, and if I need to make Digs my mortal enemy to break out of here myself, I will.

Yet again, I find myself in the torture room, my wrists hanging from the damn ceiling. They turned up the heat in this fucking room today, too. It's hot, humid and bloody miserable. Sweat covers every inch of my body like a heavy blanket and slides down my bare skin in rivulets, pooling on the floor.

Since Honey Eyes is the one who collected me, surprise ripples through my bloodstream when Digs enters alone. He silently goes to the storage closet and comes back with a bin that he sets on the metal table I was strapped to and made to come. The heat notwithstanding, I shiver at the memory.

He wordlessly pulls the contents from the bin, arranging them on the table in full view.

I can do this. It wouldn't be my first time being whipped, and I'll survive this the same way.

Tossing the bin aside, he reaches for the chain whip and spins it around in his hand. The sinister clanking of the metal rods and rings that make up the foreboding weapon reverberate through my mind like a gong being struck. He saunters over to me, my naked body already on display from where he tore through my clothes… again. This guy has a serious thing for getting me naked. Under any other circumstance, I'd be all about that.

He glides the cold metal over my hot stomach, and I have to admit that the contrast in temperature feels good.

"Do you know what this is?"

"A chain whip."

"Then you know that it moves so fast that the human eye rarely sees it coming until it's too late." He handles the metal weapon with care as he turns it over in his hand.

"Doesn't everyone know that?" I parry, keeping my voice even. Of all my training, the whips were the worst to endure, and I have the scar to prove that.

He sighs. "No, Lou, not everyone knows that. How do *you* know that?"

I attempt to shrug, but my shoulders are screaming at me, and the attempted movement only further irritates them. "I know things."

He gives me his back, returning to the table, and replaces the chain whip. The relief I feel is palpable. I loathe to consider the damage that would've inflicted on my body. Although, any repose I might've experienced is short-lived when he picks up the tightly wound snake whip, that's aptly named with its tail coming to a point, mirroring that of a viper.

I keep my face a blank mask as he approaches me, but my mind is whirring at top speed as I focus on breathing through my nose steadily so I don't make a noise. *No, not that one. Put that one back. Turn around and return it to the bin. Don't touch me with that.*

Please.

He can't read my mind because he unfurls the long whip and drags the single tail up my thigh and to my center. As he dances the twisted nylon over my skin, I start to sweat for reasons wholly unrelated to the heat.

Suddenly, the temperature in the room makes far too much sense, and I'm tempted to smile at this bastard's creative depravity. When the whips inevitably break the skin, the sweat is going to sting like squeezing lemon juice into a wound. That's a fresh layer of hell that I've already survived and never wanted to experience again.

"Do you know what this one is called?"

I swallow past the dryness in my throat and reply with as much conviviality as I can muster, which isn't much, "A snake whip."

When he slithers the whip over its tattooed namesake, I resist the urge to flinch.

To my palpable relief, he retreats to the table once more, and I realize that this is a game with rules I'm not clear on.

Seizing the cow whip, the split tails stick out of the end of its spiral like the forked tongue of a coiled reptile poised to strike, he faces me again. I swallow my apprehension as he circles me, trailing the tails over the small of my naked back.

"And this one?"

"A cow whip."

A crack resounds half a second before it snaps across my arse. I grunt, absorbing the blow, as I buck in my restraints, my eyes shuttering and my skin stinging. He hits me twice more, and I'm seething by the time he retreats toward the table.

As he reaches for the next whip, I recognize the Russian cousin to the cat o' nine tails and my eyes latch onto the rawhide embodiment of Medusa as I force my nerves to settle. I don't miss the rock-hard package he's carrying between his legs.

The twisted rawhide thongs glide over my inner thighs lightly, making me suck in a breath. It's the calm before the storm because, in the next second, he cracks the whip and the tails fly, swatting violently against the tender flesh of my spread thighs.

"Recognize this one?"

"Knout," I hiss through clenched teeth.

The thing about whips is that the small sonic boom that's created is almost as torturous as the actual whipping itself. You hear the sound just long enough prior to the sting that you can stiffen in anticipation.

I'm a ball of tension when he batters my thighs and moves onto my lower abdomen. His strikes aren't enough to break the skin, just enough to leave red welts. He circles around behind me, and I close my eyes as he begins to whip the backs of my thighs.

"Talk to me and this stops."

I can't do it, though. I can't shatter under the weight of the pain and memories assaulting me. Besides, I don't have anything to tell him. The violence wouldn't end because he wouldn't believe me, even if every word is true.

I cry out at one particularly painful blow, and he warns, "We're just getting started, so you may as well get chatty."

At his warning, I brace myself, and it's a good thing because when the tails rage against my back, I don't bother to stop the tears streaming down my cheeks, mixing with the salty perspiration dotting my skin.

He hits me several more times, each time harder, with fewer slots of recovery time between lashings. He's broken the skin. I know that because I can feel the salty sting as beads of sweat drip into the wound. My body is on fire, and I shriek at his next hit.

I could handle the broken bones, waterboarding, and burning, along with everything else he's chucked my way. None of it was *pleasant*, but I managed it. I don't know if it's because he's whipping me so soon after my near breakdown, or if it's because I truly *loathe* whippings, but I'm teetering on the edge of losing control.

As he hits me once more, the scream that leaves me sounds unfamiliar, like I'm attempting to purge myself of the agony.

"Scream for me, Lou. I love that sound. Make it again," he purrs from behind me.

I do as I'm told—though the screams I make aren't for him right now, they're for me—as he hits me several more times. I'm about to go somewhere else, desperate for more savory memories of dinners at Conall's place in Boston, having a Michelin star meal while his friends make me laugh, when the torment abruptly ends.

The whip clatters on the table as he tosses it onto the metal surface. Now that I've caught my breath, my dark soul claws its way to the surface, and I find solace in myself again.

"Quitting already? I thought playtime was just getting started?"

My teary gaze meets his shadowy thundercloud-colored irises. As he prowls over to me, I imagine he's snarling underneath that mask.

With heavy breaths, his entire aura is coated in dark ferocity. He snatches me by the throat roughly, and growls, "Is that what you want? To play? You want to be a sadist's little whore?"

I say nothing, keeping my eyes bright and locked on his, but his naughty words send a surge of wetness directly between my legs.

"Are you wet right now, Lou? Or do I need to use your blood as lube?"

Fuck, why is that turning me on?

He studies my face like it's a treasure map with all the answers, and when I don't answer, there's amusement in his tone as he informs me, "Oh fuck, you want that. You want me to smear blood all over your cunt, don't you? You want me to use my cock to coat your insides in your blood."

My voice is small, but strong when I answer him honestly. "Yes."

I have no idea if I'm going to die here before I have the chance to escape, so I have nothing to lose by telling him the truth. I may as well have some fun before I enter the next fiery realm.

Digs disappeared.

Apparently, all it took for him to leave me alone was to utter a single honest affirmation. He vanished into the storeroom, slamming the door shut behind him. It's a *long* time before that door reopens and Honey Eyes slips into the room with me.

His golden irises flicker over my nude body as he approaches, carrying a new uniform set. The color of his eyes caramelizes, the hue deepening with lustful heat, but he says nothing as he releases me from my restraints. He scans the length of my body as I don the fresh uniform, carefully ignoring the way my new welts and cuts sting as they cleave open further. As I tug on the black cotton top, Honey Eyes's attention lingers on the years-old scar left by a snake whip.

The upside to constantly having my uniform cut from my body is that the new uniforms keep me from becoming *too* dirty and disgusting. In addition to my disdain for concrete, I'm going to have a very real aversion to grime after I escape. And I *am* escaping—or at least attempting it.

Once dressed, I start for the door to presumably return to my cell, when Honey Eyes's deep, liquid voice stops me. "How'd you get that scar?"

Something about the question gives me pause, and I turn around to find both curiosity and something that looks a lot like vulnerability sparkling in his vivid gaze. The way his amber eyes glow reminds me so much of the glittery look I once had. But that was a long time ago, before I became *this* version of myself.

Maybe it's the way he's exposing himself a fraction of a degree, or perhaps it's just the fact that I was stripped and beaten after nearly unraveling, mentally, a few days prior, but either way, I find myself answering honestly. Nodding toward the metal table that boasts the variety of whips Digs brought, I say, "Snake whip."

His gaze goes steely, the molten caramel hue from a few moments ago crystalizing at my admission. "You were whipped?"

I dip my chin.

Honey Eyes's chest rises and falls evenly as we study one another in the middle of this concrete torture room. A hundred questions swirl in his gaze, but he only chooses one. "You don't have many other scars. Why not?"

I'm not sure if he's attempting to inquire cryptically about my lack of a scar where I had my uterus removed, or if he's wondering how a criminal such as myself could survive this long without having marred, storied skin depicting years of hard-fought wars.

Sure, parts of my body—inside and out—tell snippets of my life's story, but it's far from the entire tale. That's how scars work; they're fractions of a whole. They're simply the rough grooves and bark on a tree, and digging into the dirt is required to glimpse the roots.

"Not every scar can be seen," I answer instead, somewhat enigmatically. It's the truth: most of the coarse, jagged ridges of my bark are invisible.

CHAPTER 23

Sean

I've said it before and I'll say it again, *I'm so fucking fucked.*

Lou's admission jacked me up. I couldn't get out of that playpen fast enough, sending Jace in to clean up my mess, as I beelined straight for the roof for a smoke. These damn cigarettes may not be the healthiest coping mechanism, but it's this or yank on my cock for what'd probably be the thousandth hour in months.

Any semblance of calm doesn't return until my second cigarette. I knew her "*yes*" was in response to *everything,* and it hit my dick like a lightning rod. I wanted to thrust into her right then and there. But I had—*have*—no business fucking her, especially since she's not really mine. Normally, that wouldn't bother me, but for some unknown reason, I want her to be mine if I'm going to slide between those perfect thighs.

She doesn't belong to me; she's property of the United States. Sure, the argument could be made that, as a representative of the government, she's mine for the moment. But I don't want her like this. I want her mind, her body, her fight, her trust, her loyalty. I want her outside of these concrete walls. I want her of her own volition. I want her to want me because *she wants me.*

This hellhole isn't an environment conducive to getting what I want.

I let her rest for more than a week after finding her falling apart on the floor of her cell. It was all I could do to hold back the resentment and anger I felt at myself for getting her to that point. The self-loathing and regret have chewed me up this week, and I'm still waiting to be spat back out. I'm a disgusting animal that deserves to be locked up along with the prisoners below my feet. I'm no better than Kazi.

But Louhi is.

She's got a dark allure to her that reels you into her snare, trapping you there as you wait for her to feast on you. And, fuck, if I don't want to get swallowed whole.

Bringing her in for a session today was too soon—for both of us. I shouldn't have done it, even if her screams seemed to be drenched in sugar. I'm still fighting the erection she left me with, but I refuse to touch myself, no matter how much I want to. I want to bathe in the sound of her screams, letting them bubble around me, but I don't want them this way, not anymore. I want them solely for me. I want them because she *wants* to give them to me.

I only chose the whips today because I wanted to see if I could match the whip to the scar on her side, and I knew the second I trailed the snake whip up her torso that it was the culprit. She made a valiant attempt to hide her apprehension, but it still swam in her chocolatey gaze. It was that glimpse of tension that had me picking up the knout instead. I wanted so badly to reach into her mind and wrench the memories out, one by one, uncovering the source of her pain.

I'll find my way back to Lou's cell later with salve for her welts and gashes. I can't let her suffer, even if I'm supposed to. Even if I enjoy inflicting pain when it comes to Lou, the guilt still edges in, clouding my head in a blanket of thick fog.

Lou isn't a job for me anymore, despite the way I've been

treating her. Fuck, I don't even think she belongs here. I don't want to be breaking her hands, stuffing her in small iron boxes, nearly drowning her, or anything else. I want to be done. But you don't tell the government you're done. I've signed a binding contract and there's no escaping until I've fulfilled my end of the bargain. Too bad for me that won't be for another three years. However, Lou only has a matter of *weeks* until her months are up, *not* that she knows that.

I'm still waiting for Major Thompson to show his damned face so I can talk to him about Lou. I'm growing restless and anxious to share my suspicions regarding Lou to Command.

What will they do with her? Will they transfer her away, or let her rot here?

I'm powerless to kill her, though I haven't shared that with anyone. I'm past the point of being able to hold my Glock to her temple and pull the trigger or slice into her vein and watch her bleed out. I *can't*—*won't*—watch her bright, beguiling light blink out of existence.

The sturdy metal door bangs against the wall as Jace appears, the rooftop access slamming shut behind him with a resounding *boom*. He slumps into the chair beside me, slipping a cigarette free from the pack on the armrest. It's a good thing he brought more of those when he came back from the mainland, because we've been flying through them lately as we try to puzzle out what the hell landed Lou here. We're no closer to answers though, just sootier lungs.

"Just got word that Thompson will be here tomorrow afternoon." Smoke billows from his mouth, briefly dancing with my own before a breeze whisks it out to sea.

Anxiety blooms in my chest. Thompson could either have my head—Jace's, too—for not getting the answers they require, or he could hear me out, seeing things from my point of view.

The blue of the ocean stretches as far as the eye can see—then beyond that—as the waves crash against the rock face below us. It's difficult to imagine other islands and continents existing when you see the world from this vantage point. It's isolating out here, cut off from the world, stuck in an inaccessible place that no one knows about. You truly are an exile here, even if you aren't locked in a cell.

"Fucking finally," I mutter.

"He's going to be pissed she hasn't broken."

Silence falls between us like snow that I haven't seen in years as I exhale a puff of smoke. Eventually, I admit, "I think she's beginning to."

He faces me, his mouth parting in surprise, transforming his round face into more of an oval. His dark eyebrows crease and his amber eyes appear murky with confusion. "What do you mean?"

"She's not breaking for *us*. She's breaking for herself." *And that's far more dangerous than shattering for me,* I add in my mind. A cold shiver runs down my spine as the revelation blooms to life with my breath.

"How do you know?"

"Her eyes told me. She's hurting." I don't tell him about the way I found her in her cell. Something about seeing her broken on the floor felt far more intimate than anything we might have done alone together in the playpen, for my eyes only. It's why I immediately deleted the footage of her breakdown.

He scrubs his free hand over his mouth a couple of times, grumbling, "Fuck, man, she can't break like that right now. I don't—" He falls silent, sucking on his cigarette for a moment. "If she breaks right now, she's fucked. She's not giving you *anything*, even in...private?"

Gazing out at the horizon, I shake my head before dragging my attention back to him. "I don't think there's a single thing anyone could do to that woman to get her to talk." I lean forward, resting my elbows on my knees as I dig the heel of my palms into my eye sockets. "I thought if maybe I changed things up, started fucking with her—literally—she might be caught off guard enough to give me something to work with. Well, that's what I told myself, anyway."

Deep down, I know that's not why I stripped her bare, desperate to see what was underneath her tough exterior. Regardless of my motive, things have backfired epically; the beautiful woman with a steadfast resilience beneath her solid façade only enthralling me further.

His smile is conspiratorial, and I know what Jace is about to say before he ever opens his mouth, but I force myself to hear it anyway. "You like her."

"So do you," I argue, pinning him with a flat look.

He scoffs, but amusement dances in his gaze. "Yeah, I do, but not in the same way you do."

Silence swims between us, as quiet, yet thick as a school of a thousand fish gliding through the ocean beyond us. Eventually, I murmur, "She needs a chance."

He nods slowly, as if he's thinking. "How do we play this?"

If she wants to live, she needs to stay stronger now than she ever has before, giving me and Jace a chance to get to the bottom of things on her behalf. After all, it's almost January.

Time is slipping away like particles of sand through a sieve.

I hope, for both Lou and myself, that she takes my advice, turning me into her enemy.

It might be the only way we both survive this.

"We help her."

"Let me get this straight. You think we have the wrong person and she *isn't* a terrorist?" Major Thompson asks, working through the, albeit limited, information I just laid out for him. His brow pinches as he paces the length of the small, shitty office space we're gathered in.

"That's correct, sir," I state, twisting my mask between my hands clasped at my back.

"And what do you think, Marshall?" Major Thompson

questions Jace, who's standing next to me, his stance wide, mirroring my own. I asked him to join me in this meeting today since he knew almost everything I did at this point. But the thing we *haven't* discussed is whether Jace agrees with me entirely. He was skeptical at first, and while I got the impression that he had become firmly on her side by now, I can't say for sure.

My breath becomes trapped in my lungs, the weight of my oxygen growing heavier, until he reveals, "I agree with him, sir."

I resist the overwhelming urge to allow my shoulders to slump, my relief palpable. It's as if Jace just pulled some bricks from the invisible backpack I've been carrying. There are plenty of bricks left, but the removal of one or two is enough for me to breathe easier.

"I see," Thompson says, and I wonder if he does, in fact, see. "I need to run this up the chain of command. I'll be in touch. In the meantime, sit tight and find out everything she knows, *by whatever means necessary*." He stares me down as he makes this last statement, and I'm smart enough to read between the lines.

What Thompson doesn't understand is that Lou won't be telling me shit. If she hasn't started talking at this point, why the fuck would she start now?

We spend the next half hour debriefing him on a few of the other prisoners, and he feeds us the orders to terminate Solomon, an international weapons dealer and complete menace housed in Block One.

Thompson dismisses us, taking Stuco's body with him back to the mainland when he leaves on the chopper. We all went to the helipad to watch Stuco leave for the last time.

I tried to take responsibility for Stuco's death, but Thompson waved me off, telling me that he should've known better than to engage with an inmate. I don't agree, but there's no point in arguing over who owns the fault. Especially considering that the blame lies squarely with Lou and she certainly won't be apologetic.

Borman has been particularly moody since we got back—not

that I blame him—and Jace is forced to order him to chill the fuck out.

This is going to be a long week.

"Maybe we should get Lou to do this for us. I bet she wouldn't have any problem with it. Shit, she'd probably be excited," Jace mumbles from beside me. I grunt an affirmation as we pull on our masks before heading into the playpen to deal with Solomon.

While Louhi doesn't seem to wrestle with cold-blooded murder, Jace and I do. It's the least savory part of this job, yet a necessary evil, according to the government. Jace and I take turns with the eliminations so neither of us shoulder the burden alone, though that only goes so far. I've never had issues with killing people who are threats to me or those I love. If you come for me, I'll come for you tenfold.

Nevertheless, the thing with the executions of the prisoners here is that it feels murky. Every inmate housed here, including Lou, are absolute fuckheads and have all done things that should guarantee them a death sentence. Things get gray when you develop relationships—however bizarre—with those fuckheads. Solomon is one of those cases. He's been here for six years, and though I'm not particularly fond of him, he doesn't disgust me like Peter or irritate the shit out of me like Carlos.

But we've wrung Solomon dry of any information he may have at this point, so I understand the orders.

It's Jace's turn, and I lean against the back wall as he explains to Solomon what's going to happen, and the prisoner nods curtly. I'm dying to know what's going through his mind as Jace injects him with the cocktail of potassium dioxide, midazolam, and vecuronium bromide. He doesn't speak again but closes his eyes as the cadence of his breaths becomes slower, more ragged. Forcing myself to watch, as I do with every prisoner, his chest eventually ceases to move.

After helping Jace and Martinez take Solomon's body to the freezer in the infirmary, I find myself stalking down Block One. Pausing at Soloman's cell, I linger for a moment, thinking about the fact that the amount of blood on my hands is becoming so thick that I can no longer glimpse my skin. I've killed more men than an avatar in a fucking video game.

The sonorous boom of Spite's "Kill or Be Killed" saturates the prison as my feet move of their own accord, transporting me farther down the corridor, and I find myself standing at the gate to Lou's cell, salve in hand. The second I lay eyes on her gorgeous, grimy face, my somber mood lightens a skosh. Every time I'm near her, the ivory bars encasing my heart both tighten and loosen simultaneously, like being around her is a paradox. She's a delicious poison that you know will hurt you in the end, but that possibility doesn't stop you from desperately wanting to guzzle down the venom.

She lifts her head to look at me, a dazzling smirk blooming on her face, but I don't miss the way she's lying on her stomach, her knees bent and ankles crossed as she rests her head on her elbows. No matter how hard I went at her thighs, it had nothing on the way I attacked her back and ass. Even a few days later, I'm sure it's still stinging, even with the balm I've been applying.

"Just couldn't stay away, could you, Digs?"

I don't reply as I step inside her cell, shutting the door to her cell behind me, but leaving it unlocked this time. She's right, though—I *couldn't* stay away, and I didn't want to. I'm so sick of the recent plague of bitterly anxious thoughts I've been hit with. No matter what I try, my mind won't shut the fuck up these days.

However, when I'm with her, there's a mellow calmness that quiets my thoughts. Being with her is like shooting myself with a small tranquilizer. I'm sated and happy, not that I'd admit that aloud.

Crouching beside her, I carefully roll up the hem of her

shirt and tug down her pants to access her wounds. She hisses as the cool salve makes contact with the gashes slashed across her pale, olive-tinted skin. She rests her head in the crook of her elbow as I apply the balm to her perfect round ass before rolling onto her side, looking up at me with eyes that sparkle with playfulness.

Having convinced myself that I *needed* this, needed *her,* to help clear my muddied thoughts, I disregarded my better sense to stay away. From the jump, there has been nothing *clear* about this woman, but as I tend to her now, my mind has as much clarity as a perfect diamond under the microscope, free of flaw.

I would do anything for her.

She has me wrapped around her finger like a ring that she wears every damn day, yet doesn't seem to realize it. She may be locked away from the world, but it's as if her blazing mysterious fire burned like a distress signal that only I seemed to answer.

Yesterday, I had her cell cleaned again, and it's a good thing because once I finish, she stretches out on the floor, like a housecat waking up from a nap, her shoulder-length onyx hair shifting with the movement. I don't know how someone can seem so *at home* in a maximum security, torture facility in the middle of the ocean on an unknown island, but she does.

With a content sigh, her bright, mischievous gaze drops to my hip, making me swallow hard as I'm slammed with the realization of how vulnerable—and reckless—this position is for both of us. Especially with my Glock so close to her hand and my tactical knife at my thigh. She could gut me or send a couple of rounds into my chest without a second thought but, for some reason, I don't think she will.

CHAPTER 24

Sean

Subject: L. KOSKINEN
Status: TERMINATION, TO BE COMPLETED BY JAN14

I STARE AT THE TWO LINES OF THE ENCRYPTED MEMO.

Time has ceased to exist, my vision going fuzzy the longer I focus on the screen. My heart sank to my feet the first time I read it before that dread morphed into disbelief. Now I'm so angry that I can't even read the words anymore. Hands balled into fists, I lean over the shitty computer screen. Did Thompson not hear me? I'm convinced that she *isn't* a terrorist. And now I'm expected to *kill* her?

Termination doesn't seem right. I don't understand. Jace is right; there's no way she's squeaky clean, but I'd stake my own life on her innocence of most of the charges that landed her here.

I'm not capable of killing her. I won't be able to go through with that, and there's zero fucking chance that I could stand there and watch Jace do it. She's someone's *sister*. I have a sister, for Christ's sake, and if someone simply shut a door in her face, I'd disembowel them. The idea of snuffing out her light fills me with an unholy amount of rage. Fuck, I'm such a hypocrite.

The slender predator isn't giving me the knowledge I *need* to keep her alive. If only there was a way to siphon information from her, even if it meant breaking a few more rules in the process.

I've never struggled to follow orders before, but I don't know what other option I have.

What the army wants, the army gets. And right now, they want Lou's head.

Bile races up my throat, but I shut it down by leaning into my ire. Clutching the first thing I can lay my hands on, I chuck the small, empty trashcan into the wall across the room, the plastic splitting in half with the force.

"Whoa, fuck. You good?"

My gaze shifts from the broken plastic shards to meet Jace's wide-eyed gaze in the doorway, and I shake my head. Wheeling the office chair aside so Jace can look at the screen, he moves toward the computer, tugging off his mask. I know the second he's read the words because his jaw tightens, the muscle ticking.

"What do we do?" he asks in a quiet voice, still staring at the screen.

"Let's go to the roof," I declare instead. I can't sit in this room anymore. Besides, I want to go somewhere that Big fucking Brother can't watch me lose my shit more than I already have.

On the roof, I stare up at the emerging twinkling stars speckled across the night sky while Jace begins chain smoking. The sun has just disappeared, so there's still a streak of light peeking through. If I were superstitious or believed in omens, I'd probably find the dash of light in the dark sky encouraging, but I'm not and I don't.

I'm fucked. Jace is fucked. Lou's fucked.

"I can't believe that's what they decided to do with her," he mumbles.

"They must think she's a loose end and we know how much the government hates those," I explain. I should've seen this coming. Would Lou have had more time if I had never said anything?

Did I doom her to an early death? *It's true that no good deed goes unpunished.*

I should've had longer—at least another month—before the hourglass officially ran out. However, I thought I'd found a way to turn the timer back over with the revelation that I suspect she isn't the criminal we thought she was.

"Is there anything we can do?" he asks, halfway through his second cigarette.

"Fuck, I don't know. We could try talking to her, telling her what's going on. Maybe she'd be more willing to talk."

"That'd only postpone the inevitable, though, right? What would be the point?"

I sit up in my seat, running a hand over my buzzed hair, thinking about tossing the mask in my hand into the damn wind, before leaning forward on my elbows. "It could possibly buy us some time."

He falls silent, contemplating my words. We don't have the luxury of time or options. The hourglass only has a few grains of sand left.

Louhi

"Don't tell me you missed me," I chime, as Honey Eyes reappears before my cell. He's long since collected my dinner tray, so I'm surprised to see him again.

"Let's go for a walk," he replies, his voice silky smooth. I'll never pass up a change in venue, and though I'm far used to the shitty lighting and rancid stench of this cell, I still jump at every chance to escape, even for a few hours. Fuck, I'll be glad when I never see this hellhole again. I have to tell myself that there will be an *after* to all of this. Without that, my spirit is crushed entirely, and Digs might not be there to pull me out next time.

Honey Eyes unlocks my cell, and I step into the hallway. While he walks at my back, I don't see any of the other guards who are usually around when I'm being escorted somewhere, which has my hackles rising, my mind slipping into high alert.

I'm made to stop in front of the usual torture room and resist the shiver that threatens to make its way to my pussy as memories of the last few sessions in here flood my mind. *Fuck, I hope there's another one waiting for me.*

I don't have time to explore that depravity as the door swings open to reveal a stoic looking Digs sitting at the metal table in the middle of the room. Honey Eyes presses a hand to my back, encouraging me to walk inside. The sound of the door shutting ricochets ominously through the room as Honey Eyes leads me to the chair opposite his friend and my shackles are attached to the bolts in the floor. Silence fills the room as Honey Eyes takes up residence against the wall at Digs's back, his arms crossed over his broad chest.

"We need to talk," Digs explains opposite me, his forearms resting on the table.

Nothing good begins with that statement.

My gaze slides to the camera blinking in the corner of the room, and Honey Eyes follows my line of sight. A moment later, he drags a chair over, stands on it, and rips it straight from the wall.

I *swear* I hear him mutter something about it not working anyway as he stalks back out of the room like a proper assistant, leaving me alone with Digs, and shutting the door behind him.

Something about this meeting feels rather odd and my body becomes primed for a fight, apprehension needling me. I scan the rest of the room, unable to find anything else out of place, but I keep my guard up higher than usual. *What in hell's paradise is happening here?*

"Lou," Digs starts over, taking a deep breath. I study his eyes and see something new and unfamiliar lurking within the silver of his gaze. He seems unsettled, his shoulders stiff and his posture rigid, and I realize it's body language I've never seen from him.

"I need you to answer my questions."

I lean back in my seat, attempting to get comfortable as I exhale noisily. Relief slides through my muscles, relaxing me marginally at the realization that this is nothing more than another attempt to glean information from me.

The lilt to my British accent is thick as I state plainly, "Digs, we've been through this before, but in case the message has been unclear, allow me to be direct: I have nothing to say to you."

"That's just it. You don't have anything to say to me because you didn't do what you've been accused of. You don't say anything because *you don't know*."

Blimey! I'll admit that I didn't see that one coming, and I don't care for being blindsided. I didn't anticipate this tosser working any of that out either, and Mercer's going to be put the fuck out when he discovers that. Keeping my face completely neutral, I turn into a bloodhound, sniffing out what he thinks he knows.

"Is that the conclusion you reach every time a prisoner doesn't tell you what you want?"

"Drop the act, Lou. Neither of us have the time. Listen to me when I say that you *need* to tell me what you know."

Neither of us have the time. What the fuck does that mean? Is that simply a turn of phrase or the foreshadowing of something far more ominous?

Instead of asking that, I inquire casually, "And why should I trust you? The man who *tortured* me for information?"

He has the audacity to look *guilty* as my words appear to pierce him. I'm surprised that he doesn't clutch his invisible wound. After all, he does have a flare for the dramatics.

I'd be lying if I said that his regretful expression didn't have my stomach twisting a bit, though. Anguish floods his blue-grey eyes, but I refuse to let that affect me more than it already has; instead, I reinforce the walls around my heart and head.

"I don't blame you for not trusting me, and I'm not sure there's anything I can say to change that, but I want to try. What if we exchange a little honesty?"

Remaining silent, I wait for him to continue. I'll be damned if I slice open my vein first. If my chains would allow me to cross my arms over my chest, I would, if only to hide the wariness floating down my skin like fog creeping into a forest.

"I know you didn't attempt to blow up the Federal Reserve. You didn't kidnap one of the members of the Board of Governors or attempt to kidnap two more. You didn't destroy or set fire to any buildings. *Maybe* you hacked into the Fed's system and did some spying—I'm not positive there. The only thing I *am* sure about is that murder is no problem for you, so that part is probably accurate."

Leaning forward, I summon a glimpse of my cunning, vicious, sanguinary personality to the surface of my expression. He's right—murder *isn't* a problem for me. In fact, I bloody like it. I steal lives so often that I don't even really think about it other than to reflect on the pleasant memories associated with some of my more brilliant moments.

"You don't know me, Digs. You don't know *what* I'm capable of."

He leans closer, his eyes drilling into mine so intently that I swear he can read my mind and decipher the etchings on my heart. He doesn't know me, though, and if he did, he wouldn't like what he saw, *could he?*

He's right about everything except for the arson. I've set buildings, and people, on fire before, but I wasn't responsible for this attack on the Fed. I took no part in that except for some mild hacking to discover the building's plans and security protocol for Mercer. I was stupid not to find out what the hell Mercer had gotten himself wrapped up in, but it's not like we had time to sit down for tea and discuss his plans in depth. Besides, my brother is the one person I've never questioned before, although I'm regretting not pursuing that line of questioning.

I didn't even know about the kidnapping until Digs mentioned it originally, and I didn't learn who was snatched until just now. *The Board of Governors… Really, Mercer?*

"Maybe not entirely, but I know enough to know that you don't deserve to die."

"We all deserve to die."

"You may be right, but we don't all deserve to die in the next three days."

Three days? Oh, bloody shit! Is he bluffing? It doesn't *look* like he's bluffing, but that's the entire point of a poker face. And, if he's not, how the hell am I going to get out of here in three fucking days?

Damn, time is running out.

I take a breath, reminding myself that I will find a way out of here if it's the last thing I do. I will not die here. I will see Finland again. I'll wrap my arms around Mercer and kick his arse for putting me in this position.

I *have* to hold on to hope.

Hope for escape. Hope for a future. *Hope for me.*

"Answer something for me." Choosing to call his bluff, my inner serpent lifts her head, baring her sharp, bloodthirsty fangs, dripping with venomous anticipation. "What's it like?"

"What's what like?"

"Being trapped in here with me?"

His eyes sharpen as he snorts. "I could ask you the same thing. You're the one trapped with an alpha."

The bellicose smile I wear drips with the renewed promise of retribution. "Digs, you may be an alpha, but I'm an apex predator. I'm most dangerous when I'm hungry, and right now I'm bloody *starving*."

CHAPTER 25

Sean

AS HUNGRY AS THE VIPER ACROSS FROM ME CLAIMS TO BE, I wish she'd either spit me out or swallow me whole already. God knows she's been taking little bites of me from the moment she first opened her mouth in the playpen.

"Lou, I'd be fucking blind not to see you for the beautiful monster you are, and while I'm a lot of things, imperceptive isn't one of them." I run a hand down my face, only to remember the damn mask that I never thought I'd forget I was wearing. I've come to *hate* the damn thing as of late and debate removing it now.

Releasing a chest-deep sigh, I prepare to lay all my damn cards on the table. I don't have anything left to lose. There's no camera, no one to hear my next words, no one except Lou. Jace is guarding the door, but he won't be able to hear me through the thick, substantial layers of concrete and metal dividing us.

If one thing is obvious to me, it's that Lou is extremely distrusting, closed-off, and suspicious. It's a quality that's probably kept her alive this long, but now I *need* her to try to trust me. There's no hope of accomplishing that without opening myself up first.

"I'm trying to help you. You don't have to believe me, but it's the truth. I don't want to see you die at the end of the week and, fuck, something's seriously wrong with me because I *can't* kill you.

I can't fucking do it, but if it's not me, it's going to be someone else, and I'm even less okay with that. Help me help you, Louhi."

The two of us study each other, her chocolatey eyes boring into me, as if she's searching for a lie that doesn't exist. Her expression no longer holds the savagery from a few moments ago, evolving into one of wary skepticism. I don't blame her for that.

Eventually, she tilts her head to the side before righting it again and breathing, "You mean that."

Louhi doesn't understand. She can't get it through her skull that saving her life is all that matters to me, even if that's detrimental to my own existence.

"Unfortunately for both of us, I mean every fucking word." I'm not sure I've ever been more forthright about anything in my goddamn life.

Reclining in her seat, she brings her hands up as far as her chains will allow, tapping her long fingernails on the metal tabletop absently, her eyes drilling into mine and her pouty lips pursing as she thinks. "Alright then, in exchange for your honesty, I'll give you some of my own. You're correct in your assessment, for the most part. You claim that my execution is to be at the end of the week, but I think you know that I won't be allowing that to take place… at least not without dragging you down to Hell with me."

I stare into Lou's bright eyes and my mom's words drift through my head on a phantom wind: "*You can always trust your heart, even when you can't trust your head.*"

Both my head and my heart are a chaotic mess these days, and I don't think I can trust either bastard at the moment. Opting to continue with my vow of honesty, I tell her, "Go on and drag me down to Hell with you then. We both know you'll find a way to be queen wherever you go, and I'll gladly worship at your feet for the rest of eternity if only to atone for the suffering I've caused you."

Admitting to the guilt I've been wrestling with over the way

I've treated her feels good, even if I'm not all that great with apologies, especially for things like this.

I've been trained to be a master of my craft; a villain and a hero. I've been made to believe that the suffering of one can save many and I've held on to that, choosing to believe the truth and heft of those words. Lou shifted things for me, though.

Her suffering isn't worth the safety of anyone else.

"I *do* like to be worshiped," Lou admits with a wink. "But you should never apologize for the things you like. You like inflicting pain and suffering. I like killing people." She shrugs before looking down at her poor, mangled fingernails nonchalantly, like she didn't just drop a bomb.

Suddenly, this makes sense. She's never once balked at my darkness. In fact, it's never appeared to have bothered her in the slightest. Wanting to be sure I interpreted her revelation correctly, I ask, "You're a serial killer then?"

We've had a few serial killers come through here—not many, but a few—but none of them have ever acted like Lou. I'm dying to find out everything I can about the enigma sitting before me. She's so unlike anyone I've ever met.

Looking up from her overgrown, dirty nails, she smiles at me. "I prefer assassin, but if you want to get technical, I suppose I could probably fit both definitions. I kill for money, though, not because I simply feel like it, although sometimes I do. However, I don't kill for the emotional or sexual thrill like most serial killers." Her bottom lip juts out in a pout. "Assassins get a bad rap. Just because I like my job doesn't make me a serial killer."

Fuck me to Hell and back because I think I understand what she's saying perfectly. Shame over my sadistic tendencies and the darkness that lives within me remain strapped to my shoulders; but seeing her so freely accept her own proclivities reminds me that I don't have to feel bad about who I am either.

"What's your kill count?"

She smirks, her voice light and giggly when she replies, "Don't you know it's impolite to ask a lady her number."

I say nothing, only giving her a flat look, holding my breath as I crave her answer. Lifting her hand as high as her restraints allow, she waves it through the air nonchalantly, her chains jangling with the movement. "One hundred seventy-two. Actually, wait, that's not right. That guard made one hundred seventy-three."

I blink at her, disbelief rippling through me. "*One hundred seventy-three people*? You've killed one hundred seventy-three people?"

Her eyes narrow, and I know she's about to call me out for my hypocrisy. "Hello, pot. Meet kettle. How many people have you tortured?"

"Touché." I huff, mirth edging into the sound. "You've got me there, Lou. But I don't know the answer. I've never counted." *Nor have I counted the number of men I've killed at the request of the government, both here and during my time in Special Forces.* While Lou might be comfortable with the knowledge of her kill count, I wouldn't be. That would surely fuck with my valuable sleep.

As if understanding how bad counting my victims would be for my psyche, she nods slowly. Until Lou, I've never really allowed myself to stop and think about my victims as anything other than prisoners worthy of the most horrific suffering and death. I've never wanted to count them before, and if I let myself go there now, it wouldn't be good. I'd drown in that bottomless black hole.

"What happens now?"

"I don't know," I answer honestly, the rise and fall of our chests seeming to synchronize as we stare at each other. Her filthy black hair has grown out a little, and a thin layer of dirt is painted over her skin, but even through the mark this place has left on her, she's still so beautiful.

As I stare into her eyes, the tiniest glimpse of uneasiness flashes across her vision, and it grips my chest in an iron grasp. The need to comfort her, to assure her that she can depend on me overwhelms me, and I tell her, "I'm going to figure it out. Trust me."

She laughs, the sound darker than her last giggle, any trace of possible anxiety gone in an instant, like autumn eating the last remnants of summer in the blink of an eye.

"I'll prove that you can trust me, Lou." *If she'd simply give me the chance.*

Now I just need to ensure I don't let her down. I'm going to get her out of this mess and earn her trust, no matter the cost.

CHAPTER 26

Louhi

Honey Eyes took me back to my cell where I've been replaying my conversation with Digs for the last few hours. Even if I had something better to do—which I don't—I'd still be analyzing every word he said and the ones he didn't, dissecting each pause, and examining all his expressions.

I spent the first however long thinking about how he *sort of* apologized for torturing me. I come from a world where apologies don't exist and the people who screw you over die instead. Forgiveness is a foreign concept to me and not something I've *ever* granted someone. If you wrong me, that sentences you to death. I don't know what it's like to let go of the bitterness and indignation I've held toward someone other than to kill them. But as I paced the three steps forward and back—four, if I take tiny steps—within my cell, I realized I don't hold any resentment toward him for what he's done to me. Am I still irritated that he took my toenails and lit my skin on actual fire? Hell yes. But do I hold that against him? Not really. And that shocks me to my core.

There's a kinship I share with Digs. His beast is so like mine: thriving in the dark, feasting on blood and depravity, aching to be unleashed to wreak bloody havoc on the world. I saw it in his eyes as he sat across the table from me. I could also see that he's struggling to carry the shame of that darkness. I'm years ahead of him in that department, but I remember the desolate isolation that would trickle into my mind. Thank God I had Mercer to help me navigate those emotions and embrace myself for who I am. It took me years to fully accept myself and my abnormal feelings, but once I finally did, the world became my oyster. Too bad I can't help Digs find a way to get there too.

I'm not doing quite as well with the other information he divulged. I didn't anticipate him working out that I shouldn't be here, and I'm not sure how that will affect me or Mercer. I didn't want to ask about my brother since no one has seemed to work out that *he's* the one who should be here instead.

Then there's the information I chose to reveal. Something about his sincerity and the softness in his gaze had me opening my mouth and spouting truths I had no intention of sharing.

I don't know what Digs plans to do with my admission, but I've never shared my kill count with *anyone*; though, I keep a careful mental count. I don't know what I'm going to do when I hit two hundred, but maybe I'll host a party or something. *If you're still alive,* my brain supplies unhelpfully.

Lying down on the damp, moldy floor of the cell, I stretch out diagonally and close my eyes, thinking through a way of escape. I *will* stay alive.

I wasn't lying when I told him that I wasn't going to allow myself to be killed at the end of the week; I am simply too determined to see the outside world again. What I *was* lying about was taking Digs down with me if I get caught. I wanted that declaration to be true, but even as I said the words, they tasted like acid on my tongue.

What is this man doing to me?

Would Digs be willing to help me escape? I can't imagine that's what he meant when he said he'd figure it out. But what if it was? Every time I'm with him, I can't help but feel as though the darkness residing within each of us is drawn to the other like a magnetic pull. I wonder if he feels it too. Although, what if our inner beasts aren't calling to each other like I originally thought? What if it's our souls fighting and clawing to get closer? What if it's a mating call, one soul to another, and we're destined to respond?

I've never been one for fate or destiny. The only compass or divine sense I follow is my gut. She's never wrong. Ever. And right now, she's telling me that Digs is Team Lou. I should trust that, right? But that's crazy. Trusting my enemy would be ludicrous.

I'll do *anything* to secure my freedom, but something tells me Digs would have lines he wouldn't be willing to cross; I shouldn't put all my eggs in that basket. I need to make plans of my own. After all, I've always had my own back.

I've run through approximately one million scenarios at this point, but none have yielded results that don't end with me dead. I haven't begun to see nearly enough of this place to make a successful escape attempt, and that's a problem. I overheard a guard once say something about Block Ten, but I haven't seen more than this one cell block I'm being kept in, and I'm certain that was on purpose. I've only been to the infirmary, the washroom, and the torture room. That's not enough to go on for a legitimate escape attempt, and I have no choice but to nail it on the first try. Otherwise, they'll either lock me up so tight I won't be able to make a second attempt, or they'll just kill me. To make this work, I need to explore more of this place at some point in the next day or two.

Thy Art Is Murder's "Reign of Darkness" suddenly blasts through speakers, and I bob my head along to the music. It's louder than usual—and it's always at a near deafening decibel—but at least they're finally playing something I know and like. I'm nodding along when my cell door abruptly swings open, revealing three guards, the noise drowning out their arrival. Has Digs sent them? There's no way he's already worked a way out of this situation for me. If so, damn, he works fast.

Sitting up, I leer into the masked faces before me, but something about this feels *off.* On the surface, it doesn't seem all that unusual; nevertheless, my gut is screaming at me that something about this is wrong.

The guard in the center steps inside my cell, his rifle strapped to his back, a second Glock at his other hip, and a total of three combat knives, instead of the usual two. *Blimey, this is definitely wrong.*

"Let's go," he growls, and even in the low light, I can see the hatred boiling in his brown eyes.

"I don't think so," I counter, shaking my head as unease drops into my empty stomach like lead.

"It's not optional. *Let's go.*"

He's wrong. Life is full of options. Some are as simple as yes or no. Others are much more complex, like life or death. This *is* optional, though, at least to some degree.

Quickly assessing my options, I land on a surprise attack. Holding my ground, I wait until he's entered my personal space. Once he's standing just before me, I swing my head back and slam it into his forehead as hard as I can. He grunts and, with a satisfied smile, I bring a knee up and smash it into the infinitesimal balls he's got between his legs.

He doubles over, and I go for the knife at his hip, but don't get to it before the other two guards rush to his aid, one of them subduing my arms and jamming a needle into the muscle of my shoulder.

I sway on my feet, my vision hastily blurring. Just as I'm about to black out, I wonder if this was Digs's plan all along.

I'd pay good money for them to stop knocking me out. It hurts like hell coming out of that murky, drugged haze. I don't know what they shot me up with, but I can tell my arms are restrained over my head and something unyielding and firm is wrapped around my ankles. With my eyes still closed, I decide to risk curling my toes to see if they'll move without my captors noticing. Paralysis would be a problem. Fortunately for me, they do.

"You overdosed her, you fuckhead," one of the guards grumbles.

So, they want me awake.

"I'm a fucking medic; I know exactly how much I gave her, and I didn't overdose her," I hear another snap, and I nearly give away my state of consciousness by spitting at him. However, if this is the same guy who touched me on that table in the infirmary, he's got a lot more than just a little saliva coming his way.

"Fuck it. Let's start without her being awake. It'll be more fun to see her wake up to it anyway," another says, and I think he's the one I went after in my cell.

Jeesus Kristus, is everyone around here spectacularly fucked in the head?

The heat of a body steps into my personal space just as something slices through my clothes, stripping me bare. When the balmy, warm air of the room kisses my skin, I don't feel the same thrilling anticipation as when Digs touches me.

I can't help but notice the similarity of this situation and my time spent with Digs; the resemblance is uncanny. Did he orchestrate whatever is happening now? I mean, that's repugnant, even for him. But is it possible? I don't want to believe that.

Digs did say he couldn't kill me, but was he simply full of shit? I'd have been a fool to believe him, even if part of me wanted to, but based on my current situation, I can't help but wonder if it was all a lie, if *everything* was a lie.

The last of the tatters of my clothing are pulled from my body and I'm left hanging from the ceiling, my legs tied to the floor. Deciding that my eyesight would be useful right about now, my lids flutter open, and I immediately regret that decision. Three masked men stand in front of me, flipping blades in their hands.

"Glad you finally joined us. You were about to miss all the fun," the one on the left states, glee edging into his tone. But it's not the fun kind of glee that Digs gets when he's about to give in to his darkness. No, this motherfucker is just foul.

"Are you familiar with Lingchi?" the middle one asks, stepping forward, dragging the tip of his combat knife up the soft skin of my side. I get the sense that this bloke is the ringleader of this little trio, and it only makes me all the happier that I head-butted him.

"Death by a thousand cuts," I sneer, well acquainted with the ancient Chinese art of execution. I wouldn't be a very good assassin if I didn't have a vast number of tools in my tool belt.

"Then you know it's one of the most excruciating forms of torture and death?"

"Obviously." This patronizing wanker is only serving to piss me off at this point.

The other two join him then, circling me like wild hyenas. Look, I'm all for having a creative outlet, but this is not the healthiest of choices.

"We've been given orders for your execution, you know. But they never care how the prisoners die here," the one behind me jeers.

Was Digs's earlier conversation with me simply to taunt me, knowing that I'd die tonight? Was his goal all along to dangle the alluring picture of freedom in front of my face, just to add to the torture of yanking it away again via painful death?

I can feel my body going hot as my blood simmers, bubbling within my veins, and if I were to open my mouth, fire would surely flow from my lips. Betrayal scorches me from the inside out, burning my skin and melting away any parts of my heart that I, for a moment, let soften toward Digs.

Past the burning cinders, deep within the recesses of its ivory cage, my heart weeps. Shoving the ache aside, I focus my attention on my fury, letting it fuel my fire instead.

Thinking I could trust anyone other than myself was a mistake—a mistake that appears will cost me dearly.

My anger blazes more intensely than the pyre I'm dreaming of placing Digs atop, my lip curling as I imagine the smell of his flesh charring, smoldering until there's nothing but bones left.

It won't be enough.

Up until now, I've gotten the impression that Digs's sadistic tendencies were physical, not so much psychological. But I can't presume to know him at this point, so what if I got that bit wrong? What if I got *everything* wrong? What if my gut finally let me down?

My thoughts buzz like a hive of crazed wasps as one of the men slices into my shin lightly, just below my kneecap, and I hiss at the sharp sting. Another is made to my upper thigh, another to the backside of my shoulder.

Just like that, the bloodletting has begun.

Slice.

Cut.

Slash.

I bottle my screams as a gash is made on the top of my foot, a howl erupting within my chest that I trap there. My head slumps as I observe my blood dripping, falling, sliding onto the concrete. The same arsehole makes an identical cut on the top of my other foot, forcing the tears to begin sweeping down my face in a sheet of salty water.

How am I going to make it out of this?

Even as I close my eyes, trying to draw on the memory of the last time I saw my parents before their deaths, the pain seeps into my soul, blotting out the kiss my father pressed to my temple. Still, I try to recall my mother's arms wrapped around me, tucking me in to her slender body, telling me they'd be back in time for dinner, but the panic and suffering keeps the memory just out of reach.

Desolation hurts as bad as pain, and in my desperation, I assess my situation, realizing that there's no hope of escape, only to endure.

The cuts they're making are shallow, but that's how this whole thing works. These blokes clearly aren't adhering to the traditional practice of Lingchi by *removing* the more insignificant pieces of my flesh, like my arms or legs, but the result is essentially the same: maximum pain and suffering before they extract more vital pieces from my body.

Pain, sorrow, rage, and betrayal are my only companions as they carve up my body. Even if, by some miracle, I am to survive this, I'll be permanently marked with the agonizing memory of this experience, my body forever displaying the torture I endured.

Will Mercer be informed of my death? If he is, I hope he remembers to invite Conall and Viktor to my funeral.

Crouched before me, one of guards looks up, and I take the opportunity to memorize his hazel eyes, so that I'll remember them in this lifetime and the next. Mentally, I vow to come back and make the deaths of these three far worse than mine. And once they're dead, I'll begin the cycle of retribution all over again in the afterlife, making sure these three *rest with stress.*

And then there's Digs. I'll play with him until he's *begging* for death, then I'll make his eternal state of rest so fucking miserable that he won't find a moment's peace. He won't know true agony until I'm finished with him, then I'll begin again.

I'll be so bloody busy with vengeance that I won't even have time to suffer in Hell myself.

Hope springs eternal…until it doesn't, and I've just about lost it. Only a few hours ago, I was plotting my escape, optimistic that I would get the bloody fuck out of here. Not so much anymore.

The slices are coming rapidly now. Over my stomach, back, across the side of my neck. A thin cut is made to the tops then below each of my breasts, drawing a whimper of excruciation and torment from me. It's a plea for help, one brimming with emotional anguish.

For the first time in my life, my mortality surrounds me, closing in. I'm alone and scared. I've faced death and lived to tell the tale before, but now? Like this? Tied up with no way out, tortured and killed by blood loss and pain? I don't know if I'll survive that, so I release my anxiety, suffering, and loss in a bloodcurdling wail.

In the first scream that I've allowed to slip from my lips tonight, I shriek for the life I'll leave behind; I scream for the love I've never had and the days I'll never see.

I scream for *me*.

They keep slashing until I'm covered in at least a hundred superficial cuts, some deeper than others, then they jostle me around so that the wounds seep blood and tear open. My eyes drift shut as I beckon death to whisk me away from this hell and escort me to the next.

"This is for Stuco," one of them snarls as he drags the tip of his blade down the center of my chest, over my sternum. Though, I must be going into shock because an iciness crowds my senses, the pain lessening, and I hope that means the end is near.

Despondency rolls in like a dreary mist and takes up residence. Hanging my head, I attempt to increase the difficulty of pulling oxygen into my lungs, hastening death.

A violent roar cuts through the vacant static warbling in my ears, and I know without opening my eyes who it came from. I can sense him, despite the blackness creeping in. The air around me crackles and fizzes with his overwhelming presence. He must be here for the grand finale, but I don't want to give him that satisfaction. Summoning every remaining molecule of strength within me, I peel my eyes apart and drag my thousand-pound head up, resting it against my bleeding arm as I regard the blue-eyed beast filling the open doorway.

Except, I don't see a bright excitement looming in his irises as he watches me succumb to death. Instead, a dark hurricane swirls in his stormy eyes: shock, fear, and unrestrained fury spilling from every inch of him.

A whimper crawls up my throat, but I trap it there.

He came for me.

He doesn't hesitate for a single moment before yanking the man to my right from my body by the back of the neck, slamming him against the wall. In the time it takes me to blink, Digs has his Glock at the man's temple and pulls the trigger, painting the grey concrete a beautiful shade of garnet.

I had it wrong. I had it so fucking wrong.

How could I have believed he'd have been in on this? After all, wouldn't he have wanted to kill me himself?

My gut is always right, and I should have trusted her. *I should have trusted* him.

He told me to trust him, and I didn't. I've never been able to rely on anyone else before, but fuck it all, I think he may have just proven himself a worthy exception.

Something in my chest—*in the fiber of my bones*—yearns to be let loose, straining to reach for him.

For a moment, I let myself believe that he had lied. I suppose that was easier than admitting that I didn't want him to be the one who hurt me. I wanted him by my side—outside of this place.

Maybe it's the blood loss, but I want a future, one with him. I want to learn his favorite foods, and how he likes to spend his Saturdays, and how many times he's watched his favorite movies.

Another tear coasts down my face, dripping into an open cut on my cheek, making it sting anew. I'm so weak: blood-loss, exhaustion, and fear threatening to drag me under their spell, but I force my eyes to remain open.

"You'll never get away with this, Diggory," the man behind me sputters as Digs hauls him away from me. The hazel-eyed fucker in front of me dashes toward the open door, but Honey Eyes suddenly appears, his golden eyes widening as he takes in the scene, before transforming into a blaze of indignation.

He snatches the masked man before he can make an escape, holding a knife to his jugular. Dragging him back inside the room, Honey Eyes slams the door behind him.

My attention shifts as Digs positions his Glock at the guard's head.

"Wait," I whisper hoarsely, my vow of retribution humming through my weakened veins.

Digs and Honey Eyes whip their heads toward me, their weapons poised to strike.

"Wh—which one is the medic?" I ask, my need for vengeance the only reason I'm able to get the words out.

"This one," Digs supplies, turning the sod in my direction and shoving him to his knees.

"I want him," I rasp.

Digs stares into my eyes for a long moment before taking in the vast extent of my injuries and softening his tone. "Let me be your hands, your wrath. Tell me what to do and I'll do it."

Barely able to speak, I know this is as close as I can get to revenge, so I order roughly, "Take off his mask. I want to watch him die."

Digs rips the mask from the guard's head, gripping him tightly by his shoulders. The guard's face twists as he jerks against Digs's hold, but there's a slight quiver in his movements. *Good, I hope he's scared.*

"Cut out his eyes. He saw things he shouldn't."

Digs's gaze slams against mine, holding for a moment before he nods. He holsters his Glock and pulls the knife from its sheath before snapping the man's head back and carving into his left eye like it's a Christmas turkey. Gouging out his eye, he rips it from the socket, then repeats the process on the other side. The man's blood-curdling screams are so loud that I smile, despite the effort and pain.

Sounds of the soldier's agony lessen my own, the retribution nourishing my twisted soul as it loosens the iron grip that potent suffering and hatred had on my heart. I feel lighter with each cut Digs makes on my behalf.

"Remove his hands. He touched something without permission." My voice is hoarse, body trembling from the inside out as I endeavor to regain my composure.

Digs glances at me for a beat as if seeing me for the first time, but he's never seen my darkness glow like vivid, lustrous moonlight glittering across still water before. He's never witnessed the violent brutality that I'm capable of inflicting. I've seen his darkness; now he's seeing mine.

After only a beat of hesitation, he grips the guard's hand and the man thrashes, desperately attempting to yank it away, but Digs punches him in the mouth and he rocks back.

My chest squeezes in delight, like someone is gently stroking the callous scales on my heart, soothing me.

Digs starts slicing through the man's fingers, tossing each digit aside before cutting through the bones of his wrist. My feral smile grows, the joy of this man's suffering numbing my own pain.

When he finishes removing both hands, I wonder if I can ask him to remove his fucking brain since he knew too much, but ultimately decide that might be taking things a bit far, so I settle on something a little more...palatable.

"Make him bleed out."

With every slice Digs makes, the tension coiled around my muscles lessens like a sedative drip slowly leaking into my system.

He makes several strategic cuts down his forearms and steps back as we all watch the remaining blood in his body spill onto the floor, joining his discarded body parts. Everyone looks on quietly; the only sounds in the room are the whimpers from the dying fuck on the floor and screams of impending doom from the other, unfortunately still breathing, arsehole.

"Shut the fuck up and watch the show, Borman," Honey Eyes demands of his captive.

Too soon, the medic breathes his last breath, his chest going still. Just as I'm about to start in about the next fucker, Digs steps over the dead man and approaches me.

CHAPTER 27

Louhi

"Take Borman next door and deal with him," Digs orders Honey Eyes, the two of them disappearing as Honey Eyes drags the screaming guard from the room.

Digs slices through the bindings at my feet and my breaths become more rapid as I snivel, "Wait—"

Rancor sparks, tossing gasoline on my fiery need for retribution. I'm not finished with those who dared to snuff out my light. Digs ignores me, however, slicing through the rope over my head. My muscles fail me as I fall into Digs's powerful body, his strong arms wrapping around me as he catches me.

"Shut the fuck up and let me take care of you, Lou. Honey Eyes will keep him warm for you, I promise." Part of me loves that Digs is calling his mate Honey Eyes now. I hope that nickname sticks long after I'm gone from this place.

He drapes my body carefully across the table in the corner of the room, the biting chill of the metal making me grimace. My wounds pull and sting, but I grit my teeth against the discomfort. Digs disappears and returns a moment later with clean hands and a first aid kit. While I think I'm far past a first aid kit, I don't say anything as he begins cleaning some of the deeper cuts with antiseptic, making me hiss.

My eyes fill with tears—from the punch of physical or emotional pain, I don't know—but blink past them, fixing my gaze on the ceiling for a moment before meeting his gaze. "I thought—I thought you were with them."

His eyes, the color of sunlight kissing the vast ocean, soften in a way I've never observed from him. "I told you that you could trust me."

"You...you proved it," I whisper, my voice hoarse.

"I said that I would."

A warm tear slips free, sliding down my cheek as we observe each other, but I don't make a move to wipe it away. My lashes grow heavier, clumping together, as I fight the urge to let the dam break.

"I've never trusted anyone before," I admit. "Except for my brother."

His movements halt as he sets the bottle of disinfectant down next to my bare shoulder. As his masked face appears above mine, he brushes a hand over my hair, the look in his eyes spearing me right in the chest. Like a bell tolling, I can hear the sepulchral tone of my heart for the first time since my parents' death.

Would it really be so bad if I let this man in? How dangerous would it be for me to give Digs a tiny piece of myself? Fuck, I want to open for him like I've never opened for anyone.

The tectonic plates between us shift as Digs trails his hand from my head down my face, my neck, my breasts. He leans down, pulling his mask up over his mouth, his pink tongue darting out to lick the bleeding cut just above my nipple, before nipping at the tightened bud.

"Damn vampire," I hiss.

His dark chuckle reaches my ears. "I'd bleed you dry if that's what it took to be with you."

To be with you. Is that what he wants? Is that what *I* want? Bloody hell, I think it might be.

Doubt creeps in, and I pull my upper body up to lean on my forearms, my abs seeping more blood with the movement.

"I—I don't even know what you look like."

"Is that what you need? To see my face? To know what you're getting?" he asks, his voice rougher than usual.

"No." I already know I'll find perfection beneath his mask. I don't need to see his face to know exactly the man I'm getting in Digs.

"Good, now lie back." My argument now removed, I gingerly do as I'm told, and he yanks me toward the end of the table by the ankles. I choke on the breath caught in my throat as white-hot pain lances through the open wounds on my back, setting my nerve endings on fire. Curiosity and excitement bubble through me, eclipsing the pain, as my legs dangle over the end, my arse at the edge.

"Wh—what are you doing?"

"Making you mine."

I want that. I want him.

Raw adrenaline races inside my veins, my heart rate spiking at his words, jolting me to full consciousness. Desire surges through me, likely visible between my thighs, as my entire body tightens in anticipation.

He sweeps his fingers across my bleeding abdomen, making me inhale sharply at the pang, but the kiss of discomfort is overshadowed as he covers my cunt with my blood. My chest heaves as he repeats the process, dipping his fingers into the pools of blood in various places on my person before smearing it inside and out of me.

Lifting my head, I catch him tugging off his shirt that's covered in the blood of the dead guards and discard it, leaving his tan chest bare, save for the silver dog tags resting against his flesh, glinting beneath the fluorescent light. His burly physique is nothing but cut ridges and hard planes with veins slithering across them. Ample muscles give credence to his solid strength, but he's lean and lissome in a way that portrays an agility that matches his brawn.

His body is nothing short of incredible.

As he unfastens his belt, his abs tighten, bunching as he shoves his uniform trousers and boxer-briefs down past my eye line. He takes his impressive erection in his hand and strokes himself a few times, a bead of moisture glistening at the tip. I moan at the sight, my pussy fluttering. Just as I give in to the temptation to reach for him, he steps between my spread thighs, lining himself up with my entrance.

Craning my neck, I strain to watch as he slides himself up and down through the blood and copious wetness gathered between my legs.

"I told you I'd use my cock to coat your insides in your blood, but I will be the only one to make you bleed from now on. Do you understand?"

I whimper, bucking my hips, urging him to dip inside.

"I said, '*Do. You. Understand?*'"

"Yes."

"Say, 'yes, Sean.'"

Sean. Every time this man reveals something new, another brick of the wall around my heart falls away.

"Yes, Sean," I repeat, his name tasting like the most decadent dessert on my tongue. "Make me yours, Sean," I demand, dying to taste his name again.

With our eyes locked, he slides inside, drawing a whimper from me at the glorious invasion. His thrusts are agonizingly slow and methodical, every ridge and vein of his cock caressing my inner walls. He maintains his languid pace, and it's the sweetest form of torture I've endured. My eyes drift close, my fingers finding purchase on the lip of the table as he begins to stroke my clit in tandem.

It's not long before his self-control snaps, and he begins to slam into me with faster and harder thrusts, just the way I like, the dog tags around his neck jingling with his movements. His cock finds that euphoric place inside of me and assaults it with expert precision, my lashes tickling my cheeks as my eyelids flutter shut.

Just as his name flies from my lips, my eyes snap open, his expression dripping with power and possessiveness. I want to lap it up like it's the nectar of the gods, and maybe it is—the nectar of someone who's quickly becoming *my* god, anyway.

When he removes his fingers from my clit, I whine at the loss, but cut myself off when he leans over my body, grasping me by the neck firmly with one hand and clenching the top of his mask with the other. Slamming back into me, he yanks his mask off, my gaze pinned on his face as I take in his masculine beauty. And damn, he's nothing short of magnificent.

"Look at me, Lou. See who you belong to."

And I fucking do.

His clean-shaven jawline is as sharp as the knife he used to pluck that guard's eyes out. A faint, small scar runs diagonally between his left temple and the top of his cheekbone. His nose is long and strong, appearing to have been broken a few times, and his ash-brown stern eyebrows appear to be a shade or two lighter than his cropped hair. As someone who hasn't kissed anyone in years, I surprise myself by suddenly dying to feel his enviable lips on mine. They beg to be kissed.

He tightens his grip on my windpipe subtly, an overt reminder of who holds the power here, though it's not enough to choke me, as he continues to pound into me, his tags kissing my breasts. Relaxing into his grasp, my orgasm tingles on the horizon. I stare into his handsome face as we both chase the wave, my entire body coiling with the impending release.

Just as I'm about to topple into orgasmic bliss, I claim, "You're mine, Sean."

He growls a confirmation as I scream through my climax, my back arching, my fingers clawing at the table for purchase before finding Sean's back, my nails digging into his skin as he follows me into ecstasy. *I hope I scar him.*

Sean

We stare at each other as our breathing regains its normal rhythm. Lou tentatively reaches up and drags a finger down the side of my face as a small smile touches her lips. I didn't realize it until now, but I was nervous for her to see my face. I was shielding myself behind the sense of anonymity my mask provided. It felt unguarded for her to see the real me. Though, no more vulnerable than telling her my real name or claiming her as mine, I suppose.

Releasing her neck, I right myself, reluctantly sliding out of her, my cock coated in Louhi. As I stare down at the streaks of her blood still clinging to me, I smirk. Quickly, I redress myself from the waist down and slip into the storage room to grab a blanket.

When I get back, Lou has curled into the fetal position on the table and the sight makes me see red all over again.

I had been asleep when something woke me up. Unable to shake the feeling that something was wrong, I got dressed to make sure everything was locked down as it should be. I had just laced my boots when I heard the scream, immediately recognizing the sound as coming from Louhi. It wasn't the kind of scream that made my dick hard or something I ever wanted to hear again. No, this scream wrapped itself around my heart like a damn boa constrictor, nearly squeezing the life out of me. It wasn't the same scream she's made for me. This scream was different: panicked, agonizing, a sound of surrender that had me racing toward the source at a dead sprint.

Even from down the dingy hallway, her presence radiated from the room she was held in like a torch cutting through the inky night.

She lights up the dark; but much like a bonfire, if you get too close, you'll burn to ashes.

What she doesn't realize is that I'd risk a thousand infernos for her.

The tether grounding me snapped like a rotten cord weathered from years of sunlight. I've never known rage like the kind that pumped through me at the sight of Lou strung up, sliced open, covered in her own blood. However, it was the look of total defeat etched onto her pretty, blood-smeared face that cut my heart open. She had given up. She was waiting for death to take her from me. She was fucking *ready* for it. That only made me angrier, and I didn't hesitate in killing Davis for daring to make her feel that way.

The faint glimmer of herself that resurfaced when she told me that she wanted Jones for herself was the only thing that pulled me back from losing myself to the pitch-black rage nearly eclipsing my mind. It gave me pause when she said she wanted his eyes, but fuck if I didn't want to give that woman everything she desires in this world, including a set of eyeballs. The fact that she trusted me with her retribution told me everything I wondered about how Lou felt about me.

She trusts me.

That was only etched into stone the moment she said she was mine. She sealed her damn fate when she cried out that I was hers too.

"Sean," Lou mumbles, and my heart squeezes at the sweet sound of my name on her luscious lips.

Begrudgingly, I tug my mask back over my head, but forgo my shirt before answering her, "Yeah, Lou?"

"Can I kill the other one?" she asks groggily, making me chuckle as I wrap the blanket tightly around her, scooping her into my arms as I carry her from the room. I'm growing concerned about her blood loss and injuries. I shouldn't have fucked her like that, but I couldn't stop myself because I'm a bastard of the highest order.

"Yeah, baby. You can kill him," I promise as her eyes drift close.

Gently, I place her on the table in the center of the infirmary operating room. We need some privacy, and since I'll, apparently, be removing the eyes of anyone who sees her naked body, this is my only option.

When her brown eyes crack open again and she takes in the room we're in, panic transforms her face.

"Breathe with me," I instruct her, grabbing her by the shoulders and staring into her eyes. Fuck, I've gone softer than wet clay, but I don't mind so much when it comes to Lou.

"In and out. Yeah, that's it," I coach her, and when she's regained a semblance of calm, I add, "I needed to bring you in here so I can stitch you up, okay? I won't leave you."

She gives me a small nod, yet wraps the blanket around her tighter. What the fuck happened to this girl that she loses her shit every time we come in here?

Deciding that this isn't the time to talk to her about that, I ask something equally important. "Can you tell me what happened tonight? What did they do?"

I want to think they didn't sexually assault her, but I need to make sure I didn't make a royal mistake by drawing that conclusion. The fact that everyone learned that the camera had been removed tells me they chose that room on purpose, wanting to hide their actions.

When her breathing is robotic, but steady, I release her, moving to the cabinet, grabbing more antiseptic and the suture kit. Jones would've been better at this, but he's dead, and while it won't be as pretty, I know how to do it. Every soldier on the island has been trained with basic survival skills, and I guess that's coming in handy now; though I doubt the government would like to hear that I'm using my training to help an inmate, no matter how special I claim she is.

When I return to Lou, she's still in the same position, stretched out with the blanket around her. I pull up the bottom of the blanket to reveal her upper thigh, and give her a shot of lidocaine.

"Lou?" I prompt.

"They drugged me and took me from my cell. When I came to, I was how you found me. They said something about me being sentenced to die, but no one cared how they did it. That's when they began cutting me."

Despite the sickening agony she endured, relief floods me that they didn't take things further. If they had, I'd have found a way to bring Jones and Davis back to kill them again, more viciously.

She's quiet for a long time before she admits almost wistfully, "No one's ever rescued me before."

Well, fuck me straight to hell. I position my body so I'm staring down into her face and yank the stupid mask from my head once more, wanting her to see my whole face as I explain, "Louhi, believe me when I say that I'll save you every fucking time."

CHAPTER 28

Louhi

Sean has stitched half of my wounds when Honey Eyes saunters in, his hands in his pockets. He kicks the doors shut behind him, his eyes widening as he takes in Sean's unmasked face and my nearly naked form.

"Is this the infirmary or the love nest?" he teases, stalking toward the table.

"Fuck off, man," Sean grumbles, but Honey Eyes just chuckles.

"C'mon, you two look pretty cozy."

He hops up onto the table, perching next to my prone hip, his gaze skating over my injuries. His perusal isn't full of lust—though his butterscotch eyes still sparkle with mild hunger—more of a clinical assessment.

When his eyes reach my face, he asks, "How are you feeling, Lou? You look like hell."

I giggle. "You should see the other blokes. I hear my *wrath* is pretty vengeful," I reply with a wink, glancing at Sean, who snorts.

"Yeah, well, you've still got one waiting on that wrath."

Honey Eyes jumps down from the table and reaches for the butterfly bandages and begins working on the cuts that aren't deep enough to need stitches.

"You knock him out?"

Honey Eyes glances at Sean before resuming his task on my stomach. "He's back in the playpen. I held on to him until you left, but he's unconscious and *hanging out* until you're ready for him."

The stitches on my bicep tug at the skin, and I curl my lip despite the lidocaine. Sean replies, "Until *she's* ready for him. I promised her."

Honey Eyes just nods in understanding, and the three of us fall into comfortable silence, before I finally ask, "What happens now?"

Now that I know that Sean is firmly on my side, I need to know what that means for me. For us.

How the hell am I going to get out of here? Is he still going to help me? He already killed for me—twice—so I assume he's not above murder and mayhem in order to help me escape.

Deafening silence fills the room, seemingly louder than the heavy metal music that blares through the cell block. When Sean finishes the last of the stitches, he sighs. "One thing at a time, Lou. I don't know how much blood you lost, so for now, you need some rest."

Honey Eyes leaves the room for a moment, and when he comes back, he tosses Sean a pillow, who slides it under my head. As Honey Eyes drapes the additional blanket over me, panic starts to bubble in my stomach all over again. Are they going to leave me here? I can't stay in this room alone. I *won't* do it. They'll have to knock me out to make that happen.

The knuckles of Sean's large, veiny hand drift across my cheek. *Thank fuck, I didn't need stitches on my face.* "I told you I wouldn't leave you. I'll be here when you wake up," he assures me.

Honey Eyes begins to tidy up the supplies as Sean sits in a chair next to me, threading his fingers through mine. Curling my fingers over his knuckles, I relish the steady warmth of his palm. The white-hot realization that this small, intimate gesture is a first for me bolts across my brain. I know it's quite the shock to hear that

I'm not the romantic, hand-holding type. But with Sean, I find myself wanting things I've never considered before.

Things like truths and intimacy.

When I finally close my eyes, I drift off to the calming sense of safety the man next to me provides.

Sean

Jace hauls a second chair into the room and takes up sentry on Lou's other side, across from me. Silence settles over the room as Louhi's chest rises and falls in accordance with a deep sleep, the sound of the air conditioning whirling to life slicing through the quiet. This is always the coldest room on base, and I touch Lou's toes every once in a while to make sure she's still warm.

Fuck me, I really have gone soft. The version of me from even a year ago would be kicking my ass, but I can't seem to care enough to harden back up around Lou.

Chills break out over my bare chest as the cool air assaults me, but I ignore it, admiring the serenity Lou has captured in her sleep. She looks so at peace like this, despite the distress this room seems to bring her. Jace and I stay quiet for a long time, until he finally speaks in a hushed tone. "You let her see your face."

I swallow thickly. Not allowing the prisoners to see your face is a big rule around here. At best, it'd get me sanctioned, for sure. More than likely, I'd end up faced with something far worse. It's a matter of our safety—and our families'—that we don't reveal our identity.

"She knows my name, too," I tell him, laying all the cards on the table. I know there are cameras in here, but no microphones, and I'll override the recording tomorrow.

"Fuck, man. That's not good."

"About as good as killing two of my own men," I explain.

"I know this may make me as fucked as Lou, but I would've done it if you hadn't."

He didn't have to say it for me to know whose side he was on here. I don't know how she's weaseled her way into both of our cold fucking hearts, but she managed it. Though he doesn't look at her the same way I do. Even as he sits across from me, studying the venomous, gorgeous creature lying on the bed, he doesn't have the gleam in his eye that I know anyone would find in mine.

"I'm glad we got there when we did. Who knows how much longer they'd have kept her alive," I state.

Anger threatens to surge within me all over again, and I'm starting to regret that I told Lou she could kill Borman. I wish I could do it. I'd light that motherfucker on fire, watching as he burned to death. Something tells me that Lou will be far more creative, though.

Jace and I are quiet before he whispers, his lips hardly moving. "How are we getting her out of this?"

Ah, the million-dollar question.

I shake my head since I don't fucking know, and it's not as if I haven't thought about it ad nauseam. I'm running out of time. *Lou* is running out of time.

"We need a cigarette," I say in answer, signaling that we need to discuss things somewhere far more private.

He nods. "How did Borman know about the termination order?"

I scrub a hand down my face and look at him. "That's something I plan to find out."

CHAPTER 29

Louhi

When my eyelids part, Honey Eyes is gone, and Sean is no longer by my bedside. My chest tightens for a moment until I realize that I'm no longer resting on the too-soft pillow, but the hard muscle of a thigh.

Strong hands run through my hair, tugging and pulling on the midnight strands. I begin to twist my neck to look up at Sean, when he snakes a hand around the front of my neck, holding my movements captive as his husky voice chastises me. "Stop moving, Lou. I need to finish the braid."

"You're braiding my hair?" I ask, my words vibrating against his palm. He slides his hand from my neck and resumes playing with my hair.

"I thought you might like it out of your face so it didn't get into the antiseptic cream I applied to the scratches on your cheeks."

It feels good to have his hands threaded into my hair, my eyes sliding closed again as I revel in the intimate gesture. No one's ever done something like this for me, not since my mum was alive. Then again, it's not like I really *date*. I don't have boyfriends or girlfriends. Sure, I fuck…a lot, but I make sure they—or I—leave when it's over. Dating requires trust and that's not something I give freely, if at all. My line of work doesn't allow for mistakes like trusting the wrong person. Even if I found someone I wanted to date, I've had my heart closed off for so long, I don't know how to let someone in.

All that was true until Sean prowled into my life, knocking down barriers I've had in place for nearly two decades.

"How do you even know how to braid?"

Shifting so he has better access, I face the far wall, feeling him tug on the strands of my hair as he replies quietly after a beat. "I have a sister."

I'm sure he's wondering if he can trust me the same way I'm exploring those same tentative threads woven between us.

"Only a sister?"

There's a heavily pregnant pause, but he eventually answers, "Yes."

It doesn't go unnoticed that he doesn't give me their name, but I still take it as a win that I internally celebrate. I'd never go after anyone in Sean's family, but he's clearly still a little apprehensive about sharing pieces of himself with me. That's something I can understand, since I'm obviously doing the same.

Feeling the need to reassure him with his own words from yesterday, I assert, "You can trust me, you know."

He doesn't respond, but he heard me. I don't know if he believes me, but he should. I want him to know that I'd have his back and protect him like I'd protect myself. While those emotions are a first for me, they feel good.

He finishes with my French braid, and I sit up, moving to face him. He's still bare from the waist up, his expanse of muscled planes and tanned, ink-free skin on display. He must've cleaned the blood splatter from his forearms at some point, though his trousers are still speckled with the crimson spray from last night.

"How are you feeling?" he asks, and I gaze at his face, grateful that he hasn't replaced the mask. His face is even more attractive than the rest of him—and that's saying quite a lot—but I can't help wondering if he'd look *even* hotter with a dusting of facial hair and growing out his hair a tad. Although, I doubt the army would take my evaluation under consideration.

When he locks out his darkness, he appears buttoned-up, and I briefly fantasize about dragging him into the shadowy blackness with me for a little while.

After his performance last night, I have no doubt he'd more than simply survive in my world. He'd bloody *thrive.*

"Better," I answer, then after a beat, I add, "Thank you…for everything."

In my world, thanking people is much like apologizing in that it doesn't really happen. Transactions take place and you're expected to complete the job. Gratitude is expressed via payment or the fact that no one took a hit out on you.

Except, Sean isn't in my world right now, I'm in his, and I *am* grateful.

He moves to the counter, producing a disposable pre-pasted toothbrush for me. Desperate to clean my teeth again, I follow him, seizing the opportunity to brush my teeth once again.

Leaning against the counter, his arms cross over my chest as he watches me scrub my teeth clean, spitting into the sink, then brushing them again. Wiping my mouth clean with the face cloth he offers me, I savor the minty flavor lingering on my tongue.

As we stand there, our eyes stay glued to each other for several moments before he dares to run a thick finger over my defined cupid's bow and across the seam of my lips. I open for him, wrapping my lips around his finger. His eyes sharpen on the movement, and I suck more of his digit into my mouth, swirling my tongue around the pad of his index finger.

Sweeping my eyes over his face, I continue licking and sucking, waiting for the shadows to appear, but they don't. Instead, he simply retracts his thumb, gliding it over my lips once more before shoving both hands into his pockets.

Reaching into his back pocket, he pulls out his mask, tugging it on, the soldier slipping back into place as he orders gently, "We have somewhere to be."

My bare feet are silent as they pad over the cool concrete, sending a shiver through me as I follow Sean down the corridor. He holds the door open for me to the familiar room, and I duck inside.

Honey Eyes is perched in a chair in the corner reading... "Bloody hell, is that *Playboy*? Could you be any more of a cliché?"

He glances up at me, smirking, his eyes sparkling with amusement. "Not all of us get action around here, you know." He winks. "Besides, there are more than just pretty pictures; some of the articles are actually interesting."

Rolling my eyes playfully, Sean's warmth surrounds me from behind. I'm about to toss out a quip when Sean beats me to it.

"You sound jealous. Maybe you should see if Carlos is interested?"

"I'd rather stick my dick in a paper shredder."

As the two men continue to bicker good-naturedly, I turn my attention to the naked man in the center of the room, hanging from chains in the ceiling. The chains wrap under both of his arms, digging into his armpits and crossing over his chest and upper back. His arms are crossed at his lower back, bound with rope, as additional twisted ropes hold his ankles together. I appreciate that Honey Eyes took things to the extreme by essentially hanging him by the armpits and stripping him of his clothes solely for the added humiliation.

Circling the man, I poke him in the back. When nothing happens, I peer around his body, asking, "Can we wake him up? He's rather boring like this."

Sean snorts, reaching for a black case on the floor next to Honey Eyes's chair and holds it out for me. Inside, there's a needle and three vials that I'd venture contain adrenaline.

"You can wake him up, but we need to get a few answers first, then he's all yours," Sean informs me, my lips forming a thin line as I narrow my eyes at him. I don't relish the idea of letting these two have a go at this bloke first, but I suppose we all know that he won't still be breathing when I'm finished with him, so how can I really argue with Sean's order of events?

Filling the needle, I estimate the amount, since it doesn't particularly matter, so long as I don't accidentally kill him via a heart attack—that'd spoil the fun prematurely.

Plunging the needle into the side of his shoulder, I depress the plunger. A few beats later, he's gasping, filling me with giddiness and zeal.

"Hello, doll," I chime as I flash him my most reprehensible smile. Now conscious, he attempts to wriggle free, but the clanking of his chains is simply the soundtrack of his death.

Ignoring the vitriol he's spewing like a faucet, Sean comes to stand beside me, and I nod reluctantly, backing up to stand against the wall, sulking a bit as they take their turn.

Based on my own experience in this room with them, I knew that Honey Eyes and Sean worked well together. Able to view things through a more objective lens now, their seamless partnership is nothing short of impressive. They alternate asking questions and removing fingers and toes without batting an eye. The two men seem to communicate nearly telepathically, anticipating the other's next move.

It's comical how quickly a guard in a government-run torture prison buckles under the torture inflicted on him. *Wimp.*

When Sean and Honey Eyes learn all they want, they step back, droplets of blood speckling their bodies from their masks to their sand-colored boots.

Sean nods at me, and I trod toward the shelves containing the various tools, perusing my options. When I spot a block with various knives stationed on the bottom shelf, I pluck a fillet knife from its slip, testing the sharpness of the blade against the pad of my thumb. *This will work.*

The world around me—the audience, the room, the entire bloody prison—fades away as I stand before the sniveling man, his face bloody and bruised. Lifting the blade, I trail the tip over his skin much like he had done to me, only I press a little harder, a stream of blood appearing in my wake, leaving me transfixed by the way his skin parts like water for me. It's been so long since I got my hands dirty. I fucking missed it.

Breathing deeply, I soak in his terror, committing it to memory so that I might bask in it later. I missed the feeling of exacting retribution.

I've mastered my craft so that I'm now able to be highly selective in the jobs I accept at this point in my career. I have more requests in my encrypted inbox than I could realistically take in this lifetime and the next. It wasn't always that way, though; there was a time where I took every job, regardless of the risk. However, I made sure I became the best in the business, so that I could be able to choose which hits I wanted to accept and reject.

The guard I killed in the infirmary was the first target I haven't been paid to eliminate in years. Nonetheless, he provoked me, and I wanted to remember the way bloodshed felt.

Standing before this man, I recognize a difference. This is vengeance I haven't tasted in *ages*. This is compensation. This is punishment. This is justice.

I drag the blade over his chest and look up into his ruddy brown eyes, parroting his words mockingly. "Are you familiar with Lingchi?"

He doesn't answer, not that I expected him to—continuing his wails and curses—so I tell him, "You seem to be a bit rusty on your ancient torture methods, but that's alright. I'll fill you in." I don't typically talk theatrically with an overabundance of hand gestures, but I make a point of waving the knife around when I speak to this wanker.

Borman won't shut the fuck up and listen to me, though, testing my patience. Fed up, I glance behind me to request a gag, when Honey Eyes saunters past me, shoving a dirty-looking rag into the captive's mouth, growling, "Shut the fuck up and listen to her."

A grateful smile sweeps across my face as Honey Eyes stalks past me, returning to his post against the wall at my back.

Resuming my one-sided conversation with the soldier, I explain, "As I was saying, death by a thousand cuts means something different within various Chinese dynasties, but they all contained the *removal* of flesh, in some capacity, something you seem to either have forgotten or not have been aware of. Luckily for you, I'm somewhat of a slow-slicing expert, and I'll try to keep this process as authentic as possible for you. I'm partial to the methods of the Qing Dynasty, so that's what I'll be adhering to."

He screams into his gag, the sound pure delight to my ears, as I cut through the flesh of his left pectoral, then his right, tossing the skin and muscle tissue I removed aside, suddenly grateful for the adrenaline coursing through him. I want him alive for every painful moment of this.

I continue the cuts I made in his chest down toward his ribs, exposing the top portion of his ribs, again lobbing the flesh on the ground. I must admit, there's something about seeing the inside of someone's muscles that's fascinating to me. Maybe in another life I might have been a bloody coroner.

I've only killed someone by slow slicing once—because it's tedious and incredibly messy, not because I don't like it—but I find it particularly poetic this time around.

Stepping behind him, I address the flesh on his upper arms, confident that my time with this tosser is coming to a close. I doubt he'll survive much longer, especially since he's already gone silent, his wet face and the shallow rise and fall of his chest now the only indication of life. He's long since pissed himself and his head hangs forward, resigned to his fate.

Circling my prey, I stop to remove the flesh from his thigh, when I notice that he's fading faster than I anticipated. Making one more slice before gripping him by the hair, I yank his head up so that he's looking at me. I'm not sure if he can actually *see* me at this point, yet I still promise, "See you in Hell and we'll pick up where we left off."

Two more strategic cuts before I know he's gone. In accordance with Lingchi, I exchange the fillet knife for a hatchet and remove his head.

A satiated calmness slithers through my veins lazily as I relax for the first time since I regained consciousness to find my wrists and ankles shackled by the bloody government.

"Fuck, Lou."

At the sound of Honey Eyes's voice, I turn around, a very real smile on my face. It's the only indication that the hungry viper within me is well and truly fed for the first time in months. It's Sean who catches my eye, though.

As we study one another, I observe the cloud of darkness encasing his blue irises, and he continues to hold my gaze as Honey Eyes adds, "You're one scary woman. Remind me to never get on your bad side."

Reluctantly, I drag my attention from the man systematically crushing the walls around my heart and slide my gaze to meet a pair of golden-caramel eyes, letting triumph seep into my smirk.

"I'm the best for a reason, Honey Eyes."

"I believe you."

I glance around the room, noticing the blood and gore covering my surroundings. Thankfully, Borman was positioned over the drain, so at least some of his bodily fluids disappeared, but there's still a mess.

"Would you like some help tidying up a bit?" I ask. Under any other circumstance, I'd call in my crew, or leave it, depending on the situation; though I'm not above getting my hands dirty by cleaning up my own messes.

Honey Eyes just shakes his masked head and states, "I've got it. It was worth it just to see you in action."

Sean brushes past me and ducks into the storage room, but returns in a flash, carrying *another* fresh uniform. *Do all the prisoners fly through these uniforms as quickly as I seem to?*

"Let's get you cleaned up," Sean mutters, and I wave to Honey Eyes before following him to the shower.

CHAPTER 30

Louhi

STEPPING INSIDE THE EMPTY WASHROOM, SEAN LOCKS THE door behind us before placing the clean uniform on the counter and moving to a cabinet on the left wall.

After setting the stack of towels he retrieved on the counter, he reaches for the hem of my shirt. The blood-soaked cotton fabric glides over my skin as he tugs it over my head and our eyes catch the moment my top disappears. Without breaking eye contact, I hook my fingers into the waistband of my pants and shove them down, stepping out of them.

Naked before him, I tug off his shirt, tossing it out of sight, reaching for his belt next and unfastening it before unclasping his trousers. He growls, the sound a warning that I don't heed as I attempt to thread his belt through the loops at his waist. I freeze when his hand shoots out, his fingers wrapping around my wrist tightly, making me smirk as I watch the shadowy tendrils appear in his vision.

"Lou…" he cautions, but I suppose I'm impervious to any red-flag warning at this point. He's awoken something insatiable within me, and no matter how much he gives me, I want more.

When he moves my hand away, I pout openly at his denial, but he just chuckles. "So fucking desperate for me, aren't you?"

I nod slowly, capturing my bottom lip between my teeth. I'm already wet, my pussy aching for him. I wish he'd dive between my legs to see for himself.

Faster than a viper's strike, he spins me around so that I'm now facing the mirror, my back to his front, with both of my hands now trapped within one of his at my stomach. My chest heaves as I take in the sight of us together.

He leans down, meeting my eye in the mirror as he murmurs into my ear, "Will you be quiet while I feed you my cock?"

A grin spreads across my mouth as I nod. He straightens, a deviant smile consuming his face as he replies, "We'll see."

Clearly, he doesn't believe me, but neither do I.

A shiver wracks my body, his words providing a challenge I plan to meet head-on. He bends once more, his breath cascading over the shell of my ear and floating across my cheek as he whispers, "Are you nice and wet for me?"

His question skitters down my body until the answer floods me as my pussy flutters, and I stifle the groan rumbling in my chest.

"I bet you are. You're always ready for me."

Without another word, he pulls his belt free of his pants and wraps it around my wrists, pulling it tight. I suck in a sharp breath, our eyes meeting in the mirror as I test the restraints.

By nature, I am *not* submissive, though I did try slipping into that role once. It didn't end well. I may or may not have *accidentally* killed the man who told me to "crawl," but I gave myself props for trying it. Life is short, so you have to give everything a whirl at least once.

After that experience, and before I met Sean, I'd go to extreme measures to make sure I was never in a position of submission or vulnerability. Now, I find myself itching to let go entirely.

Passing him total control would allow me a freedom I'm unfamiliar with. It's a feeling I find myself apprehensive about indulging in.

Stepping between me and the sink, he grabs a face cloth, running it under the faucet and adding soap. Turning back toward me, he glides the warm cloth over my face, the dingy white towel now tinged with dirt and smears of blood.

The rough cloth erases more of the grimy film coating my skin as Sean carefully cleans my face. His face is stony as he works, focused on the task at hand as he cleans every inch of me. I want to reach up and run the pads of my fingers across his tanned skin, mentally mapping the grooves, lines and planes of his body as I explore him.

But I'm trapped.

While he works, I memorize each freckle on his flesh, the shade of his skin, and sketching the pattern of his veins in my mind. The dog tags around his neck sway and clink softly as he moves, like seductive wind chimes.

He turns, rinsing the cloth and beginning again as he cleans my neck and chest, navigating the cuts. The rough fibers prickle and tease my flushed skin. When he drags the cloth over my pebbled nipples, I close my eyes, leaning forward as I silently beg for more. When he doesn't give me what I want, I frown, frustration curling in my belly as it mixes with raw need.

"Spread your legs," he commands once he's cleaned my stomach and arms.

Pinning him with a defiant look, I don't move. As much as I'm inclined to submit to Sean, I like fighting him a little, too.

He meets my stare, arching an eyebrow as if to ask if I'm sure I want to test him. "You're behaving so well, Lou," he tells me, running a fresh, warm cloth over my weeping cunt, rubbing it over my clit. "It'd be a shame if you lost out on the opportunity to get fucked the way you want because you couldn't do as you were told."

Curling my lip a little, I spread my legs.

A satisfied hum vibrates in his mouth the moment my legs spread. "That's my girl."

Why does that sound so right, so good, to be his girl? Why does that declaration have my clit pulsing?

He takes his time washing the entirety of my legs and feet, careful of the numerous cuts and bruises on my skin before moving onto my back with a fresh cloth. When he's finished, he tosses the rag into the empty sink basin with the other soiled cloth.

When he reaches for a third cloth, my patience snaps like a brittle twig. "Aren't you done yet? When are you going to *feed me*?"

I'm starving for him; I *need* him, I *want* him. Like a cock-junkie, I'm desperate for a hit of his delicious pleasure, his wicked pain.

Instead of answering me, the corner of his mouth lifts as he rounds me, the cloth in hand.

He seizes me, yanking me back so that I'm flush with his front, my hands trapped in front of me. The tail of the belt gently swats my pussy at the same time he shoves the cloth into my mouth.

"Now, Lou, I'm going to feed you now."

Fuck, finally!

I whimper into the rag as he dips his hand between my thighs, slipping two fingers inside. "Fuck, you're drenched."

A muffled cry permeates the washroom as the pad of Sean's thumb flicks over my sensitive clit. I pitch my hips back, seeking his cock as his other hand grips me by the back of the neck, shoving me forward forcefully, bending me in half. His other hand abruptly leaves my pussy, yanking my restraints as he lifts my joined hands. It's not until he's threading the belt around the faucet in front of me that I realize what's on the menu.

Bound, gagged, and completely at his mercy, my cunt drips with savage lust.

With heated, rapt attention, I lift my gaze to watch in the mirror as he makes quick work of shedding his remaining boots and clothing. I whine into the fabric when my body blocks the sight of his throbbing erection as he steps up to me.

"Quiet," he barks, the dark tendrils swallowing his gaze. With my next heartbeat, his hand comes down across my arse in a brutal hit. Biting down on my gag, I brace myself as he spanks me again.

"This is for not trusting me," he snaps, and I whine into the fabric, shifting my weight.

His hand cracks against my heated skin once, twice more. "This is for thinking I'd have been in on what those assholes did to you."

My instinct is to roll my eyes, though I know I probably deserve this paddling; however, I don't have the chance to so much as frown as my eyes are suddenly rolling to the back of my head on their own as his thick cock slides between my legs.

Then, he's fucking me.

His pace is brutal, punishing, harsh in a way that's gloriously sweet. Wiggling my fingers, I attempt to gain purchase around the metal faucet, to no avail, eliciting a cry of frustration and ecstasy into my gag as Sean promptly begins to hit my G-spot.

Tingles spread through my limbs as my head starts to go fuzzy, on the brink of my orgasm.

"I love watching your greedy cunt eat my cock like it's starving."

I shriek into my gag as I clamp down around him, unable to control the small spasms he's summoning from me. He hits the ball of nerves inside me over and over again. Grabbing my braid with one hand, he yanks my head back so that I'm forced to watch him in the mirror as he fucks me to within an inch of my bloody life.

At this angle, I catch the smirk crawling over his face as his thumb and forefinger move to pinch my nose, making my legs tremble at the intensity.

"You weren't quiet," he remarks, his breaths strained. "Should I still allow you to come?"

I can't help it, I wail into my gag, nervous that this might ruin me, that *he* might ruin me.

Please, please let me come, I beg him with my eyes. *I need this, I need you.*

He releases my nose and yanks out my gag, and I guzzle in air as he slams into me again while stroking my clit. "Scream my fucking name when you come, Lou. Remind this hell who's making you feel like you're in heaven."

My head empties of thought, my limbs convulsing, and I come hard, chanting his name like a mantra.

He comes inside me with a grunt and tremors continue to wrack my body as I come down from the high. He withdraws from me, releasing me from my restraints and hauling me back into his arms before my legs collapse beneath me. Hauling us both onto the counter, I curl into his chest, my cheek resting against his silver tags, as the cadence of our breathing attempts to regulate.

Plunging a hand between my legs, he scoops the beads of cum that have dripped from me and shoves them back inside. Twisting my head, I find his face, confused for a moment. Since Honey Eyes knew, I assumed he was aware of my missing reproductive organs due to the exam that I did *not* consent to having, but what if I'm wrong. "You can't get me pregnant."

His eyes search mine with vigor, and I hold my breath until he smirks. "I know, but that doesn't stop me from wanting to stay inside of you even after I've left."

A real, authentic smile inches across my face. I'm beginning to understand his fierce possessiveness. I've never been proprietorial about someone before, but the more Sean worms his way into my heart, the more that feeling consumes me.

The urge to kiss him overwhelms me as he sweeps a hand over my hair, cupping the nape of my neck, but before I can lean forward and capture his lips, he presses his lips to my forehead and changes the subject. "Why don't you have a uterus?" he inquires, his tone soft and curious.

I blink up at him once, twice, before swallowing thickly. *Can he handle the truth? Will my heart remain intact after slicing open that scar again?*

I must stay silent too long because he leans forward, gripping my chin, forcing me to look at him. "Promise to tell me someday, Lou. I can wait until you're ready."

His ability to read me, to say the right bloody shit at the right bloody time, is uncanny.

"I promise. Maybe over a glass of wine."

He scrunches his nose, making me titter. "Whiskey then?"

His face contorts in obvious distaste, and I roll my eyes. "*Jeesus Kristus,* what do you drink?"

"Beer. Not really a liquor guy." *Bloody figures.*

"I could go for a beer occasionally, but I'm mostly a wine connoisseur. Although, I do like a good sipping vodka from time to time," I reply, thinking of the last time I had a good sipping vodka at one of Conall's incredible dinner parties that he throws, featuring world-renowned chefs. "It's a good thing that your beer will go with my dream menu of juicy lamb chops, roasted turnips, or glazed peas and carrots, maybe even both."

Running his hand down the short length of my braid, he asks, "Are you one of those women who pairs her wine with her food too?"

I smile as I shrug nonchalantly. "Of course. You get the full flavor profile that way."

He chuckles, his chest vibrating against my body. "Beer goes with everything. More importantly, what the *fuck* was that menu? *That's* the food you dream of eating?"

I smirk. "Today it is, but that's because it pairs nicely with the red wine I can't stop thinking about."

"Turnips, really?" He grimaces. "It's disturbing to know you dream about root vegetables."

I laugh, the tension in my neck marginally loosening, but it's short-lived. We fall silent, our breaths echoing off the tiled walls in time with water dripping from a leaky showerhead, the jaws of reality slowly yawning open, thoroughly prepared to bite into our momentary bliss.

Though we don't say it, we both hold the other tighter, seemingly desperate to cling to each other as uncertainty looms over us like the calm before the storm.

CHAPTER 31

Sean

LOU GLARED AT ME AS I LOCKED HER BACK IN HER CELL, BUT I couldn't very well have her roaming around the base freely while I talked to Jace. That would've caused instant chaos in the prison, and I'm already swamped with the damage control I need to do. Thankfully, Borman didn't have time to fuck shit up *too* badly, but I still have a lot to account—I mean, lie—for.

I tried to ease the sting of putting Lou back in her iron and concrete cage by giving her extra food and water, which didn't quite have the desired effect, but it's the best I could do at the moment. The parting look she gave me is all I see with every blink and shutter of my eyelids. I don't blame her for her renewed sense of skeptical distrust and suspicion, but I couldn't explain myself to her, not now. I'd be dubious as fuck of my behavior if the roles were reversed.

Something has happened between us. I'm done deluding myself into thinking otherwise. At best, I'm smitten with Lou. At worst, I'm swimming blindly into foreign waters without knowing how to fucking float.

"What did Martinez say when you talked to him?" I ask Jace, bringing the cigarette to my lips, the bright sun streaming onto the rooftop through a break in the cloud cover, evaporating the tendrils of smoke corkscrewing toward the sky.

"Only that Borman showed him a memo from Thompson saying that he wanted him to ensure Louhi was terminated by Friday. I don't think Martinez knew jack shit about Borman's plan with Davis and Jones, though."

"She was never their favorite inmate, and they hated her even more after she killed Stuco, so I'm not surprised they took matters into their own hands. How'd you explain to Martinez what happened to those three idiots?"

He lifts a shoulder casually. "I told him they underestimated their opponent and Lou killed them." Taking another drag of his cigarette, he adds on an exhale, "It's the truth, more or less. I wouldn't want to fuck with her. I've seen a lot of shit, but I've never seen anything like what she did to Borman. I hate to say it, but she was a damn artist with that blade."

A rough, gritty chuckle rumbles in my chest as I nod in agreement.

He's right. She *was* an artist with Borman's body as her canvas; I was enraptured by her craftmanship. Her skill level is something enviable and the way she carried herself with lethal elegance was fucking enchanting.

The power seeping from her made my dick hard. I don't typically get off on watching the suffering inflicted on someone else if it doesn't come directly from me, but I'll be damned if watching Lou didn't make me harder than stone. It wasn't what she was doing either; it was simply *her*.

She makes me hard.

Deviating from Lou's impressiveness, I steer the conversation back to the more pressing issue. "Why did Thompson send Borman that memo in the first place?"

"Do you think someone tipped him off that we'd...have a hard time with that order?"

"That's what I'm thinking, but who? If it was Borman or one of his *friends*, then the issue has been dealt with."

Jace leans back in his seat with a sigh. "If it was anyone else, we've got a big fucking problem. Which way do you lean?"

I run my fingers over the short hairs covering my scalp as I think through my answer. "I lean toward Borman himself." Lowering my voice, I add, "But we need to get her out of here, especially if that someone else is still breathing."

Smoke slithers from Jace's mouth, both of us falling silent. Seagulls caw in the distance, the air feeling denser than usual with a storm looming on the horizon. The humidity is stifling here on the best of days, but this afternoon, it feels overtly oppressive.

I don't know how long we sit there in contemplation before Jace admits quietly, "I deleted the tapes in the infirmary."

Whipping my head toward him, I mutter, "Thanks. It was on my long-ass to-do list." I pause for a second before asking, "Did you watch the footage?"

He snorts. "I saw enough to know I needed to erase them immediately and not sit around and wait for it to get stored on the government's servers before you had time to get to it."

The shift within myself is blatantly obvious to me, considering my first thought is concern and rage over the idea that someone could've seen a very naked Lou, not what would happen to me or my career over fucking an inmate.

I can't pinpoint when it happened, nor is it worth analyzing, but I think I fucking love her. It's the only explanation I have for why I'm willing to throw my own goddamn life away for hers. Maybe I'm an idiot for wanting to protect her soul, her body, her breath with everything I've got left to give her. If I rot in Hell over the decisions I make, so be it. It'll have been worth it for just twenty minutes with Lou.

I trust Jace implicitly, and if he said he deleted the footage, I damn well believe him. It's one less thing for me to worry about, and for that, I'm grateful. Considering everything going on, thank fuck Jace was forward-thinking.

Jace nods and we fall back into a companionable silence, his head tilting back to watch the steel-colored clouds slide around the sky. I'm nearly done smoking my second cigarette when he speaks again, his voice barely a whisper on the wind. "Let me guess...you have a plan."

When I glance at him, the lines on his face are tight with tension. I'm sure if I were to look in a mirror, I'd find those same lines on my face tenfold.

"Yeah," I breathe.

Leaning back against the wall opposite Lou's cell, I simply watch her. She's sleeping now, curled up in the fetal position, finally having succumbed to the sleeping pill I slipped into her water earlier. Despite leaving the music turned off for the night, I don't think she would've rested without it, no matter how much she needs to in order for her body to heal.

I never thought I'd say it about a prisoner, but she looks out of place in her cell, reminding me of a caged animal in a zoo. She doesn't belong here. She belongs in the wild, roaming free, leaving chaos and carnage in her wake.

Clenching my fists at my sides, I resist the urge to barge through the iron door and take her against the wall, regardless of the smell of piss, putrid grime, or literal fucking shit on the floor. Even asleep, her dark magnetism draws me in.

I wanted one last look at her. I couldn't help it.

CHAPTER 32

Louhi

I CERTAINLY DON'T RECALL FALLING ASLEEP, BUT WHEN I WAKE, it's with a lurch. The usual heavy metal music isn't screaming through the speakers; instead, the high-pitched wail of a siren blares, vibrating the concrete around me.

Sean. Where is he? If this were his hairbrained, wild attempt at busting me out, he'd come for me, right?

Bolting upright, I rub at my eyes with the base of my palms, aiming to eliminate the thrum of a headache that pulses at the base of my skull. Getting to my feet, I move to the barred door and try to peer through the metal rods, but when I grip them, the gate shifts.

Thoughts swirl like a cyclone in the pool of my mind, threatening to drown me. Shoving past my concerns about Sean and the full reason behind the siren's howl, I focus on myself. I can worry about the rest later—Sean included.

I need to get out of here. Now.

I don't know what witches are casting spells in my favor, but may the fucking gods and goddesses bless them. They deserve to hit every green traffic signal for the rest of their lives and find heaps of money on the ground each time they step outside.

Forever an opportunist, I tug on the bars a bit, and without much effort, the hinges swing toward me. Through a lull in the shrieking siren, I catch the distinct sound of metal grating against metal, alerting me that I'm not the only one taking advantage of this situation. Nonetheless, a little company won't stop me from capitalizing on this moment.

Cautiously, I slip from between the concrete and the door to my cage and step out into the corridor for the last time—they'll have to kill me before I'm ever locked behind those iron bars again. Never again.

I glance at the camera that I'm unsure is operational now that hell seems to have broken loose—literally—and I blow a kiss at the shiny round spyglass, *just in case.*

Exhilaration spirals through me, and I'm practically bouncing on my toes as I make way toward the mouth of freedom. Liberation feels so close that I can almost reach out and touch it with my fingertips, longing to seize fresh air, free will, and the taste of my favorite foods. I'll do anything necessary to ensure that escape is clenched tightly in my grasp.

I've taken a handful of steps down the poorly lit hallway, when the door to the cell at the end creaks. My spine straightens, body coiling to strike. I've always chosen war in a fight-or-flight response, and this will be no different, no matter who emerges. That cell has only ever been vacant when I've passed it, mistakenly assuming no one was housed there.

My mouth falls open before spreading into a grin when I see none other than Kazi Akintola step from the cell.

Last time I saw Kazi, he had long black hair that reached his shoulder blades, shaved on one side. Now, he's as bald as a Sphynx cat. That makes my blood heat for him, not because Kazi and I are necessarily mates, but because he had perfect, enviable hair that dared you to comb your fingers through it. If I liked his hair, I could only imagine how much he loved it.

Fuck this place and absolutely fuck Sean if he's the one responsible.

His neck is still thick and beefy, but his bulky, behemoth build is slimmer than I remember. He's a massive man at six-foot-seven, maybe taller, but he hasn't been able to keep up his muscle mass. I'm sure the size of the cell impacted that quite a bit, making me grateful for my smaller stature.

Reminding me so much of a bear, Kazi's never been afraid of a fight, using his size and brute strength as a weapon. You'd have to be a poor sod to end up in a hand-to-hand scrap with him. He doesn't lose. Though, Kazi's weight loss will put him at a disadvantage when trying to escape now, and the snake living within me bares her fangs. *Viktor is going to be bloody pissed when he sees Kazi.*

Though I'm relieved to see him, I'm not the least bit surprised to learn he ended up in a place like this. His morality isn't a shade of grey, its pitch fucking black. While I won't pretend to be good or moral, at least kids and animals are a hard limit for me, even if they're my *only* limit. I'm not sure Kazi could say the same.

With a genuine smile on my face, I call out, "Kaz!"

He whips in my direction, a scowl on his face and a growl vibrating in his throat at my use of his nickname, but I continue speaking as I saunter toward him casually. "What the bloody fuck are you doing here? I thought you were dead."

Resisting the urge to chuck my arms around his shoulders in an embrace, I stop a few paces from him. I can't imagine Kazi being the hugging type, but fuck is it nice to see a somewhat familiar face. The gaze he pins me with is distant and icy, and I suppress the shiver of glacial coldness I'm hit with. His dark eyes narrow on me as he takes me in fully and his lip curls slightly at whatever he sees. While he's one terrifying motherfucker, he doesn't frighten me.

"I'm sure you aren't the only one. How'd you get here?" he asks, the lilt of his accent thick. The timbre of his voice is more abrasive, hoarser than I recall it being, and I wonder what the fuck they did to him.

"Favor to Mercer," I reply succinctly, not wanting to show too much of my hand. He'd understand my sense of loyalty, considering he shares a similar connection with Viktor, but my trust only goes so far, so I shift the subject. "We should get out of here."

Just then, two guards round the corner, coming to a screeching halt when they find us in the hallway. At once, they charge us. Kazi takes the guard closest to him, knocking him out with a single punch to the face before the man even has a chance to reach for his Glock.

The other guard comes at me, fast, his gun already in his hand. I anticipate his move, and when he lifts his arm to get a shot off, I duck beneath it, swiping his utility knife as I brush by. Stepping around him, I drag the blade across his throat. *Easy peasy.*

When I turn back around, Kazi has the other guard's knife embedded in his chest.

He nods at me, the cords in his neck stretching with the movement. "Go."

My eyebrows pinch and my lips thin. "You're not coming with me?"

"I have a few things to take care of first."

A wild, unrestrained smile takes over my face. I know exactly what he intends, and I can't say I blame him. And now that he's mentioned it, I have a vindictive vow of my own I need to uphold.

"Speaking of, do you know which cell Carlos belongs to?" I ask, swiveling my head down the hallway in the direction of the other cells.

"Cell Two. Make it hurt."

"Always."

I spin, taking a few steps toward the second cell. When I get to the entrance, I turn back toward him. "If I see Viktor first, I'll let him know you're here."

He nods solemnly, telling me that he'll do the same, because let's face it, Viktor is going to be the first call either of us make—for entirely different reasons. Kazi disappears down the corridor just as I step into Cell Two and sneer at the sniveling, broken man in the corner.

"Hello, Carlos." I don't have the time to do this the way I want, but I'm a woman of my word so I approach the man cowered in the corner, gripping his oily dark brown hair and jerking his head up to look at me. "It's time to learn to be quiet."

Wordlessly, I move to clutch his chin and squeeze his cheeks until his mouth pops open. With my other hand, I grab hold of his tongue. Stepping to the side of his body, out of the *majority* of the spray, I slice through his tongue with the dead guard's blade. Crimson mist showers the air, the black fabric of my uniform absorbing most of the scarlet dots littering my body.

His sobs are so loud that they out-pitch the siren as I wipe the blade on his soiled uniform before darting from his cell. He'll either bleed out or he'll live without a tongue—either result I can live with.

In the hallway, I snatch the Glock from one of the dead guards, slinging one of a rifle over my shoulder and heading for the exit—wherever the hell that is.

CHAPTER 33

Sean

I stare at the blinking red light that's been flashing green as long as I've been stationed here, now indicating that the system is down.

Closing my eyes for a moment, I focus on breathing to the rhythmic cadence of the siren wailing through the prison.

Breathe in for four counts, breathe out for four counts.

Inhale. Exhale.

I've lost count of how many times I've told myself that this is the right thing to do—for Lou, anyway. I've accepted the risks. There's a possibility of peril for myself, for Jace—even for Louhi—and I'm positive that a lot of the fuckheads residing behind their own bars will meet their end tonight. While I'm more settled about the inmates' deaths, it's putting the guys who work for me at risk that leaves a sour, acrid taste in my mouth.

Most of them don't deserve the chaos landing in their laps. I couldn't warn them, couldn't tell them to make sure they're armed more heavily than usual. They're on their own.

Not that they'd take anything I said into consideration anyway—not now.

I've betrayed each of them, committed treason against my country. I've broken the code and smashed through it with a battleax.

"I thought you were going to meet me at the rear exit." I whip around to see Jace in the doorway, his chest heaving like he just ran here, before adding, "We've got to get to the boat."

Dammit, I must be running later than I thought. As I stared at that switch, my fingers hovering over the plastic that would unlock the cells, I swear every one of my senses was alive with the ticking of the clock. All I needed to do was flip the lever.

But while flipping the switch meant Louhi's freedom, it also meant lives lost. It meant putting nearly forty prisoners and even more of my men in Death's grasp. That's a heavy weight to bear, even if parts of this place and job don't bother me nearly as much as they should.

Clearly, as evidenced by Jace's presence, I've lingered a bit too long before eventually shutting off the power.

Nodding, I scan the control room once more before taking a step in his direction. "Did you unlock all the exits?"

He snorts. "Yes, Dad," he replies derisively, rolling his wheat-colored irises, and though I can't see the rest of his face through his mask, I know he's grinning.

It's not a foolproof plan, by any means, but it was the best we could do with a few hours' notice. Jace was to unlock the exits while I shut off the power, and we both pray that Lou steals someone's mask and uniform, allowing her to get her fine ass to the other side of the island.

Our plan hinges on Lou's ingenuity and craftiness, but we've laid the groundwork for her, opening all the doors—metaphorically and literally—for her to escape. I've never seen the assassin at work before, but Jace reminded me that if she was a shitty hitman, she would've ended up here far sooner. If it's to be believed that she's flown under the radar after killing one hundred and seventy-three people, then she should have no problem escaping this place.

Right?

The pressure of the situation is so thick that it threatens to choke us out, so I grasp at levity with sweaty palms, retorting, "Last time I checked, you didn't have a dad."

Jace laughs openly. "Well, neither do you, asshole," he remarks as we approach the doorway, needing to get the *fuck* out of here.

She'll be fine, I remind myself.

Gunfire rattles in the distance, sobering us both as my gaze cuts to Jace, who simply dips his head in a nod as if to reassure me that she'll be fine.

As soon as we step into the hallway, Martinez is there, his cocked Glock trained on my chest. His brown eyes blaze with hatred and disgust, and I can't say I blame him. I'd want to shoot me, too, if I'd found out my commanding officer was a treasonous fucker.

"Martinez," Jace starts in an attempt to diffuse the situation. "You don't want to do this."

"Like fuck I don't," he spits, his eyes twinkling with truth. "I didn't believe Borman when he said that you had a thing with Koskinen." He snorts, his finger curling around the trigger, ready to press the lever at any moment. "None of us really give a shit if you're fucking her. We're all fucking the inmates."

"Not all of us," Jace mutters next to me, his proclamation laced with horror, not jealousy, and I am right there with him—with the exception of Lou.

Ignoring Jace, Martinez barrels on. "If only you'd have thought with your head and not your dick, you wouldn't have to die, but you fucking deserve to now. How could you do this?"

How could I do this? Easy, I could, and would, do anything for Louhi.

Although, he's right about one thing. I *do* deserve to die for what I'm doing. I deserve to die for everything I've done—the torture, suffering and murder I've inflicted—here. I deserve to die for not being the man my mother raised me to be.

I deserve to die for choosing my heart over my head.

As if my hammering heartbeat was some kind of detonation timer, it counts down—*three, two, one*—the concrete hallway suddenly splattered in blood, carnage, and death.

CHAPTER 34

Louhi

THE SPRINKLERS SURGED TO LIFE AT SOME POINT DURING MY wanderings of this maze. Three wrong turns and four murdered soldiers later, I'm *still* lost in this labyrinth of concrete. I'm soaked, aggravation chewing at my bones, threatening to consume me. *I just want* out. *Is that too much to bloody ask for?*

As I take another corner, my body slams into one of the guards. I half-expect to find warm honey eyes or irises the shade of steel staring back at me, but the dark brown shade I'm met with is foreign to me. We observe each other for a beat before I lift the Glock, pressing it against his chest and pulling the trigger—twice. Bending down, I loot his person for additional ammo, muttering a curse for not thinking to ask—or torture—him for directions to the fucking exit. Now he's dead and I'm left with increasing frustration with this network of concrete corridors.

I'm not sure how long I prowl about for, but I end up killing two prisoners and one more guard before shoving on a door and stumbling outside into fresh motherfucking air. *Finally.*

I gulp down the salty, wet air like a dying woman, my heart mauling my ribcage with the ferocity of its cadence. I've lost the memory of the last time I breathed oxygen this fresh, so I stand there for a moment, taking in as much as humanly possible. The air feels heavy with the potential for rain—*of course*—and I fill my lungs to the brim several more times, taking in my surroundings.

There's barely enough light to make out the razor wire along the top of a seemingly smooth concrete wall in the distance, but it's there. Two large, heavily manned guard towers stand at the corners, with a mammoth gate in the middle. Soldiers line the wall and man the gates. In all, there's maybe twenty or thirty of them. I didn't realize how many men were stationed on this base in the middle of hell, but it's more than I would've guessed.

A guard halfway between me and the gate turns in my direction, and I dart to my right, making myself flush with the wall, hoping that at least one of the few palm trees between us hides me.

Stifling a shiver of excitement, I take inventory of the rifle slung over my shoulder, the Glock in one hand and the knife in the other; I know I'll never make it by attempting to shoot my way out of this. Nor will I be able to simply walk through the gate undetected.

Blimey, this is bad.

I have a sinking suspicion that they stationed additional guards here to pick off prisoners as they emerge from the main exit, and I was lucky enough not to have chosen that door. My assumption is confirmed when four prisoners burst through the door at that exact moment and are met with shouts and a spray of bullets flying toward them. All four of them slump to the ground, their blood pooling on the ground.

Where is Sean? Or Honey Eyes?

Scanning the yard, I don't see them, yet it's hard to know with certainty, considering the mask every guard wears. While I'm convinced that I'd recognize the build of Honey Eyes, I'm confident I'd *feel* Sean from a lifetime away. My magnetic draw to him borders on something tangible, the electrical charge bouncing between us enough to detonate a bomb.

Something bad must've happened to them; that's the only explanation for why they haven't found me. I've gotten the impression that Sean's either in charge—or close to it—so it would make sense that if he's been attacked or killed, the sirens would be going off and mayhem would've ensued. My heart squeezes at the thought, but I shut out those thoughts. I can think about the gaping hole his absence will leave me with later. Right now, I need to get the fuck out of here.

Peering around the corner of the prison my back has been slithering along, I see that the building ends at a cliff's edge. More walls, razor wire, and guards are present, though, so I can't just make a run for it and jump in the ocean—which wouldn't be ideal, but it'd be better than dying from a bullet shower. I gnaw on my bottom lip as I think through my limited options. Suddenly, an idea hits me, a grin flitting over my face.

Keeping my movements small, I inch back toward the door I had exited, praying to those damn witches that the door will open without drawing attention to me and their bloody spells must hold because it does.

Figuring that the majority of the guards stationed here are in the prison yard I just came from, I make a beeline toward the back of the prison that backs up to the cliff. Keeping my ears on alert for other footsteps, I hold the Glock at my side, my finger ready to press the trigger. *It's a good thing Sean didn't break that finger.*

The hems of my uniform pants are soaked as my bare feet slosh through the few inches of water now pooled on the concrete floor. My eyes dart around frantically as I duck in and out of hallways, attempting to navigate the maze. Eventually, I spot what I'm looking for: rats.

Following the scurrying rodents, I slip down one corridor and another. The rats will know the most direct path to dry land and safety, so I'm with them.

Sprinklers overhead continue to spit water in a barrage, adding to the chaos of the steady, ear-splitting shriek of the siren thundering within these walls. Through the havoc, my ears pick up on a scuffle not far behind me and I don't spare a glance as I pick up my pace, making two more turns, first right, then left.

The rats and I halt at a dead end, standing before a solid metal door, my heart rate skyrocketing as I contemplate my options. Thankfully, the rats save my arse once again.

I'm rooted to the spot, the water sloshing around my ankles, when I notice that the door is standing slightly ajar, barely wide enough for the rats to slip through. Shouts ring out behind me, followed by the telltale pops of gunfire, and I don't think twice before rushing to slip inside.

I shut the door with a soft *snick* that I'm sure can't be overhead over the bedlam taking place. Swallowing thickly, I stare at the three drainage pipes on the wall ahead of me. They're old—*really old*—obviously harkening back to the original footprint of this place—whatever that was. The rats are jumping the few short inches into the drainage pipes along with the water and slipping away. Rats are little warriors, though, and I have no doubt that they're surviving whatever drop awaits them on the other end.

Muffled shouts and voices rumble from the other side of the door, and I decide that I have to *go*. I either leave now, or I die here. There's no third option and dying here is *not* a possibility for me.

Gulping down the hard mass lodged in my throat, I trudge through the shallow pool of water and choose the pipe on the far right on gut instinct. The pipe can't be more than twenty—*maybe* twenty-two—inches wide, and I know the fit is going to be bloody tight.

Choosing to go headfirst, I rip off the medical tape wrapped around my fingers and place the rifle into the drainage tunnel, crawling in behind it, keeping the Glock in one hand, abandoning the knife altogether. The guns will survive the water, and I suspect they'll prove more useful in the end—at least that's the direction my gut leans.

Tight was an understatement. It's unbelievably compact, and even though I don't suffer from claustrophobia, I'd be lying if I said this wasn't affecting me. Forcing measured breaths, I focus on the freedom waiting for me on the other side of this pipe.

The weight of the severely limited space, the scent of stale, soured water—which I find far worse than the smell of piss and shit in my cell—and the sensation of the rats pattering across my legs, back, arms, and the weapons in my possession all press down on me heavily. Breathing through my mouth, I attempt to calm my racing heart.

Salvation is close enough to touch. I will not die in a drainage ditch. I will kiss the lips of freedom again.

Under vastly different circumstances, I'd find the determination to persevere of the hearty little rodents skittering past me awe-inspiring, but right now, it's difficult to reach that same conclusion. The silver lining is that if something were to happen to me in this pipe—like choking on the rotten smell until I die—at least the rats will be fed. *Fuck, that's a morbid thought.*

Moving as quickly as I can, I shove past the thoughts of death, rats, and rancid smells, inching through the pipe. The warm light from the room in which I escaped has all but faded, but I'm not sure how much farther I have to go. Things are darker in here than a bolted, long-abandoned closet, only an inch or two to spare on either side of my shoulders as I shove the rifle along, gripping the Glock in my right hand. Eventually, faint light dances ahead, and I scramble desperately to reach it.

Tucking a hand on the inside of the strap of the rifle so the water doesn't carry it over the edge of the pipe, I squeeze the handle of the handgun tightly, unsure of what might await me. Slowly and carefully, I poke my head out of the end of the tunnel and breathe in fresh air as I consider my next move. Craning my neck, I look down, my eyes expanding to twice their size, stomach twisting, as I take in the hundred-or-more-foot drop to the ocean below. But that's not what would kill me; it's the jagged rocks that would send me straight to Hell.

Glancing to my left, I immediately eliminate that as an option. The cliff face is too smooth, with nowhere to gain purchase. Water spews from the other two pipes, too, and navigating that constant flow of water would be an issue with fatal consequences. *I didn't make it this far just to die in a torrential waterfall.*

Swinging my head to the right, I'm confident that's my road—or climb—to freedom.

Still resting on my stomach, I inch out a little farther so that my head and neck stick out of the pipe. Like a snake emerging from her den, I stretch my arms out of the hole and pull the strap of the rifle over my head. With the rifle now resting diagonally across my back and the barrel facing my feet, I ensure that the safety is still on. *I'd hate to kill myself accidentally after all the trouble I've gone through.*

I slip the grip of the Glock into my mouth and momentarily thank Sean for the cock sucking he had me do, because the handle of the gun is nothing compared to him. I spin around, methodically pulling my torso out of the tunnel. With my core engaged, I reach above me and grip a rock, my bare feet now resting on the bottom of the pipe. Using my abs and shoulders, and the adrenaline coursing through me, I hoist myself up and out of the hole. *Thank fuck I've been working out in my cell.*

Standing in the pipe's opening with water flying around my ankles and dropping to its new home in the ocean below, I make my next move. Still facing the rock face, I reach to my left and grip another rock, my left leg swinging out, my toes gripping the rock I've chosen.

The pinky and ring fingers on my left hand are still broken, but the gravity of the situation makes me numb to the pain, though I'm still careful not to press my weight on them. Cautiously, *so bloody cautiously,* I maneuver myself to the next rock, and the next, and the next.

I'm beginning to think I've lost the plot. While I'm not afraid of heights, this might be one of the most reckless and nerve-wracking things I've done, and I've done some *wild* shit in my twenty-nine years. One wrong move and I'm a dead woman. If the dark rain clouds overhead choose to unburden themselves, I'm dead. If a guard finds me here, I'm dead. If the Glock falls from my mouth—which is beginning to ache—and hits my foot, knocking me off balance, I'm dead.

When I see the edge of the cliff, I latch onto the sight of freedom with an iron grip, reaching for my next purchase and the rock beyond that.

CHAPTER 35

Louhi

I MAKE THE LAST FOUR MANEUVERS AND PRAY TO ALL THE GODS, goddesses, and witches that this is the end of my rock-climbing career.

My abs, jaw, shoulders, fingers, and toes are screeching at me, but I ignore the dull, pulsing discomfort as I hoist myself up onto the grassy top of the cliff…on the *outside* of the prison walls.

I manage to suppress the fizzy bubble of glee threatening to leap from my throat, though I allow the grin after pulling the Glock from my mouth, flicking the safety off and gripping it tightly. There's only about a foot of space between the cliff's edge on my left and the prison's expanse of concrete on my right. As hard as it was to scale the rock wall, I know my journey off this island is far from over. That was simply step one.

There's a guard tower up ahead, and I assume someone is manning it, though I can't quite tell. The grass is taller on this side of the wall, so I choose to lie down on my stomach and army crawl—*oh, the irony*—and inch my way toward the tower.

With no way off Exile Island from this cliff, I need to get to the other end of this landmass in order to make a better plan. Plus, getting as far from this prison as possible can only work in my favor.

Maneuvering around this tower and the next is my only option. It's still preferable to taking my chances in the prison yard, though.

On the ground up against the concrete wall, I crawl toward the tower slowly, my thoughts drifting back to Sean, and a nagging ache takes up residence in my chest.

What happened to him? Is he dead? Why haven't I seen him?

Without the time, firepower, or energy, I won't be able to search for him now. I need *off* this island—one way or another. Once I have my freedom, I'll find out what happened to him and can come back for him, if he's still alive.

I check myself. *Come back for him?* I'm bloody delusional to think that I'd come back here or try to rescue a man from his own government. Besides, it's not like he loves me or something. Trust doesn't equate to love, does it? Although, I've never been in love, so how would I know if someone loves me? Sean and I clearly had an intense connection, but is that love?

My mother's advice regarding love slips into my mind like a key into a lock.

. . . He'll only enhance your shine. The love he has for you should be so bright that when you see it reflected back, you're nearly blinded by it. Every day should end brighter than it started with a man that loves you.

Does every day end brighter than it began with Sean in my life?

I mutter a silent curse at the stark realization that it bloody fucking does. I've been locked in a cell for twenty-something hours a day, made to piss, shit, and sleep all in the same area, and only allowed out for torture sessions and the *rare* shower. Even *with* the torture, I closed my eyes each day with a sense of safety and optimism that shouldn't have existed. Maybe it was the fact that I felt as though my soul was looking into a mirror, breathing to life feelings that have been in hibernation until now. He lightened the load of each breath I took inside those concrete walls and the idea of something having happened to him upsets me far more than the death of a prison guard should.

Vittu! I think my mother was right, and I'm not sure what to do with that information. I loathe to admit it, but I suppose all of this means that I'll be coming back to Ex-I, after all.

But what if he's dead? Refusing to entertain that notion, I shove that idea aside. Even as my inner beast whimpers at the prospect, I won't let myself go there. Not now. I can spiral later, when I'm curled up in a real bed with my perfect pillow tucked under my head.

Near the tower, I risk craning my neck to glimpse two soldiers posted there and I make myself smaller, praying like mad that they don't look down. On my belly, I snake around the squared base of the tower, and when bullets don't sprinkle me with holes, I let out the breath I was holding.

I continue through the tall grass down the adjacent side of the prison toward the next tower, sparing small glances over my shoulder to verify I haven't been spotted. The guards seem to be focusing most of their attention on the center of the prison yard, picking off and subduing the prisoners that attempt an escape. Though I can't see through the thick concrete walls, I can hear a cacophony of gunfire and shouting over the wailing siren and crashing waves. It's obvious that whatever is happening in that yard is the purest form of pandemonium.

I hope Kazi gets out.

When I finally reach the last guard tower, I'm riddled with the impeding freedom within my sight, but inject a sense of calm into my veins so that I don't do anything hasty.

At the base of the tower, I scan the environment ahead, making my next plan. There's a copse of trees and smaller bushes up in the distance, and I need to get to those for cover. However, there's nothing but dirt in front of the entrance to the prison; nothing but dirt standing between me and the vegetation.

I narrow my left eye and arch my eyebrow in intense concentration. Glancing up at the guards in the tower, I wait until they turn their attention toward something in the yard and sprint for it.

Maybe forty feet from the bushes and trees, shouting and more gunfire ensues somewhere behind me and I run harder, faster. My legs burn with the exertion as I push myself to run as fast as I can, ignoring the way the barrel of the rifle batters violently against the space between my spine and my side.

Flinging my body into the bushes, I catch my breath while I listen. My splash into the bushes wasn't exactly silent, but I'm hoping it went undetected amid the chaos ensuing on the island. While I don't hear anyone running after me, I don't risk a peek. Instead, I grip the Glock in my hand tightly, making sure the safety is still off as I crawl forward between the bushes, keeping my ears wide open.

Vines and cords of branches dart out, scraping the bare skin of my arms and ripping at my filthy uniform trousers, but I do my best to disregard their presence as I briskly navigate them. When a particularly thorny limb scrapes over one of the deep cuts on my back through my shirt, I suck in a sharp breath, gritting my teeth through the sudden sting.

Undeterred, I keep moving forward, tendrils of blood now sliding down my bare arms and the hand gripping the Glock, making my grasp slippery. The tropical trees and vegetation are still thick, and I use that to my advantage, knowing that my inky hair and black uniform will help me blend in, especially now that the sun has evacuated completely.

Frantically looking around, I assess my surroundings. Based on the sounds of the ocean coming from my left, I know I'm still relatively close to the water. What I don't know, though, is how wide or long this island is, which puts me at a disadvantage. My only plan is to keep going until I can't go any farther. I have to assume there's a boat somewhere. It'd be highly unlikely that the soldiers stationed here would have no way off this hostile landmass.

I see the guard half a second before he comes at me from my right, tackling me to the ground. The breath is knocked out of me as I land on the rifle and hard tangled branches, making my back shriek.

Cruel, vile eyes stare down at me, and I know that if I were to rip the mask off this soldier's face, I'd find a snarling man foaming at the mouth beneath. Without a thought, I bring my knee up, jamming it into his thigh as a growl vibrates within his chest.

He holds his combat knife to my throat, and I smile.

"You're not getting away. Why the fuck are you smiling?" he grunts.

"I always smile in the face of death, darling."

With a scoff, he presses the knife more firmly, warm blood now slipping down the side of my neck. "At least you recognize death when you see him."

My smile grows, a light giggle trickling from me like rain dancing on tin. "Simply because I see death doesn't mean I'll meet him. I'm not so easily claimed."

His beady eyes narrow on me before he shakes his head, clearing his expression. "You're fucking crazy."

"That's not very a nice word." Lifting the Glock clutched in my hand to his soft side, I pull the trigger. He howls, but I'm able to roll out from beneath him before getting to my feet and planting another round in his skull.

With the Glock still in my hand and the rifle at my back, I run from the scene at a breakneck pace. I'm sure the sound of my gunshots just gave me away like a beacon of light in the dark. *I miss my silencer.*

Dodging trees and stocky bushes like my life depends on it—and it bloody well does—I race for freedom, darting left, then right, leaping over roots and the random rocks that crop up.

I don't know how long or how far I run, but my muscles and bones are pulsing, aching, and cramping by the time I see another cliff. My heart sinks to the abyss of my soul at the sight.

CHAPTER 36

Louhi

Taking a deep breath, inhaling the humid night air, I close my eyes and try to think. I'm not even at the edge, and I can tell that the drop will be as steep and treacherous as the one I came from. Letting my gut guide me, I veer right, avoiding more tropical vegetation. More gunshots sound in the distance, and I grit my teeth.

Adrenaline and sheer determination spur me onward and dispel any possible uncertainties. The taste of freedom is so close and I long for a sip.

I dash through the trees as fast as I can until I hear the low thrum of voices over the sound of the crashing waves. Crouching down behind some bushes, I'm sure I haven't been spotted, at least not yet. As quietly as possible, I eject the magazine from the Glock and count how many rounds I have remaining—*nine*. Replacing the magazine, I begin to crawl forward on all fours between the branches and heavy foliage.

Getting as close as I can, I peek through the leaves on the bush in front of me and see…*a beach*. But more importantly, my eyes lock onto a bloody *boat*. With a way off this God-forsaken island, I squint to make out only two men standing by my means of escape.

I unstrap the rifle from my back and thread the barrel through the branches as I lie on my stomach on the ground, getting cozy.

This could easily be my favorite position in the entire world: lying on the ground with the butt of a rifle nestled in the cushion between my shoulder and chest, my finger hovering over the trigger, my breaths coming evenly as I lean forward and observe my target in the viewfinder. Through the scope, eyebrows pinched, I watch the two masked men. As I take in their familiar builds, my entire body locks up, recognition taking hold. Potent relief washes over me like the salty water sliding up the sand.

"Sean," Honey Eyes declares, his voice barely audible over the waves slapping against each other, but his words and the solemnity of his tone reach me. Honey Eyes and Sean face each other, the surf threatening to cover their boots as the waves swim toward them.

"If you do this, you won't just be a deserter, you'll be an enemy of the State. Is she really worth that? I want you to be sure," Honey Eyes asks, and my lungs trap my intake of oxygen, refusing to let it go as I anticipate his response.

Sean doesn't so much as hesitate before stating, with unwavering and impenetrable confidence, "She's worth everything. She's worth more than my life."

My mouth parts in a radiant beam that I can feel in the depths of my soul as carbon dioxide whooshes out of me. *He bloody loves me.*

Just as I'm about to climb to my feet, I hear Honey Eyes speak again. "What if she didn't make it? What if she doesn't come? I better not have killed Martinez for nothing. Sucks that he had to die, you know, he was one of the better ones."

Even from this distance, I catch the anxiety woven into his voice, and it makes my heart squeeze. *Bloody hell, I really need to lock that organ up again. She's going to get me into trouble.*

"She'll make it," is the only thing Sean says, but it's enough to have me stretching to my full height, swinging the rifle back over my shoulder as I saunter toward them.

"Hello, darlings," I chime casually, drawing their attention, the Glock dangling at my side. Both men whip their heads in my direction as I slip between the bushes and descend the sandy slope toward the beach.

"You're here."

"Of course, Honey Eyes. When will you stop underestimating me?"

Then, I shift my attention to Sean, who has turned to face me fully. He tugs off his mask, crumpling it in his fist, shoving it into his friend's hands. His face is marked with relief and something else, something almost light and sugary that my tongue is desperate to taste.

Just as I come to a stop before the two men, thunder cracks in the distance, and I tilt my head toward the sky. The air is thick with the threat of a downpour, and I don't think we have long before that storm is upon us.

Still in his mask, Honey Eyes tilts his head to the side and narrows his gaze on me. "Wait, how did you get out?"

"Drainage pipe."

"The one that leads to the cliff?" Sean clarifies, speaking for the first time since I made my presence known.

His eyes are wide and disbelieving as I smile broadly. "That's the one."

"Fuck, we figured you'd kill a guard, put on his uniform, and walk out the front gate," Honey Eyes explains. "That was our plan, anyway."

I shrug. "I suppose that *might* have worked, but I've never done things the easy way. Besides, the path I took was far more impressive."

"I won't argue with that," Honey Eyes admits, and I wink at him.

"You ready to get out of here, Lou?" Sean inquires, and I bounce on my toes, practically skipping toward the boat anchored in the ocean not far away.

I've just begun wading into the chilly water as Sean's low register rings out from behind me. "Tell my mom… Fuck."

Frowning, I spin around to find him running a hand over his buzzed hair, his profile etched with determination. He stands on the beach, his gaze locked with Honey Eyes, the surf spilling onto his boots. If I had to describe his expression in two words, I'd choose despair and grief.

In light of what I overheard them say on the beach, I didn't consider that Sean might be…coming with me. *Abso-fucking-lutely not.* I don't want to be the reason he abandons his family, his career, his entire bloody life. *I'm not worth that.*

"Fuck, Sean. You're not escaping with me, are you? You can't. You'll be a criminal. Let me go alone."

I've barely gotten the words out before he's stomping toward me. I march back toward the beach, meeting him where the water laps at the sand, both of us glaring at one another, our breathing heavy. I don't know what I plan to do to keep him from chucking his life away, but if I have to shoot out his kneecaps to stop him, I will.

"You don't get it, Lou. I can't let you go. I spend every damn day with criminals anyway, so it only makes sense for me to become one."

Those words hang between us as I let his declaration drag me under the tide. Who am I to stop him? I'm a huge believer in free will and the freedom to make your own choices in life—even if they're idiotic. If this is the choice he's making, am I so hypocritical as to try to stop him? However, I would like to fully understand the motivations of his actions. '*I can't let you go*' doesn't quite cut it for me.

Softening my tone, I ask, "Why are you really doing this?"

"Because I like being a defector and enjoy being hunted by my own government." Sean's sarcasm is wholly unappreciated as it drips like thick molasses from his tongue.

"No," I declare firmly. "*Why?*"

He sighs inordinately, the exhale audible over the bellow of the ocean around us. "There's not another option for either of us.

There's no other way out. But even if there were, I wouldn't take it. I'm with you, Lou."

His fists clench and unclench at his sides as evidence that he will fight me tooth and nail to get on that boat, but it won't come to that. I won't be stopping him, not when my heart and gut are begging me to escape with him. It feels *right* to let him come along. It feels *right* to be with him.

Dipping my chin in a solemn nod, I turn in the direction of the boat, trudging into the ocean, ignoring the way the salty water makes my cuts sting. He loves me, even if he hasn't said it. He's choosing *me*. And if I'm being honest with myself, I've chosen him too. With my back to him, I find myself smiling a real, honest smile.

"Lou, hold up," Honey Eyes calls, and I shift toward the beach once more. *Bloody hell, we have* got *to go.*

He bends at the waist and pulls off his boots, tossing me one, then the other, and I nod gratefully. I'm still barefoot in my black prison uniform, so these will be useful.

"Take care of my friend, Lou."

"With my life," I reply honestly. Wading through the ocean, I can still hear their conversation, though I don't turn around.

"Tell my mom that I love her. Tell her...tell her that I took her advice and that my head couldn't be trusted," Sean requests. The sorrow in his voice is heavy like too-thick cream, but I take a deep breath and bite my tongue.

I can't possibly imagine what Sean's about to go through, abandoning his family and Honey Eyes.

"I'll tell her," Honey Eyes promises in return.

The water floats around my ribs, and I'm almost to the boat—*to my means of escape*—when I hear some small splashes behind me and Sean speaks again. "Watch out for Callie, too. Don't let her think the worst of me."

"I won't."

There's a long beat, the sound of more water sloshing, followed by Sean's admission in a low, quiet register that barely reaches me over the roar of the vast ocean. "I love you, man."

His mate chuckles, replying slightly louder, "You've gone fucking soft, bro, but I love you, too. Now, get the fuck out of here."

Water laps around my chest as I toss the boots I've kept dry into the boat. Before climbing aboard, I submerge myself, letting the water wash over me, cleansing me as I smile into the sea. Hoisting myself over the side of the dust-colored quad engine offshore boat, it's obvious that we'll be adding theft to our list of crimes tonight.

Sean climbs in a few moments later, and I gaze at the shoreline as I wring out my hair, calling out curiously, "Hey, Honey Eyes, what do you look like?"

He chuckles boisterously enough that the sound reaches me. "I'll show you next time I see you."

"Deal. Do me a favor, yeah?"

Cocking his head to the side, he shouts over the waves, "You mean, *another* one?"

I giggle, yelling back, "Look out for Kazi, will you?"

He shakes his head and replies, "You two *would* be friends."

A laugh trickles from me as I tread on wet feet toward the cockpit, still smiling, where Sean starts the engine.

Standing next to him as the motors kick on and the boat begins backing away from the island, I explain gently, "Sean, if you come with me, know that you'll be walking into *my* world."

While I won't deign to try to talk him out of something he wants to do, I want to ensure that he knows what he's getting into by running away with me. His future won't look anything like his past.

He shifts his attention to me long enough to confirm, "Your world is mine now."

Sean's bare forearms flex and his jaw ticks as he maneuvers the boat, and I have to admit that he pulls off the whole *criminal-on-the-run* look way too well.

CHAPTER 37

Louhi

I DARE TO LET OUT THE BREATH I'VE HELD CAPTIVE FOR MONTHS. Sinking into the seat behind Sean, I slip my feet into Honey Eyes's too-big boots. When I sit up, my attention toggles between his back muscles pinching and flexing and the island drifting further away, unsure which sight is more alluring.

"Where are we anyway?" I ask.

"Three hundred miles off mainland Hawai'i."

"What's your plan?" I wonder aloud.

"My plan only gets us to Hawai'i."

I smirk smugly at his back and chime, "Then it's a good thing you brought me along."

He snorts, and we fall silent as we coast over the waves. Rain begins to trickle slowly from the sky, dotting the water around us like pockmarks.

"So, I take it the alarm and sprinklers were your doing?"

Facing away from me, he shouts over the rain, motor, and waves, "Yeah, Jace—Honey Eyes—packed the boat with supplies and moved it to the beach yesterday, and I set off the emergency system and disconnected the power that locks the cells. Then we made our way out here separately under the guise of hunting down escaped prisoners and met up about half an hour before you got there."

At this point, it feels odd to refer to Honey Eyes by anything other than the nickname I've given him, so I ask, "Is Honey Eyes going to get in trouble for any of this?"

"He shouldn't. We blamed the murders of Borman, Jones, and Davis on you, and he'll pin your escape on me. They'll definitely question him, but he'll be fine."

I get to my feet, taking shelter under the Bimini top next to Sean to get out of the drops of rain steadily beating down. I sat there longer than I probably should, letting the sky's tears soak my face. It's been so long since I enjoyed the feeling of being outside, no matter the weather. The cleansing didn't hurt either.

"That's fairly devious, Sean," I tease, placing a hand gingerly on his bicep. "Perhaps you belong in my world, after all."

He smirks, but before he can reply, spotlights glide over the boat. My eyes hit Sean's face like a bullet, and he rushes to answer my silent question. "Under all of the seats."

Racing to the seat I vacated, I lift the cushion to find a knapsack full of weapons. *I love an arsenal.* I toss him a Glock that he catches and pull a loaded magazine from the sack. I swap the half-empty magazine that was loaded into the assault rifle that I brought onto the boat with me into the sack and load a fresh one.

Crouching down, I aim the rifle over the stern at the boat full of men chasing—hunting—us. As I look through the scope, waiting for a clear shot, curiosity and concern seep into my skin like lotion and I call back to Sean, "Are you going to be able to shoot at your own men?"

"They aren't my men anymore." His tone has a bite behind it that I don't miss.

"So, if you need to kill one of them, you can do it without hesitation?" I'm challenging him on this, because it's not simply his life at stake here. I haven't come this far, only to die because the man next to me has a crisis of conscience. There's no room for that here. I need to be able to trust Sean with my life and safety. He's proven that so far, but having to kill his men—his mates—is entirely different.

When he doesn't answer me as quickly as I'd like, I glance over my shoulder at him, my mouth open to snap at him, but he lifts his handgun and immediately fires two shots in the other boat's direction. *Actions speak louder than words, I suppose.*

"When I said I was with you, I meant it."

I smile, looking back through the scope as I map out a plan. I wait one beat, then another before ordering Sean, "Take a hard left."

The other boat returns Sean's fire just as he follows my instruction, and the second the engine comes into view in the scope, I fire four rounds, knocking out each engine. Sean speeds away again, and I fire a few more rounds at the other boat, just for fun. With the gun and my attention still trained on the boat in the increasing distance, I admit, "I won't doubt you again. Trust is…hard for me."

He doesn't respond, though I know he heard me.

Once the other boat is out of sight, I move to seek shelter from the rain in the cockpit.

"Lou," Sean says mildly, "This will never work without complete trust in each other."

I nod, swallowing hard. The two words that leave my lips are a phrase I've never spoken to anyone in my adult life, and I find them incredibly difficult to form. "I'm sorry."

He studies me, and I can just make out the silver of his eyes, even swathed in the dark cloak cast by the sky. "Don't be. Just tell me this will work. Tell me I didn't just throw my life away for a woman who doesn't trust me. Tell me that I didn't just wreck everything by loving someone who can't return the feeling."

My eyes bug out of my bloody skull and my breath catches. Locking my gaze onto his, my voice is tender as I reply honestly, "You didn't. You make every day end brighter than it began. I'm with you too, Sean."

It's the closest I've ever come to telling someone I love them.

My chest burns, but it doesn't hurt; instead, it feels like someone ignited my heart, lighting up the darkness that's resided there for so long.

He sets his Glock in a small cubby to the right of the wheel before reaching out and cupping my cheek. With his skin against mine, the gesture feels like everything wholesome and right in this world. I swear I can hear our breaths over the breaking of the surf and the howling of the stormy wind, and I know that my heart is hammering faster than the rain pelting down around us. When I obliterate the miniscule distance, I snake a hand around the back of his neck as our lips crash like the waves around us.

His soft lips feel like home, like safety and warmth. I deepen the kiss, parting for him to gain access to my mouth, desperate for more of him. When his tongue sweeps inside, he tastes like deliverance, and I indulge in that delicious freedom like fine wine.

He feeds me his proclamation from earlier, love now dancing on my tongue as his hand glides down my back, welding us together.

I've never coveted love before, but now that I have Sean's, I've been transformed, irrevocably changed. Or perhaps that's simply because I might love him, too.

Right there in the middle of the Pacific Ocean, on the run, standing on a stolen boat with a man who lied, disobeyed, and killed for me, I feel more at ease than I've felt in the whole of my life.

There's no escaping this connection.

There's no escaping *him.*

His kiss communicates everything his words don't, and I let the moment cocoon me in its warmth, basking in its heated glow.

When our lips finally part, he dips his head once more, connecting our lips in a gentle, chaste kiss before murmuring, "So perfect."

My heart soars, and I smile when he pulls away, a genuine display of joy and comfort written on my face as I tumble into the chair next to him.

Silence falls between us as I look around at the vast open ocean.

The hum of a motor cuts into the dreary night and with another sigh, I get to my feet, stalking back to where I left the rifle at the rear of the boat. Sinking down, I look through the scope and call out to Sean what I see. "Two boats gaining on us."

He guns it, and the adrenaline from a few hours ago is waning, leaving only ire in its wake to fuel me. Real freedom is so close, and the idea of losing the fight fills me with anger.

Remembering a story of mythology my father once told me, I find myself wishing that I could summon Syöjätär to fight our enemies, but the Finnish mythological goddess of snakes isn't here. She's not sitting on a rock in the middle of this ocean combing through her hair, waiting to be summoned to go to war for us. She's not turning her snakes upon the men after us. But I'm not Louhi, the Finnish goddess of death, calling upon her daughter for aid. I'm only Louhi Koskinen, mortal woman and assassin. There's only me out here and the fiery rage coiled inside me. Well, and Sean.

As soon as the first boat is within range, I fire a shot and a soldier in the boat drops. I pick off a second, third, and fourth. Two more men remain, the rocking of the boat making this more challenging than it would be otherwise.

There aren't many things I enjoy more than pulling triggers, except for sleeping with *my* pillow and *maybe* creating a unique death for someone. As I slip a new magazine into the rifle, I take a breath and zero in on my next target.

I finally get another shot off and when only the boat's captain is left, I leave him for Sean. When the other boat is finally within view, I begin the process anew. Bullets whizz past me, some lodging themselves in the side of the boat, one landing in the cushion by my calf, but I ignore them all as I pull the trigger again and again.

After what feels like forever, one boat retreats while the other is left floating without anyone living to man it.

"How much farther to the mainland?" I inquire over the patter of rain.

"About one hundred and seventy-five miles."

Bringing the rifle with me, I make my way back to the seat next to Sean and get comfortable.

"You're pretty good with that thing," Sean remarks, nodding to the rifle at my side.

"I've been a sharpshooter since I was eighteen."

Folding my legs underneath me, I survey the dark open water surrounding us. "If you could choose a single weapon in the world, what would you pick?"

His head slides toward me and his eyebrow cocks. "Seriously, *that's* what you want to talk about right now?"

I lift a shoulder. "Why not? It's not as if we have anything better to talk about. Call it getting to know each other."

He rolls his eyes, which makes me smile, but he answers, "Handgun, if I have unlimited ammo. If not, then I guess my utility knife."

"Your Glock or something else?"

"Probably a Glock. They're simple and reliable."

He's right about that. They're made of far fewer pieces, making them easier to disassemble and reassemble. But like most things, if you treat them right, they'll do right by you.

Thinking of Conall and Viktor, I muse, "I have a friend who opts for a Desert Eagle and another who always carries a .44 Magnum."

"Based on the caliber of those weapons, I'm going to go out on a limb and assume those aren't *law-abiding* friends?"

I titter softly. "Not exactly."

He nods, but I can see the beginnings of a smile tugging at the corners of his lips. After another beat or two, he sighs, "I'm almost afraid to ask, but what weapon would you choose if you could only have one."

"Brilliant question."

He hits me with a blatant *what the fuck?* look, uttering, "It was *your* question."

"So?" I respond with a shrug. "It's still a brilliant question."

His chuckle is loud, free, and I find myself following suit. It's nice to see him laugh, since stoicism and graveness seem to be his default.

"Believe it or not, I'm not picky. Put any sort of weapon in my hand and I'll smile. But if I *had* to choose one, it'd be a rifle, specifically a .338 Lapua Magnum. Although, when it comes to my work, I've been gravitating toward poison lately. Not because I don't want to get my hands dirty, but because I love the way it eats people alive from the inside out. It's violent and exhilarating. I can slip it to them, watching them unravel and succumb to the toxin over the span of hours while they have no idea what's happening to them."

I'm not entirely sure why I revealed all that information. Perhaps it was a gesture of trust, though maybe it was a test. I wanted to see how Sean would react to a truth like that. He only nods, though, his expression unreadable.

"Does it bother you that I'm an assassin?" I ask curiously.

Slowly, he slides his gaze toward me, the action highlighted by the dim lights of the dashboard of the boat. Almost imperceptibly, he shakes his head before clarifying, "Lou, I'm walking into this thing with you with my eyes wide open. I know who you are, and I'll never stop you from pursuing the life you want. Besides, the lines between right and wrong are blurring more for me every day."

Unlike most people, I grew up with a warped sense of right and wrong. Morality is rooted entirely in the perspective you have, and I shaped my own stance long ago, but Sean needs time to evaluate exactly what his view on that subject is.

I nod in understanding, turning to face the ocean, so he doesn't see the smile on my face, my heart fluttering wildly in my chest like a trapped moth.

CHAPTER 38

Louhi

We coast across the inky ocean for the next couple of hours, uninterrupted. Both of us consumed with our thoughts, we don't speak much to each other. The rain has been stuttering on and off, but it's gracing us with a break at the moment.

I'm soaked to the bone with rain and seawater, and there's a very good chance I'll wind up ill after this entire ordeal, but I don't mind because *I'm free*. Though things are still far from over, the granite rock that was perched on my chest has been removed, and I'm basking in the luminescent glow of liberation.

Glancing at the man who saved me when I couldn't save myself, I can't imagine being with anyone else, not even Mercer. I don't know where my brother is or why he didn't come to get me like he promised, but I intend to find out. He'd never abandon me to a fate worse than death, so I'm sure he has a good excuse. I need to get us to safety first, though.

Without Sean, I don't know what would've happened to me, but I'm grateful I didn't have to find out. He got us off that bloody island, and I'll get us the rest of the way to true freedom, by any means necessary.

Mainland Hawai'i finally comes into view on the horizon, and Sean mutters, "I hope you have a fucking plan, Lou."

I peer at the clock on the boat's computer, noting that it's still the middle of the night, which is something I'll take full advantage of. My head flicks to Sean, and I let my smile give him all the reassurance he needs. I can prove my dependability, just as he's proven his.

Sean slows the boat as we approach the island, flipping off the headlights, and I mentally run through our options. There are a few ways to go about this and all of them are highly illegal.

"Get us close to the base," I order him under my breath, a clear decision playing in my mind like a favorite song. Ex-I will have alerted the military base here of our escape and I'd be willing to bet that they'll assume we'd head for the other side of the island, but that's not what we'll do. Sean gives me a wary look but swings the boat in the opposite direction, and my suspicion is confirmed knowing where Sean had been headed.

Keeping my voice to a breathy whisper, I explain, "We need to steal a car, ditch our clothes, and get to a payphone."

He nods, pulling up to a dock as quietly as possible, as I pull a knapsack containing a small arsenal from the storage compartments. Slinging the sack over my shoulder, we disembark from the boat. Sean ties off the boat as I fish a Glock from the sack, gripping it in my right hand. From beside me, Sean loads a fresh clip into his handgun and shoves it into the holster at his hip.

His entire demeanor, especially combined with his uniform, screams, *I'm in the army*. It's hot, really hot. While that's usually a look for Sean that bloody does it for me, we can't afford for either of us to get distracted and make a mistake now.

This is far from my first time escaping a dangerous situation, but the stakes have never been higher. Step number one is getting the fuck away from this military base.

Scanning the car park as we approach, I spot a bike at the far corner and smile. My eyes flick to the camera on the corner of the nearby building and duck my head as I beeline for the sporty red and black Ninja, Sean hot on my heels.

Making quick work of hot-wiring the bike, I climb on and wait for my backpack to take his position behind me. He glares at me, his left eyelid twitching as he rallies some restraint and climbs behind me, grumbling, "Why do you get to drive?"

"Everyone knows that the person who hot-wires the bike gets to drive the bike."

He growls in my ear, and I laugh as I gun the gas, speeding into the tropical, humid night. Practically speaking, since he's in his uniform, Sean will blend in far better near the base than the girl in the black uniform, so it makes the most sense for him to drape his body over mine. At least I'm telling myself that's the primary reason, *not* that I want him to touch me.

I've been gulping down breaths of freedom from the moment I escaped Ex-I, but as this bike zips down the open road, the unbridled weightlessness I experience is something I relish to the fullest.

Hitting the gas harder, Sean leans forward, wrapping his thick, muscular arms around me tighter and I smile to myself. I continue to bob and weave, taking random side streets, being considerate of the weight distribution on the bike. The wail of a siren in the distance pierces the drizzly night, making Sean stiffen behind me, but it could be police, ambulance or fire. To be safe, I yank the bike down a dark alley, parking behind an industrial-sized dumpster. While we wait it out, I mutter, "Got any coins? A Quid or two?"

"Uh, no, who carries loose change anymore?"

I gnaw on my bottom lip as I ponder our options. The lack of money, specifically change, poses a problem, but we can work around that.

When the wail of the siren grows faint, I whip back out onto the road, my eyes darting around, taking stock of my surroundings. Suddenly, I spot a payphone outside of a dodgy petrol station, but the cameras fixed on the building would make stopping risky, and without any coins, it'd be pointless. It'd take me too long to make the phone operable, anyway, and that's assuming it'd be possible at all.

Cameras all around the city are picking up images of us, and I curl my lip as my frustration gnashes its teeth. We need to ditch the bike, we still need a change of clothes, and I need to make that bloody call.

Eventually, the ocean comes into view up ahead, and I hang a left, backtracking a few blocks, and park the bike in a neighborhood, facing the other direction.

I whisper, "We're on foot from here."

We duck in and out of backyards and car parks until we reach the sandy shore. On the beach, I locate a phone booth to our right, far behind a lifeguard stand and just before a sand dune crests, but without change, it's bloody useless.

Inclining my head, I indicate that we should try walking in the other direction. We navigate the beach for what seems like forever before we spot a group of teenagers enjoying a night swim.

Tugging on Sean's shirt, we drift backwards before falling to our stomachs on the sandy dune covered in a weighted blanket made of grass and vines. The sky overhead is still thick and full of additional rain, bathing us further in gloomy darkness.

The four teens—two boys and two girls—are scampering around the beach, drinking from cans and laughing loudly. Their clothing spills from their bags like a candy container that's just been busted into, overflowing with sugary temptation as I eye their belongings like I'm addicted to sweets.

"I need you to steal their shit, specifically their clothes and any spare change they have," I whisper to Sean.

"Why me?"

"Because I'm in this bloody prison uniform and you're in your military uniform. They'll trust a bloke in the army."

"Why can't we just ask to borrow their phone and ask them nicely for their clothes?"

I turn my head toward him, resting a hand on his forearm braced on the uncomfortable ground next to me. "Sean, love, you're not in the same world you were twenty-four hours ago. You now exist in a place where you're on the run. Calls can be traced, fingerprints lifted, witnesses questioned. I need to make a call that can get us to safety, but we need to operate under the assumption that those teenagers will turn us in, so the less interaction we have with them, the better. We only need enough money for a one-minute call."

His moonlight eyes dance like the morose thundercloud brimming with lightning and rain above us as he gazes back at me and I smile, delighting in what I see within them. He nods, and I squeeze his forearm a moment before he climbs to his feet.

You couldn't pay me to go for a night swim in these waters, with the threat of sharks below the surface, but it doesn't seem to be fazing the teenagers as they splash drunkenly about seventy yards out.

Sean's gait is confident as he approaches the haphazardly strewn clothing and belongings. He plucks up as much as he can carry and stalks back toward me, undetected. None of the beachgoers appear to have even noticed that Sean was there at all, which is shocking. A shriek comes from the ocean, but Sean doesn't break stride or glance back at the sound. Peering around him, they don't seem to be shrieking because they spotted Sean, but for some unknown reason that would only be logical to a person utterly tanked. Until Sean returns, I monitor the four teens giggling and playing among the waves, oblivious to the danger lurking amid the grass.

I snake backwards a few feet before righting myself just as Sean reaches me. When we're far enough from view and the massive dune stands between the teens and us, Sean drops a few coins into my outstretched palm.

"We've got two bucks," he informs me, which is far more than we need, but I won't complain.

He clutches the new clothes as we retrace our steps until we reach the payphone. I slip into the booth, unsurprised when Sean wedges his way in behind me, out of abrasive sea air.

Sea air whistles the tune of freedom as it batters against the exterior of the booth.

I'm free. Free to find Mercer, free to learn the truth of why he didn't come for me, free to take a bubble bath with a glass of wine in my hand, free to live my life.

Free.

Holding my breath, I dial the numbers I memorized in case of an emergency I hoped I'd never have.

When a deep male voice answers the phone in Russian, I assert, "Viktor, it's Louhi. I'm collecting payment."

CHAPTER 39

Sean

Lou immediately switches from English to something Slavic—Russian, I think—and after a rapid-fire conversation, she hangs up the phone, her face arcane as we back out of the booth. I didn't even know she spoke Russian until just now and it makes me wonder what other languages she can speak fluently.

Louhi Koskinen is a never-ending, seemingly unsolvable mystery.

I frown, my eyebrows slashing down so far that they damn near eclipse my vision as she makes out like a bandit—which, I guess, she is—for the wooded, overgrown area to our left. While it only takes me a few long strides to catch her, my head buzzes with the need for answers and my hands twitch to do something, *anything*. As soon as we're under the cover of the trees and vegetation, I grip her arm—not hard, but firmly enough that she knows I'm not fucking around—and spin her to face me.

Slanting her head to the side, her almond-shaped eyes seem to glow with the gift of freedom. However, now that she's free of her prison, I wonder if I might be entering mine.

"What the fuck was that? Who did you call?"

She arches an eyebrow at me like she can't believe I'd ask such an asinine question, but I've never been on the run before, and I don't like feeling in the dark in this situation.

I'm spiraling. I've been out of control for far longer than I'm comfortable with. The stakes of the situation couldn't be higher, the pressure biting down on my chest in a death grip. When she doesn't respond right away, I entreat her, my voice scratchy and low, "Lou."

Her name hangs between us like a noose swaying in the breeze, unspoken words and questions braided into the rope. *Are we going to survive this? Will I have given up everything just to lose her in the end?*

Anxiety threatens to strangle us, killing us slowly as we die a painful, excruciating death. As I fight the urge to give life to those dark thoughts, she slips her hand into mine, our fingers intertwining like roots on an ancient, steadfast tree.

"Fucking talk to me," I implore, and her expression softens, morphing into something bordering on apologetic.

"*That* was our ride out of here. He'll be here at noon tomorrow."

"Who is '*he*?'"

A beat passes before she breathes, "Viktor Novikov," like I'd know who the fuck that is.

My face must clue her in to my ignorance, and she explains, "The Pakhan of the Bratva."

I remember Jace mentioning her father's ties to the Bratva, but what the *fuck* is a *'Pakhan'*? "In motherfucking English, Lou."

She gives me a small, sheepish smile. "Viktor is the head of the Russian mafia, like the Godfather or Capo is of the Italian mob."

Taking a deep, centering breath, I remember that this is the life I signed up for with Louhi. This is her world and these are her people.

"What did you mean when you said you were 'collecting payment?'" I ask, my voice the only sound over the roar of the distant ocean and the steady buzz and chatter of insects.

She pulls me deeper into the wooded area, until we're enveloped by the condensed, flourishing verdure, her face alight with the glow of freedom. "I did a…sensitive job for him a few years ago, and at the time, my gut told me to demand a favor as payment instead of money. I just cashed that in."

"And, he's what? Sending a plane? A boat? Where are we going?"

Stepping into my space, she tilts her head back as her free hand snakes up the front of my uniform, gliding over the camouflaged-printed cotton and nylon before settling around the back of my neck, dragging my head down to meet hers. "He's sending his plane. It'll pick us up and take us to Russia."

Even before her lips dance with mine, I know she's attempting to feed me the comfort I so desperately need; the reassurance that we'll make it off this goddamn island.

Louhi presses onto the balls of her feet, her lips skating across mine for a moment. Restraining myself, I wait, briefly letting her lead, opening for her as she explores my mouth. It's not long before my tether breaks and I melt into her, cupping the back of her head as I deepen the kiss.

Lou's lips taste like the right choice, a good decision, like *love*.

As our mouths tangle, I can almost feel our souls coalescing, intimately knitting together and binding us to each other permanently. We kiss until our surroundings seem to vaporize, leaving us the only two people left in this world.

Pressing her closer to me, I slide our joined hands around the small of her back. As the waves in the distance crash in a hypnotic rhythm and the bugs sing their song around us, I lose myself in Lou, in the slice of freedom we're sharing, one that's hopefully not temporary.

Our bodies connect as I tug on her braided hair, my movements becoming more frantic as we claw and scrape at each other's clothes, shedding them. When Lou is left in nothing but the black cotton prison uniform top, I rip it down the middle, discarding it in the shrubbery.

A heartbeat later, we're frantically swallowing one another's cries and moans, fervently filling each other with everything we've never voiced aloud, reminding the other that we'll make it out alive—together.

Our fears will not hang us.

Enraptured by the spell cast by the moment, we aren't in control, giving our bodies the ultimate authority. The threads connecting us feel stronger than steel, our shared respect and trust weaving a beautiful pattern into the fabric of our hearts.

As we come down from our highs, Lou slides a hand up my chest, resting over my hammering heart, her dark eyes full of sincerity as she whispers against my lips. "There's a darkness inside you, Sean Diggory, and I'm going to dance within it."

My gaze roves over her beautiful face before I knit our lips together again, like two links in a chain being permanently connected.

When we come up for air, I drop my forehead to hers, palming her soft cheek. "To Russia," I repeat her words quietly, hoping to sound surer than I am, begging the ice flooding my veins to go undetected, even as my mouth goes dry. I swallow, attempting to make the hard lump in my throat disappear.

I knew this was going to happen. I talked it through with Jace at length when we were plotting a way to help Louhi escape. I knew what I was giving up. But you can know something is coming, prepare for it even, and the stark reality still manages to slap you in the face.

Right now, the gravity of my decisions clamps down around my chest, weighing a thousand tons.

I've deserted my life, my career, my friends, my family. I'm a *traitor*.

And I've done it all for the woman in front of me.

TO BE CONTINUED

AFTERWORD

Before you turn into Louhi and consider stabbing me for that mild cliffhanger, and leaving you with a plethora of unanswered questions, please sheath your blade. I'm thrilled to inform you that the culmination of Sean and Louhi's story will be featured in *Enemy of My Heart*, which will conclude The Enemy Duet.

If you enjoyed this book, I'd be honored if you'd leave a review or told a friend about it. Reviews mean the world to me and allow me to actively pursue my dreams of storytelling. Thank you!

ACKNOWLEDGMENTS

If you'd told me three years ago that I'd be publishing a book, I wouldn't have believed you. I don't have a background in writing like many of my wonderful fellow authors. While my foray into writing looks different, I find that incredibly beautiful. It's never too late to discover your dreams and desires. My passion for writing and storytelling is new, but it burns red-hot, nonetheless.

I tell you all of that to thank you, friend, for reading Enemy of the State. You will never understand the depth of my gratitude for making my dreams come to life as you turn each page of this book. Thank you!

A million and ten thanks to my husband for encouraging and supporting me—and adamantly rejecting the idea of me giving up. Thank you for being my best friend and for showing me the kind of love I thought only existed in fiction. Thank you for letting me write through Thanksgiving—fine, every holiday—when I said I wouldn't, and for feeding us both when time lost all meaning. You are more than a dream come true and I'm entirely undeserving of your love and kindness, but baby, I'm keeping you forever. Thank you for your unconditional love. I love you and your perfect heart. I'll find you even in death.

Lisa and Stan, my cheer squad, thank you...for, quite literally, everything. Thank you for adoring this story and its characters. Thank you for being my friends, for encouraging me to pursue new dreams, and for loving me so well. Perhaps the days of me gabbing nonstop about Louhi and Sean in the backseat of the car and over the dinner table are finished, but likely not. I could never have done this without you. I love you both. I'm sorry for all the expletives.

Mackenzie, I *would* follow you over the edge of a cliff. Thank you for taking a chance on me, a girl who rarely has any idea what the hell she's doing. Working with you will never lose its luster and I'm privileged to know you. Thank you for metaphorically holding my hand and making me giggle my way through edits. That camera scene—you know which one—is entirely for you. I fucking adore you.

Haley, to say "thank you," seems lame. I have an undying love and appreciation for you—now and always. Thank you for your countless hours of assistance, book chats, and squealing over Louhi's unhinged behavior. The way you've embraced Louhi, Sean, and especially Jace, from the very beginning has set my soul on fire. You are a gift made of pure starlight. Knowing you is a delight and a half. Thank you for all you've done to help me make this book a success. I'm sorry that you can't get rid of me, even if you try. I love you, book lover.

Ashlee, thank you for creating such a gorgeous cover for me. Working with you has been such a "pinch me" moment and I'm so grateful to you. Thank you for not kicking me in the shin for being chaos incarnate.

Danielle, there would be no book without you. Thank you for encouraging me to write that first book two years ago and for cheering me on ever since. There aren't words to adequately express my gratitude. You've truly changed my entire life. Thank you for enthusiastically reading all my books, even the shitty ones, and for being my friend. I love you eternally.

Rebekah, thank you for everything! From dishing about plots over salads to laughing our asses off about Louhi doing Louhi things—on *and* off the page—you've stood at my side for every second of this book. Thank you for not letting me burn out and for loving my characters as much as I love you.

Annie, Darby, Kayley, Dani, and Maisie—thank you for being my friends, for supporting me, and loving me so well. While I'm sure that none of you were shocked to find that I wrote a scene with nipple clamps and rice, thanks for still looking me in the eye without so much as a blush on your cheeks. You guys are solid friends for that.

Stacey, thank you for making the inside of my book so beautiful. Working with you was a dream. Thank you!

Virginia, thank you for waving your magic wand over B.H. Eastwood. Tarantula Studio has made my branding dreams come true. There aren't enough adjectives in the English dictionary to describe my gratitude, so I'll just say thank you for lending me your expertise. You're truly one of the kindest people I've met, and you've got a forever friend in me.

While I sincerely hope you never read this book, thank you, Mom, Dad, and Ry, for your love, patience, and years of encouragement. I finally found what I want to do with my life. I love you.

ABOUT THE AUTHOR

B.H. Eastwood writes scorching hot romances that will have you on the edge of your seat and clutching your pearls. She lives in the southern United States with her husband and their aged Golden Retriever.

When she's not obsessively spilling her brain onto the page, you can find her banging her head at a metal show until she's nearly concussed or curled up with a book, preferably on a gloomy day.

Although, no matter where she is or what she's doing, you can rest assured that she's thinking about the precious stories smoldering in her brain.

Connect with B.H. Eastwood on
Instagram, @authorbheastwood,
or through her website, www.bheastwood.com.

Thank you so much for reading!

Printed in Dunstable, United Kingdom

64735390R00170